The Mercian Chronicles
BOOK 1

Sword & Fire

P.J. Reed

published in 2023
by Lost Tower Publications
P.J. Reed asserts her copyright over this collection of her work.
P.J. Reed is hereby identified as the author of this work in
accordance with Section 77 of the Copyright, Designs, and Patents
Act 1988.
This book is sold subject to the condition that it shall not, by way
of trade or otherwise, be lent, hired out or otherwise circulated
without the publisher's prior consent in any form or cover than that
in which it is published.

Cover Design: SelfPubBookCovers.com/billwyc

ISBN: 9781805173663

Lost Tower Publications

Sword & Fire

ONE

Name - Meloc
Location - Welfasten
Allegiance - Mercian Warbands

The grey, smoke-filled, mist clawed its way down the valleys from the northern mountains. It turned the air cold, causing the outlying farmsteads to fade in and out of the view of the ill-equipped local militia who patrolled the town walls.

To the north, the distant outline of Stonefall Fortress stood silhouetted against the horizon, a symbol of strength and hope. The villages of the lands to the east were abandoned, their inhabitants fleeing in panic as the Dunmuir invaded under the cover of darkness.

The city walls strained under the weight of the terrified villagers. The refugees sat huddled together, as they clung to what few possessions they had managed to grab in the fractured minutes it had taken them to realise the Dunmuir army had invaded the Eastlands. They sat in a shocked silence, broken only by the cries of the children too young to understand their plight. The cityfolk joined their silence, hiding in their houses, praying the invaders would somehow sweep around them and war would not come to their town.

Wooden shop signs creaked in the strangely frosted winds, which blew grey snow across the city. Stilted, barked orders rang throughout Welfasten as the militia drafted every able-bodied man and youth to patrol the city wall and defend the hastily made barricades which had been strung across the streets. The great oak town gates situated beneath the walls of the guard tower had been closed. The huge crossbeam had been slotted into place, fixing the gate into the thick stone walls of the citadel, and were to remain closed for the foreseeable future by the command of the Order of the Wergend.

The latest wave of displaced villagers had gathered outside the city gate, begging to be allowed inside the safety of the city walls, until the sky had darkened, and their hope of sanctuary was lost. During the night they fled, their path lit by Vana, the ever-shining Star of Mercia, as they hoped for a kinder welcome further west.

The town's watchfire sat in a crystalline bowl situated in the centre of the red brick bridge, which arched across the roof of the guardhouse. The fire had been lit when the first refugees had flooded into the town. Its red flame a warning to all that Welfasten was in peril. The guards had stood watching northwards all night, waiting for Stonefall Fortress to light its fire in answer and prepare to defend the lands of the Midheim.

Hidden under the shadows of the watchfire, at the bottom of the towering grey guardhouse, was a row of tiny, black-barred windows. Cityfolk could pay one copper coin to look through the bars and see the latest collection of criminals, vagrants, and daemonkin to have stumbled into their city.

The anxious faces of the prison row's latest inhabitants peered through the iron bars. Whispers on the row warned that if Welfasten was to be invaded, they would either be left to rot in their cells or executed in case they joined with the Dunmuir invaders. An 'X' with a small circle nestled in the top of its crossed lines had been crudely painted under the barred window furthest from the guardhouse door. It was a warning to the god-fearing locals to avoid looking directly at the monster inside.

A dirt-stained young man sat on the floor in the corner of his cell, silently staring into the dusky sky. He shivered as he felt the presence of myrkir; an insidious, lurking dark magik.

Something evil had arrived. It lingered on the edge of the city, in the shadows just beyond the walls.

The warlock frowned, squinting through the shifting darkness. He looked for a guard's shadow moving under his cell door and satisfied he was unwatched, whispered the *Leith* spell under his breath. His body jolted as he felt the galdor energy pulse through his body. The warlock's large cobalt-coloured eyes widened fractionally and transformed as flames of amber filled his pupils, casting fire shadows across his grey brick cell. His vision flew to the lands north of his prison.

He saw the pine woodlands that covered the Witian Foothills burning in the night. Masked horsemen with billowing black cloaks drove their horses through the glowing embers of cindered villages.

'But where is the Northern warband?' Meloc muttered, as he rubbed the rash of black stubble across his chin. If the guards did not allow him a razor soon, for the first time in his life, he might be sporting a beard. The young warlock frowned. He was not completely sure that he could even grow proper stubble, let alone a real beard.

Meloc squinted at the scene unfolding in his head as a black spot moved too quickly down the snow-covered sides of Stonefall Mountain. The spot came nearer. Meloc saw two huge black wings silhouetted against the snow. A cloud of powdered snow leapt into the cool air with each beat of its wings.

He watched in alarm as its dark grey eyes glinted hungrily at him through the darkness.

Someone had summoned a heryfin.

The outer wall of his cell imploded inwards, and the daemon bird hovered momentarily in front of the cowering warlock, hungrily assessing him. The heryfin flapped its black wings once and lunged at the warlock. Its two-inch iron talons missed the warlock's face by inches, as he dived across the cold stone floor and rolled underneath his narrow wooden bed. The bird thudded on top of the bed and began to peck through the wooden bed boards. The warlock covered his head with his hands and watched in horror as a jagged hole ripped through the wood. The scratching stopped for a second, Meloc glanced through his fingertips and gasped as he saw an unblinking, soulless eye staring back at him through the hole. The heryfin lifted its head of shining black feathers, opened its hooked, black beak, and let out a high-pitched caw which echoed throughout the prison row.

Some of the prisoners cried out in fear at the sound, recognising it as the bringer of myrkir.

The heryfin growled, its beak cracking through the bed board, aiming for the warlock's eyes. Meloc screamed and covered his eyes with his hands.

The *Leith* spell collapsed.

The daemon bird shrieked and disappeared.

Cautiously, the warlock opened his eyes, which had returned to their unnatural cobalt hue. He breathed a sigh of relief and lay panting against the cold stone floor, blinking sweat from his eyes. The sorcerers of Dunmuirlun watched for ripples in the pathways in the galdor energy throughout the Two Kingdoms. Anyone in Mercia, who was able to control the energy was a potential threat to Dunmuirlun, and in the months prior to the invasion many of the magikborne had disappeared. Meloc had come to Welfasten to warn the town chief of the evil presence growing in the darkness and the disappearances of the Mercian magikborne. He had not even made it past the guardhouse. The invaders were coming, and he could see no point in refraining from magik.

The cell door flew open. A thin, blue-cloaked Wergend officer, strode into the cell, followed by two worried looking gaolers. The officer's stern face hidden under the brow of a bronze helmet and dented nose guard. He looked down at the prostrate warlock in disgust.

'What happened here?' he ordered in a softly accented voice as a huge black feather floated gently past his face.

'I slipped,' Meloc said, looking up at the officer.

'Get him up,' the Wergend ordered.

The two gaolers dragged Meloc to his feet and held him up in front of the officer.

'I doubt that. You have obviously been communicating with daemonkin, I can smell it in the air,' the officer said. 'He is still joined to the galdor path. His unmynistering must have failed. Restrain the daemon.' The Wergend began to chant his anti-daemonic creed.

'Get away from me, you wyrm-ridden idiots. You have no idea what's coming for you!' Meloc shouted, 'I need to speak to Chief Feitar!'

'Your threats have no hold here, warlock-scum!' the Wergend growled and nodded to the gaolers.

Four rough hands grabbed the struggling warlock. Meloc was thrown onto the remains of the wooden bed. Two pairs of thick, iron shackles hung from posts situated at either end of the bed. The silent guard hit Meloc's shin with the flat of his sword. The warlock grunted and tried to pull away from the grip of the prison guards. The thick set guard grinned and pressed tightly on Meloc's wrists, while the smaller but wider guard stretched the daemon's arms above his head. The Wergend officer slapped the pair of shackles on the writhing man's wrists.

'Get off me, you animals!' Meloc shouted. He concentrated hard, trying to feel the galdor path with his thoughts but the Wergend's chant had blocked the way. The warlock cursed and kicked out at the guards. The guards caught hold of his flailing feet and pinned them down as the Wergend Officer shackled them to the posts at the end of the bed.

The officer unclipped an iron wristband inscribed with glyphs Meloc could not read from his belt and bent it onto the warlock's wrist. Immediately, Meloc stopped struggling as he felt the galdor energy drain from his body.

'There… he should cause no more problems. Send a messenger hawk to Eldingar Tower. The unmynstering did not work on this warlock.' He grabbed Meloc by the hair and stared intently into his eyes. 'I can see he still possesses some daemonry. He will need to be cleansed again. See to it, immediately.'

'Yes, Captain Kasian.' The gaolers saluted, and the officer left the cell.

'As I sees it, we'll all be dead before the hawk returns, an' our shift ended at sunrise,' the thickset guard stated.

'Aye,' said the other, his face taunt with fear. 'Let the day watch do it. We will die soon anyways, may as well die drunk an' happy than fighting the Dunmuir horde.'

'Aye,' said his friend. 'Let us choose our own deaths.'

The guards left the cell and Meloc heard the three sets of heavy iron bolts slide over his door. 'What about my breakfast?' he yelled, expecting no reply.

TWO

Name - Anders
Location - Stonefall Mountain
Allegiance - The Mercian Warbands

The autumnal air was scented with the smell of decay, damp earth, and decomposing leaves. Captain Anders opened blood-shot green eyes and groaned as the early dawn light filtered through the twigs of a twisted oak and bore into his skull. Gingerly, he touched his forehead. The wound had dried during the night. He raised his head and peered down at his stomach. This cut was worse. The sword had slashed straight across his stomach and was still damp with blood.

Anders cursed as he lay and shivered in the icy morning air. The ground felt frigid and sharp against his bare back. He clenched his fist and felt drying leaves crumble under his touch.

He was still alive but slowly bleeding to death and freezing. His armour, undershirt, and weapons were gone. They must have thought him dead and stripped him of everything before they dumped his corpse into the ditch.

He half-smiled.

It would take much more than a slice to the skull to kill him.

He was far too hard-headed and narrow-brained, as Chief Thorvald often stated when he sent the warrior on yet another punishment duty. Patrolling the stone road eastwards from Stonefall Fortress and Devoran village was a task for a recruit, not a seasoned warrior. It was the most uneventful patrol from the fortress. Until last night, when a band of ill-assorted bandits had dragged him from his horse and tried to gut him.

He covered the gaping wound in his stomach with a mud-stained hand and struggled to stand. The stones dug into his bare feet. The bandits had stolen everything except his loin cloth.

Anders sighed.

It was going to be a long day.

He grabbed one of the pale oak roots which twisted downwards into the hole and pulled his body up the crumbling sides of the ditch. A sharp pain tore through his stomach as his wound ripped apart. A trail of blood began to trickle from the wound. Anders ignored the pain. With one last pull, he reached the top of the ditch, grabbed a tuft of overhanging mountain grass, and hauled his body over, landing on top of the bank.

Anders lay there panting as he watched the ambers of dawn turn to blue. The sun would be up soon. He had to move, but first he needed to staunch the bleeding. Anders scoured the wild grass for his clothes. None had been left unwanted and discarded in the undergrowth. That was the problem with bandits and battle-pickers; they stripped the clothes off the bodies of the fallen before they were even cold.

Anders staggered to his feet. He grabbed a handful of dock leaves growing at the foot of a tall ashling tree and pressed them against his wound, then he walked back through the trampled undergrowth to rejoin the long stone slab road.

Stonefall Fortress towered majestically above him. The pale orange sandstone blocks of its battlements stood out proudly against the stark, white mountain peaks of the Witian Mountain range, protector of the northernmost reaches of the kingdom of Mercia. Its tall towers were lost in a grey haze which hung over the top of the fortress like a fallen storm cloud. Anders shivered.

Something felt wrong.

It was a three mile walk back to the fortress but if he was blessed with good fortune, the early morning horse messengers would be riding and once they had stopped laughing, might even give him a ride back to the fortress.

Anders staggered along the road.

The frozen morning air whistled through the rolling green tundra, but he felt hot. Drips of perspiration fell from his forehead, and he blinked them from his eyes. He looked down at his stomach. An ominous touch of red had spread beyond his wound. Anders frowned and whispered a prayer to Tyr, protector of all who served in the great warbands. He needed to get to the fortress quickly and be healed, before Mein, the black spirit of death, collected his soul. The touch of Mein or the creeping death took more warriors than enemies' blades ever did. Anders knew he had not earned enough glory to enter the Valholl; the hall of the glorious dead, which was promised to fallen warriors, and he refused to die and go to the other lesser lands of the dead. His forefathers would disown him.

A family of rooks cawed loudly and took flight.

Anders squinted into the shadows between the trees which lined the narrow road. A flash of sunlight pierced the branches of an ancient oak which scattered shadows across the grass. He scanned the undergrowth for flashes of enemy metal armour and sword lurking in the bushes and shook the thought from his head. The poison was beginning to affect his mind. He needed to get the fortress.

Ahead, the ancient stone road divided.

The main road stretched over the brow of the hill and disappeared as it fell into the valley. While a newer, well-used mud track split from the road. Anders took the path to the right which led into the lowest reaches of Stonefall Mountain.

The track wound upwards, snaking between the tough grass which clung to the mountainside and the faulted white stones whose galdor crystals glistened beneath the rising sun. Anders shielded his eyes with his hand as he passed a deep seam of crystals which irradiated with a burning opalescence. Once past, he quickly touched the blue-lined guard rune with the skewed blue box which was tattooed onto his forearm, to ensure he was protected from the unpredictable magik of the laying stones. Bands of fir trees stood dark green against the muted green of the mountain scrub grass. A breath of freezing air blew down from the mountain rippling the branches of the firs, leaving a trail of frosted grass and branch in its wake.

Anders shivered as the ice fall touched his naked flesh and ice flecks formed across his body. He heard the sound of great wings in flight and pushed strands of unkempt, long sandstone blond hair from his face as he squinted into the lightening sky. High above him the huge grey-scaled wings of a frostdrek flapped majestically together as the beast flew over the crest of the mountain. A wave of tiredness washed over him as his frozen body suddenly felt warm.

'I will not become part of the mountain,' Anders whispered as he stumbled onwards.

The mountain path twisted through a wall of towering rocks which formed a natural ring of protection around Stonefall village. He breathed a sigh of relief as in the distance a cluster of wooden roundhouses came into view.

'I have been attacked. I need aid!' Anders shouted towards the huts. His cry for help was unanswered. Anders pressed the leaf harder to his wound. The hairs on the back of his neck prickled with a warning, as if he were going into danger.

However, Stonefall was the seat of his father's lands, it was impregnable. The fortress had held firm against both homegrown bandits and various raiding parties ever since the defeat of the Dunmuir army at the great battle of Stonefall Steps in the time of his great-grandfather. He called out again. The wind whistled and somewhere a door slammed shut.

Anders trudged past the Great Hall, the biggest structure in the little settlement, with long wooden walls and a high thatched roof. Usually, the hall bustled with the village business, arguments, levies, and heavy drinking. However, this morning it stood silent. Anders frowned and looked for a weapon. Abandoned in the grass was a jagged rock. He picked it up and entered the building.

The hall was deserted. Several rough drinking tables had been upturned and several ale jugs lay broken in the straw which littered the floor.

There was a loud crash, and something charged through the open doorway.

Anders spun round, raising the rock above his head, ready to strike the intruder but stopped.

'My Lord, thank the gods you are still alive. When you did not return last night, your father sent me out to find you!' Sorimire thumped Anders on the back.

The rock fell from his hand as Anders collapsed forward onto his knees.

THREE

Name – Meloc
Location – Welfasten
Allegiance – The Mercian Warbands

Hunger gnawed at Meloc's stomach.

He had not eaten since yesterday, when a bowl of greying porridge had been carelessly pushed through the slit cut in the bottom of the reinforced wooden and iron-slatted door.

A frosted wind blew through the glassless window. Meloc looked up and frowned. For an instant the black iron bars glistened white with ice crystals before they melted to nothing.

'Dragons' breath,' the warlock muttered, 'Just when you think things can't possibly get any worse, they invariably do.'

'In case anyone is interested, that was the breath of a frostdrek. The Dunmuir have summoned their dragons to war, and we are all about to die!' He shouted and rattled his chains loudly against the bedframe. Usually, the noise brought the prison guards immediately to his cell. Meloc waited for the sound of running feet and the unimaginative angry yells of

'Silence warlock-scum' from the guards.

He could hear nothing.

A feeling of unease rose from his stomach. He whispered an invocation to Brokkir, the forbidden god of metals, and began to twist his hands in the manacles, trying to soften and stretch the heavy metal circles.

The cell door swung open.

Meloc rattled his chain noisily. 'It's about bloody time you came. I bet it's well past lunchtime now!' he yelled, trying to turn his head round to see who stood in the doorway.

'Get your own bloody lunch, daemonkin,' a guttural voice growled.

Meloc frowned. It was not the voice of one of the prison guards. 'Who are you? Come inside and make yourself known.'

The voice laughed, 'Well, well you're a little fyrdrek aren't you? You 'ave a big ol' mouth for someone chained up so.'

Meloc pulled on his chains, trying to squeeze his wrists though the manacles.

The voice laughed. 'You'll not be gettin' through those without a pick, magikboy. Allaric check him fer valuables.'

A fair-haired youth, dressed in brown tattered clothes walked cautiously towards the restrained warlock. The cell door clicked shut.

'But he's daemonkin, Tabor. I don't want to touch 'im. He could turn me into something odd or make me grow an extra leg.' The youth stared at the warlock in horror.

'You don't 'ave to touch him. Just grab his carriables. I'll 'ave that fancy wristband for a start an' check his rags for coin.'

'But that's 'is anti-magik band. If we take it, he'll get back in the galdor field an' magik us into something bad,' Allaric whimpered as he stared down at Meloc.

'Does it look like 'ee could magik us into anything? He's all tied up, you bloody idiot!' Tabor growled as he grabbed his cellmate by the face. 'Wergend wristbands go for six gold coins on the black market. Now get it and his money pouch too while you're rummaging him.'

Gingerly, Allaric leant over the prostrate warlock and felt around the top of his grey trousers looking for his money pouch. Meloc swore loudly and twisted to one side.

The youth overbalanced and fell against him. The touch of the daemon's skin against his was too much for the youth. He leapt off the bed and fled.

Tabor tutted. 'Bloody amateurs,' he moaned. 'If you want anythin' done proper, do it yourself.'

He walked over to the bed and yanked the iron band from the warlock's wrist. 'This will make some good coin,' he grunted. Meloc tried to wriggle away from his touch but could do little to protect himself from the thief. Tabor's eyes narrowed as he saw a flash of brown cord around Meloc's neck. He tore open the squirming warlock's green tunic open to reveal a small leather pouch on a leather throng.

He ripped the bag from Meloc's neck. Coins chinked together. Tabor grinned and grabbed the warlock's face with a dirt-stained, calloused hand, 'Not so poor as you seem, huh? Daemonborne scum.'

'You have got what you want. Now, for hels' sake release me. The city is in danger I must speak with the chief.'

'Aye, the city is in danger… from the likes of you,' Tabor hissed and pulled a small wooden spoon from the frayed sleeve of his dark brown tunic. Its end had been carved into a spike.

'You will bore me to death with your dronings, sooner than kill me with that little spoon,' Meloc said raising one fine black eyebrow.

Tabor grabbed Meloc's forehead with one hand and pressed his head into the bed boards, gripping the spoon in the other. 'Let's see how much menace you will be with no sight,' he hissed.

Meloc yawned.

Tabor roared with rage and punched him in the face.

The cell door opened and Allaric burst back inside. 'Some

bloody dogooder must of 'eard. The guards is gone and called for the Wergend Captain. He's coming. I can feel it in me waters an' he won't be leaving any prisoners alive; you mark my words.'

'Scitte!' Tabor swore. 'I'll leave you to 'im,' he grabbed hold of Meloc's hair and smacked his head against the bed board. A drop of blood ran down from the corner of his mouth.

'I doubt you will live long enough to complain about yer supper. Let's get out of this rathole.'

Tabor and Allaric rushed from the cell, their footsteps echoing in the silence of the abandoned prison block.

Meloc licked the blood from his lips and grinned. His left arm was free from its wristguard. '*Sumargaldor*,' he whispered. Instantly, he felt the warm, slightly electric presence of galdor as amber flames began to dance around his bed. A black energy oozed from his body as it sought out the amber. They touched, sparking, and crackling as they formed an energy bridge as he re-joined the galdor field. The galdor rushed through his body. He swallowed as a wave of heat and nausea surged through his body and the room began to spin.

The fingers of his left hand tapped a code against the bed.

The manacles on his ankles and wrists fell open and rose snakelike from the bed. They hovered in the air for a second as their ends untwisted themselves from the legs of the bed. He twisted his hand to the right.

The manacles flung themselves against the cell wall.

Meloc sat up and swung his legs over the side of the bed rubbing the red sores on his wrists as the dizziness subsided. He stumbled over to the only other piece of furniture in the barren room, a three-legged stool upon which the guard had thrown his threadbare, grey cloak; so old it contained more holes than material. Meloc pulled the ends of the cloak together and pinned it under his chin to gain as much warmth as the frail cloth could provide. The same tainted cross that marked his cell doorway was sewn on the left breast of the cloak: a warning to the good citizens of the city to keep their distance from the unnatural monsters that walked among them. Meloc crouched down on the cell floor as he took a leather pouch from a pocket hidden within the lining of his cloak. He opened the pouch and shook out a tiny piece of metal which glowed slightly in the shadows. It was marked with a rune depicting the lower half of a vase turned on its side, *petthro* – signifying the power of that which is hidden.

'Magik reveal yourself,' he whispered and touched the metal stamp.

The metal hissed and melted on top of the stone floor, reforming into the shape of an iron wristband. Meloc grinned and snapped it around his right wrist. Another form of protection for the good city folk.

The wristband felt warm and hung too loosely on his thin, pale wrist but it would help to protect him from the prying eyes of the fearful locals.

Cautiously, he opened the cell door and peered around it.

The dark stone-walled corridor seemed deserted; there was no sign of the guards. He checked the next cell, it was empty.

The prison row was deserted but would not be for long?

The Wergend soldiers would return. Meloc shivered in the coldness of the thick stone corridor. He pulled his hood over his head, hiding the unnatural paleness of his face and walked through the empty guardroom and out into the dazzling sunlight of Welfasten city.

Meloc slipped into a maze of back streets so narrow that the upper stories of the wooden buildings clinging to either side of the street almost touched. Little daylight reached these streets, and he went from shadow to shadow, avoiding eye contact with the inhabitants of the back alleys.

A deep, long howl echoed through the alley.

The warlock froze, listening with his head cocked to one side. Meloc felt the giant dog's footfalls across the alley, its breath heating the cool morning air.

'Faen!' he swore. His disappearance must have been discovered already and the Wergend summoned. A werhound would pick up his scent easily. He had to find the nearest galdorhus, a secret, rune-protected safehouse for the magikborne, and hide there until the search had left this quadrant. He rubbed his palms together and blew across them. His breath blew amber highlights across the grey shadows. A series of blue footprints appeared and walked down the alleyway. The first prints disappearing as the newest appeared.

A low, menacing growl hung on the air.

Meloc cast a furtive look over his shoulder and hurriedly followed the remaining footprints. The footprints led to a narrow alley which opened onto the central space of Welfasten city, Martur Market.

The market was in the central square of the city interior, housing a motley collection of wooden carts jostling for space on cobbled streets carpeted with litter, mud, and decaying food. It formed a bustling hub of excitement and noise: with people haggling over prices, women gossiping about the latest imagined scandal and little children running amok, merrily screaming at the top of their voices. The barking of the city dogs added itself to a cacophony of chickens, sheep, horses, and cows, all voicing their excitement at being part of the inglorious chaos of the market.

It was a place warlocks and other undesirables tried to avoid during daylight.

Meloc pulled up the hood of his cloak covering his pale face and unnatural eyes as he hurried across a deserted street and into the market. Immediately, he sensed something was wrong. Instead of excited noise and laughter, he felt a wall of anger. Hungry men armed with staffs, pitchforks, and anything they could use as a weapon, stood in groups shouting at the traders, demanding the food which must be hidden as there was none to be found. Women with young children hanging around their aprons wore worried expressions, trying to work out how to feed their starving children. A cart was overturned and smashed against the cobbles, but no food was found hidden in secret compartments underneath. The shouting grew louder, and desperate men started fighting each other. A cart was set alight and red flames shot into the night sky, showering the square with tiny red fire sparks which lit the fallen straw which covered the cobbles.

Two huge, red striped werhounds leapt from the alleyway running east of the market. They stood snarling as the people caught between the hounds and the fire screamed and

ran towards the main market entrance.

A unit of Wergend stood in a semi-circle around the exit, checking the panicking people for signs of daemonic aberration. A man screamed and ran towards the tall officer watching proceedings, his cloak on fire, begging for aid. The officer signalled to the crossbowman at his shoulder. The crossbow pinged and the man fell to his knees clutching the red stain covering his chest. He collapsed onto his face as fire took hold of his corpse. The mob paused and stumbled, some going forwards into the ranks of the Wergend, while others preferred to take their chance in the burning square.

A figure rushed across the square, his hood falling from his face to reveal the sharp, pointed features of an alfri. The Wergend yelled as one and sent a volley of arrows in its direction. Each arrow missed its mark and pinged against the cobbles as the alfri nimbly leapt from the cobbles onto the nearest house roof. Some of the arrows skidded into the crowd and there was a high-pitched scream as a well-dressed woman was shot through the leg.

A thick grey smoke billowed through the square and the fires burnt unseen through the greyness. A guttural shout sounded above the chaos as the Wergend ran down the road to try to catch the fleeing alfri before she left the rooftops. Relieved and choking, the mob surged through the entrance gates and vanished back inside their houses.

Meloc breathed a sigh of relief. His way was now completely clear of peasants, the Wergend, and city guards.

'People can say what they like about the Wergend, but they do have their uses,' Meloc declared as he watched as the light blue cloaks disappeared around the street corner. His stomach rumbled so loudly he feared the werhounds would hear him. He needed to find food before his body began to fail him.

His cobalt eyes narrowed as he saw a shadow move by the rubbish piles. A rat. He cast a furtive glance over his shoulder and slid the iron band from his wrist. His eyes glowed with amber flames and a bolt of white flew from his outstretched arm. The rat went rigid and fell to one side. Meloc dashed forward, grabbed the stupefied rat, and stuffed it down his shirt.

The blue footprints stopped outside an abandoned wooden

shack, its broken door barely hanging onto its hinges. In the bottom corner of the door, unnoticed by the general population of the city, someone had carved a rune depicting the lower half of a vase turned on its side, a *Petthro*.

Cautiously, Meloc opened the door. Nothing began to smoke or hiss. Relieved he slipped inside the shack and placed his hand on the door and whispered, '*Laessa.*' Immediately, a bronze bar shot out from each plane of the door fastening it to the doorframe. While the broken pieces of wood and torn fabric scattered around the room reorganised themselves into ornately carved furniture. The hated iron wristband was thrown carelessly towards a wooden chest, disappearing into the pile of dirty rags. A fire appeared in the grate and Meloc hung a black cooking pot over it, adding to the mixture an array of overpowering herbs to disguise the smell of one finely diced rat.

'If I have any more rat,' Meloc muttered, 'I will probably grow fur and start licking myself.'

The warlock settled into a comfortable cushion lined wooden armchair. A glass of wine magically appeared in his hand. He sipped at the soothing liquid and his eyes began to close.

FOUR

Name - Hamarr, Lord of the North
Location - Stonefall Fortress
Allegiance - The Mercian Warbands

The war drums beat through the foothills surrounding the mighty fortress. Their low ominous beat a warning of impending, inevitable doom. Death was coming, he could feel it. Lord Hamarr stood on the Eastern parapets watching the columns of black approach as arrows pinged and thudded against the stone battlements around him. A few of the warbandmen caught in the open screamed, their bodies impaled by heavy, black arrows. Their mail coats no match for the Dunmuir longbows.

'Archers away and make every arrow hit their mark,' Hamarr commanded, as the Stonefall archers shot into the Dunmuir forces massing around the fortress. His faded blue eyes scanned the land beneath the fortress. The enemy forces stretched from Stonefall to the foothills of the Witian Mountain, their black armour covering the green of the grazing lands in a dark shadow. The Dunmuir forces would take the fortress through sheer mass of numbers. His men, brave as they were, stood no chance against such overwhelming odds. Stonefall Fortress would fall and with it all the north-eastern lands.

Hamarr clenched his jaw but said nothing.

The first three lines of the Dunmuir consisted of the grey faces of conscripted lowlanders, their numbers bolstered with peasants and slaves from the Dunmuir borderlands. They were dressed in slatted black leather tunics, leather helmets, and were armed with knives, clubs, and axes. Only their leaders carried swords, which they proudly waved towards the fortress as they stalked between the lines. Although ill-equipped and ill-trained, the lowland men were savage. Years of starving on the edges of the Dunmuir Plains had changed them into something less than men. Their jaws and teeth had strengthened and enlarged, so they could rip skin from muscle and crunch through bone. Their tastes had increased to include man flesh, while their bodies had leathered and bulged with knots of muscle.

Lord Hamarr gripped the hilt of his sword tighter. The lowland lines would have to be destroyed before Stonefall fell. The least he could do was to save the women and children under his protection from such a savage death.

Beyond the lowlanders were the massed ranks of the main Dunmuir force, the black mail coated Dunmuirherr. They formed in squares of a hundred strong which stretched to the edge of his sight. They were trained soldiers, well-equipped and merciless, but at least they were still human. They would slaughter everyone they met. But death by their sword, would at least be quick.

The horsemen of the Draigar Brigade weaved in between the two sections of the army like war wraiths. The riders' faces were hidden under heavy, black, round-topped helmets with nose and ear guards, fastened by leather chinstraps. Their cheekbones protected by thick bands of leather. Lord Hamarr had fought against them in the earlier summer skirmishes, and he was glad their soulless, grey eyes were covered.

Their battlehorses were huge sunless black beasts, their souls twisted by a gnawing hunger for human flesh. Fire sparks exploded underfoot every time their hooves struck the land. The horses screamed and snorted smoke as they cantered between the lines, creating a smoky trail, which hung across the battlefield, obscuring the farthermost units from his view.

Strapped onto the flank of the horses were two-handed battle swords, which no ordinary man could lift.

If the Northern warband stood firm against the lowlander rabble and died in battle with the guards or the Draigar, they would fall as heroes and enter the Sumorlands – the lands beyond the living world or even enter the exalted halls of Valholl.

Hamarr closed his eyes as he whispered a prayer to Tyr, God Protector of the Northern warband.

'Ready the oil!' he ordered the sergeant.

Sergeant Thorne beat his chest with his fist and bowed. He marched across the battlements calling to the soldiers. 'Let's give the stinking Dunmuir dogs a bath in Stonefall oil! Make ready the barrels!'

There was a loud cheer as his cry was taken up and rang around the fortress wall. Great wooden barrels situated on ledges beside the battlements were manhandled into the gaps between the parapets. Chains were attached to the sides of the barrels and clipped onto the metal rings which had been hammered into both sides of the pouring gaps. The guards prised the lids off the barrels with their knives.

'Barrels secure!' they shouted signalling by raising their fists, then ducked behind the raised battlements as another arrow fall rained onto the fortress.

'Release the oil!' Hamarr roared.

The guards heaved the barrels forward; the barrels caught on their chains, pouring their contents away from the wall but covering the ground in viscous, black oil.

Inaudible grunts and shouts rose from the ground below the fortress as the lowlanders, panicked by the falling oil, broke their lines, and stumbled backwards. The Draigar screamed at the men to hold their ground and unclipped long black whips from their belts. Their battlehorses reared up onto their back legs, lashing out with their iron-capped hooves as the lowlanders huddled in groups caught between the raining oil and the Brigade.

'Archers light your arrows,' Hamarr commanded.

The archers wrapped oil-soaked cloths to the tips of their arrows and plunged the tips in the flaming torches which illuminated the battlements. The arrows caught fire on contact with the flames and the archers fired them into the oil below.

There was a loud roar as red flames leapt across the oil-soaked ground. The warbandmen on the fortress cheered in delight as the forward ranks of lowlanders screamed as they were caught by the fire, the rest fled into the woods as they tried to outrun the flames.

'Well done, my Lord,' Sergeant Thorne grinned.

Lord Hamarr smiled back. 'Stonefall Fortress will not fall without a fight. We have a few more tricks yet. Make ready the catapults.'

'Yes, my Lord.' Thorne bowed. He turned and yelled to the catapult masters situated on the great towers of the fortress, 'Ready the catapults.'

'Yes, Sergeant!' answered several voices, their faces lost in the acrid grey smoke which poured upwards from the ground surrounding the fortress. The warbandmen began to cough and choke.

Hamarr covered his mouth and nose with his scarf as the smoke clawed at his throat.

A muffled shout came from the black squares of the Dunmuir guards, and the war drums beat out an order across the battlefield. There was a thudding sound as the front five rows of each square knelt.

'Faen!' Thorne exclaimed and peered through the battlements. An arrow pinged off a stone an inch above his head.

Hamarr took hold of the collar of his undertunic and pulled him back. 'Have a care sergeant, I would not lose you in this battle.'

Thorne blushed and lowered his gaze. 'I am sorry,' he muttered.

Lord Hamarr's lined face softened, and he slapped the sergeant on his back. 'Your courage makes me proud... my son.'

Thorne smiled and glanced at the archers who sat nearest them. They grinned and whispered to their fellows. The rumours around Thorne's birth were true. He was the illegitimate son of the King and the maid from Fastness.

'Keep your focus,' Hamarr growled, the hairs on his arms rose and sweat seeped down his back as a cold wind blew across the fortress walls.

'What is that, my Lord?' a fresh faced, young archer pointed to the machine at the centre of each Dunmuir formation.

The wooden machines stood as high as a horse and were built on a T-shaped base. At the front of each machine was a thick wooden cross piece. A long piece of wood protruded from the cross piece; its centre hollowed out to hold an equally long iron siege arrow. A magazine box situated on the revolving wooden track behind the crosspiece fed arrows into the holder. Two men turned a heavy wooden wheel situated on the side of each machine. Slowly, the crosspiece raised upwards its trajectory fixed on the eastern battlements.

'Siegebows,' Hamarr replied as he felt his heart sink. They had destroyed the Dunmuir forces at the battle of Stonefallsteps. The same technology that had saved them in the past was being used against them. The Dunmuir had learned from their past mistakes.

'Archers fire on the siegebows, make them burn!' shouted Hamarr.

'Burn them to the ground! Fire at the crossbows!' ordered Thorne, standing next to Lord Hamarr.

An arc of fire arrows whooshed through the grey sky and scattered across the battlefield. Several hit the three crossbows located nearest the Fortress. A slight amber glow flashed through the wafts of smoke. The arrowheads pinged from the machines and fell burning onto the mud.

Hamarr shook his head. The design had been improved. They were now protected by the spells of the Dunmuir battlemages. Only the Mercian warlocks could counter their spells and save Stonefall, but they were still dining in luxury at Fregna Tower. He clenched his fist and thumped the stone of the battlements.

'Fire everything we have at them!' Hamarr roared. The wind became stronger and whistled around the battlements, pulling at his plaited beard and long hair. It was ready to take him to his ancestors.

Another volley of Mercian arrows soared through the sky.

The fortress guards threw broken stones and bottles over the battlements, while the warband men drew their longswords and waited patiently.

A groaning, whirling sound rose from the siegebows as the machinists turned a handle and the track began to groan into life. Heavy iron arrows dropped from the munitions box, the siegebow ropes were pulled taut and then released. Ten great arrows soared through the sky.

More and more followed as the siegebows reloaded automatically. The arrows formed the shape of a black claw high in the clouds and fell as one, smashing everything that lay in their path. Stonefall Fortress shook under the impact. The heavy iron arrows smashed holes through the curtain walls, sending stone and dust high into the air. Everyone defending the fortress fell against the footways, some screamed as they were pinned beneath blocks of falling stone. Others made no sound. Their eyes and mouths fixed open as their crumpled bodies, impaled by siege arrows, were smashed against the fortress walls. Then the arrows stopped falling.

For a moment, there was silence.

Hamarr lay face down against the pathway, covered in a layer of dust and small stone. In the distance, he heard the sound of wooden siege ladders slapping down against stone.

He closed his eyes and waited for death.

FIVE

Name - Hamarr, Lord of the North
Location - Stonefall Fortress
Allegiance - The Mercian Warbands

Time seemed to stop. Sound was suspended. Clouds of dust and smoke billowed from the space where the centre of the fortress curtain wall had once stood. Hamarr rubbed the dust and grit from his eyes, and groaned as he saw the smoking remains of the eastern parapet. The few remaining archers fired from jagged gaps which had been punched through the stone battlements. All around him lay the smoking detritus of war - splintered arrows, helmets, and broken bodies - some still crying out in pain. Blood dripped from the wooden footways which ran along the fortress wall.

Hamarr looked upwards. The flag of Stonefall, a white mountain on a field of green, flapped in the gusting wind. Its lower fastening broken, it would soon be free, carried on the gusting wind to safer parts.

Get up! A martial voice inside his head ordered. *You are not dead yet.*

Hamarr pulled himself to his feet, the walls of the fortress spun and a drum inside his head began to pound. Cautiously, he felt the back of his helmet. It had cracked open to reveal a deep, bloody cut.

A dirty grey hand appeared through a gap in the battlements. Its owner leapt through the hole.

'Faen!' he groaned.

Death would have to wait.

Hamarr lunged, his sword piercing through the leather plate

of the lowlander. The lowlander grabbed the blade of the sword and stared at Hamarr; its grey eyes wide with shock. Hamarr withdrew his sword. The lowlander slumped onto his knees, dark blood oozing from the wound.

'Help me!' the lowlander whimpered.

Hamarr kicked the lowlander back through the hole and the man fell screaming.

Immediately, his place was taken by another lowlander as they swarmed over the damaged walls.

'Hel!' Hamarr swore. They were being overrun.

An arrow whizzed through the smoke and struck Hamarr in the chest. He staggered backwards, his hands clutching at the arrow. Hamarr gritted his teeth as he tried to pull the arrow from his chest. It was stuck, the barbs of the arrowhead had fastened against his ribcage.

His hands slipped as blood trickled down the arrow shaft. A drop of blood splashed onto the wooden floor as the northern wall exploded.

The shockwave reverberated throughout the fortress. The eastern wall staggered under the force of the explosion. Wood and stone shards flew upwards in a mushrooming cloud of fire, smoke, and dust. Then rained down upon the remains of the fortress. However, the eastern curtain wall remained standing.

'Retreat and regroup along the inner walls,' Hamarr ordered. The cry was taken up around the smoking fortress.

The creaking of an opening portcullis gate grated through the screams of injured soldiers and the sounds of falling rock.

'Faen! The western defences are destroyed,' Hamarr growled as he peered through the clouding smoke.

Heavy footsteps and guttural orders, shouted in the rough dialect of the lowlanders, echoed through the smoke as the

Dunmuir horde broke through the western inner wall and into the inner courtyard.

The villagers hiding in the courtyard screamed in terror as the Dunmuir began their slaughter.

'The western walls have been breached. We have been betrayed,' Hamarr said as he looked around the fortress in despair, 'My god, why have you forsaken us?' He collapsed onto his knees.

A tall, dirty figure with flowing red hair, matted with dried brown blood appeared, dodging between the fires, on the smoke-filled battlement. He wore an old green robe over grey woollen trousers and ancient leather boots. The figure carried the remains of the regulation round wooden shield of the North, its white and green quarters covered in brown dried blood and black scorch marks.

'Well, my heir, you are late and ill-dressed as always... where is your mail coat and sword?' Hamarr whispered as he clutched at the arrow in his chest as he fell backwards onto the shaking floor.

'Father! No!' Anders cried out as he knelt and cradled his father's head in his arms. 'I'm so sorry I'm late. I met insurgents on the night patrol. They must have been an advance force. We fought and I was left for dead.' Anders lowered his gaze as he blinked the tears from his eyes.

Hamarr stared up at his son and shook his head. 'Or did you get drunk and gamble everything away again?'

Anders blushed and opened his mouth to protest but no words came. He did not wish to argue with his dying father.

'Lord Hamarr!' Sergeant Thorne screamed as with a two-handed slice, he removed a lowlander's head from its body, jumped over a fallen Stonefall archer, and skidded on his knees to his father's side.

'Father, you are hurt. Do not fear I will carry you to the healers,' Thorne whispered, looking in horror at the blood pooling around his lord's body.

'It is too late for me, Thorne,' Hamarr whispered smiling up at him. 'Give me my sword. Do not despair. I am happy for I will die a warrior's death and the halls of Valholl await me.'

Thorne smiled back at his father and helped him sit so his back was propped against the posterior wall. He pressed the great sword into Hamarr's hand. 'I will protect your body with my life, and we will enter Valholl together,' Thorne replied as he stood up and raised his shield.

'I will protect you too Father!' Anders replied grabbing a fallen short sword as he knelt next to his half-brother.

Hamarr held up one shaking hand. Thorne grasped it, wiping the tears from his eyes with his sleeve.

'Ah Thorne… my son,' Lord Hamarr said as his eyes began to glaze. Blood trickled from the corner of his mouth. 'Save who so ever you can but send word to the King. Before the sun sets Stonefall Fortress will fall, and the north will be taken. The King's Guard must burn everything north of the Vimur River. Let the eastern scum march on our ashes and starve.'

Hamarr's faded blue eyes opened slightly as his soul left his body.

Thorne reached forward and closed his father's eyes as he whispered a prayer for his ascension to Valholl.

Anders stood up. His face ashen. Even in death, he had disappointed his father. He staggered backwards as an icy chill spread through his body.

Somewhere close by a grey-faced Dunmuir lowlander

roared as he brought a studded mace down upon a dying warbandman as the grey army surged through the fortress.

Thorne leapt forward to meet the lowlander. His sword crunched through the black Dunmuir breastplate. The soldier stopped in mid-roar and looked down at his stomach in confusion as dark blood began to pour from the jagged cut in his chest.

Anders felt his body move on its own as he ran forward and kicked the soldier hard in the stomach. The dazed soldier tumbled backwards over the battlements. His death scream lost amid the hungry roars of the swarming horde and the crash of stone on stone as the remains of the Western Tower collapsed.

'Northmen to me!' Thorne shouted, as he raised his sword above his head and turned it sideways, his blade pointing towards the mountains. The surviving warbandmen gathered as they watched the grey faces of the Dunmuir foot soldiers pour over the battlements.

'The Fortress is lost, to be avenged another day. Night watch, go to the women and children in the Moaning Caverns beneath the Keep. Lead them through the tunnels and head for the ruins of Einsamall Tower beneath the Grey Mountain. There is nothing there that warrants the attention of the Dunmuir army.'

'But sergeant, there is nothing in the Grey Mountain for us either, we will starve in the Greylands,' a huge warbandman called out, the left side of his face hidden beneath red battle scars.

'Nonsense,' Thorne smiled, 'a fit warrior like yourself shouldn't have any problem looking after the needs of our women.'

The warbandman grunted and signalled to the remaining Night Watch and ran towards the Southern Tower. Its entrance broken and bellowing grey smoke.

'The rest of the north follow me. The Eastern Tower still stands. We will draw the eyes of our enemy upon us and fight our way through to the tower. Those who survive must make for Fastness Fortress to inform the King of our misfortune.'

A low muttering came from the remaining warbandmen, and several shook their heads.

'I was born in Stonefall, and I plan to die here.' A voice called out from somewhere.

There were grunts of agreement.

Anders ran his hand through his matted hair and stepped forward. 'We men of the Northern Warband have pledged an oath of allegiance to the King. Stonefall will soon fall and then they will come for the King…'

'Good!' a disembodied voice called out and the men laughed.

Anders threw his knife into the face of a Dunmuir foot soldier as it climbed over the battlements. The soldier fell forward. Blood seeping into a grey circle around its head.

'Swordmen make for the Eastern Tower. I will remain here with the archers to cover you. The men of the north do not forget their honour or their King.'

The warbandmen nodded. Their faces grim.

Sergeant Thorne gripped Anders' sleeve. 'I will remain here. You go. You are the rightful heir to Stonefall.'

Anders shook his head. 'No, you must leave me to my glorious end. At least in death I can bring honour to my house.'

Thorne nodded. 'Die with honour, my Lord,' he whispered

as he gripped his half-brother's forearm. Thorne released his grip and raised his sword high above his head.

'Warband on me!' he shouted and began to weave a path through the fires and broken bodies heading towards the Tower. The remains of the warband followed him.

Anders was left alone.

A screeching sound came from beyond the clouds.

'Faen!' Anders cursed as he squinted into the grey smoke-filled sky.

A breeze swirled around the fortress. It picked up the pieces of straw, splinters of wood, and dust that lay scattered across the battlements. The screeching came nearer. The straw and splintered wood blackened to soot. The stones of the fortress steamed. The Dunmuir foot soldiers climbing over the battlements screamed as the skin burnt away from their hands. The bows of the archers and the shields of the swordsmen burst into flames and then turned to ash and was carried away by the thundering wind which almost took the men from their feet.

'What magik is this?' Thorne screamed as the wind threatened to blow him from the battlement. He grabbed hold of a stone. Instantly, his hands reddened as he screamed in pain.

A huge black shadow crossed the courtyard.

Time seemed to lengthen and slow.

Anders found himself falling backwards watching as Stonefall Fortress stood illuminated by fire as the southern battlements exploded.

SIX

Name - General Vargal
Location - Stonefall Fortress
Allegiance - The Royal Dunmuirlun Forces

Pillars of smoke billowed from the fires raging inside the fortress and mushroomed into an organic, grey cloud which spread quickly across the dying land. The cloud base flushed red, illuminated by the glowing scales of the fyrdrek as its mighty wings cut through the smoke.

The drek's crimson eyes flashed brightly against the dull sky. Its elongated neck swayed from side to side, as it searched the mountainside for survivors. The fyrdrek's red stomach flushed amber as a deep rumbling sound came from within. The beast opened huge jaws to reveal rows of serrated gleaming white teeth and screeched its roar across the smoking land.

Each flap of its wings created a vortex. Trees bent and snapped in two, their branches flying into the mountainside. The cooking fires of the Dunmuir were instantly extinguished. The soldiers, who were resting in groups after their victory looked up in alarm.

'Ah! Here at last… I see our air support has finally arrived,' whispered the preternaturally tall General sitting on top of a huge black battle horse. His quiet voice warned of a hidden menace. He sipped a flagon of wine, while he watched the drek circle through the sky.

'Move at your peril men,' he warned.

The fyrdrek swooped lower, drawn to the smoke of the fires. Its wingtips almost touching the heads of the group nearest the fortress. One of the soldiers jumped up in alarm and ran towards the blackened skeletons of the fir trees. The rest of his group sat clinging to one another, as the drek stopped circling and hovered above them, its unblinking eyes watching them as if it were choosing its prey. With one beat of its wings the fyrdrek lurched forward, neck outstretched, and caught the fleeing soldier in its fang-lined snout. There was a crunching sound and blood dripped from the corners of its mouth. The drek tossed its head upwards, the body flew into the air, and fell into the outstretched mouth.

The fyrdrek roared at the men who fell to their knees. A sudden wind blew from the mountains, tugging at the drek's wings. It roared once more and flew eastwards along the mountains.

'And so, the weak will be culled,' mused the General, to no one in particular.

There was a crash as the Eastern Tower collapsed onto the inner courtyard. An explosion of dust flew into the air and hung for a minute, like a white shroud covering the dying fortress. No shouts of panic rose from inside its walls, only the screaming silence of the dead.

Four lowlanders approached the camp. Their clothes still smoking from the raging fires. The men had tied grey scarves around their faces, to protect themselves from the clawing, caustic smoke that spread across the mountainside.

'Here's the body, my General.' The bigger lowlander bowed and nodded to his companions. The corpse was unceremoniously dropped face down on the ground.

'Very good,' replied Vargal. He kicked the corpse with the black metal toe of his boot. It flopped onto its front.

The General stared down into the swollen, blackened face

of Lord Hamarr and smiled.

'So, Hamarr, you did indeed fall to the Dunmuir sword as I predicted. Your hubris was indeed bigger than your might, as I suspected. Strip him of his mail coat and helm. Then, tie his body to the gates of the fortress. It will serve as warning to those who dare to challenge the might of Dunmuirlun.'

'But my General, we have just carried his body all the way from the fortress. We are tired, we need some food and rest,' said the lowlander.

'Nonsense,' sneered the General. 'Strong lowlanders like yourselves can work for hours without respite, but if you feel that you can't do your job properly, I will release you from your sufferings and find a unit better equipped for the task.'

The lowlanders stiffened and bowed to the General. 'Er… Oh no, my General, we only live to serve you and… the King.'

The corner of Vargas' mouth twitched. 'What news of the lordling Anders?'

A younger lowlander untied a battered helmet from his thick leather belt. The faceplate had been sliced in two, there was a large dent at the top of the helm.

'Begging your pardon, my General, but this is all what was left of him.' He held the helm towards the General, his hands shaking.

The General laughed quietly. 'Well, well… the line of Stonefall has finally been wiped from the royal scrolls of Mercia. Put the helm on a spear. Next to his father's body.'

'Yes, my General.' The lowlanders bowed as they wearily picked up the body and trudged back towards the remains of the fortress.

Vargal watched as they disappeared into the smoke and smiled.

Stonefall Fortress, the indestructible protector of the Witian Mountain Pass, had fallen, the gateway to the remaining free lands of Mercia, had been opened. No one in the kingdom would be powerful enough to stop the advance of the Dunmuir.

Vargal signalled to his servant who was kneeling in the mud before him.

'Bring me my Stryx, now!' he growled, wrapping his billowing black cloak tightly around his body. The chill wind turning his skeletal face lighter grey as he frowned down upon his resting troops.

The servant bowed and walked over to a cart; its cargo hidden under sacking cloth. He pulled the cloth to one side to reveal a row of wooden barred cages. Its inhabitants both animal and human glared at him through the bars. The servant shuddered as he unlocked the cage of a large grey-winged creature with a revolving head, and two huge unblinking eyes, which hung upside down from the roof of its cage. Gingerly, the servant put his hand in to grab the leather thongs which criss-crossed the creature's body. The bird twisted its neck to one side and pecked through the boy's hand. The youth screamed and quickly wrapped his bleeding hand in a dirty rag.

'Stryx to me!' Vargal commanded, a smile twisting across his grey-tinged lips.

The bird dropped from its perch and swept out of its cage, unfurling two sturdy wings which flapped together once and landed on Vargal's outstretched arm. 'Well, my feathered monster, now you've eaten, take this message to the King.'

He placed a sealed parchment in the canister strapped to the birds back which was almost hidden by the bird's thick feathers. He hurled the bird high into the smoky air. The bird screamed as it circled its master once and then flew high eastwards over the lower mountains.

Vargal surveyed the ruined fortress with satisfaction. He would return soon and with greater forces. Nothing could stand in the way of his march on Fastness Fortress, the capital of Mercia. He snatched a flaming torch from two cowering foot soldiers. Between them knelt a dark blue uniformed warbandman.

'It was not a complicated order to follow soldier. If it is edible take it, if it bleeds kill it, and if it is burns put it to the flames,' he whispered menacingly at the soldier.

'Yes, my General, but this one says he's one of us.' The soldier bowed and pulled Sergeant Sorimire's head up by his hair.

General Vargal stared at the soot-blacked face of the Mercian with disgust as he flicked a piece of grey soot from his cloak.

'Please General. I have served you well. Without me the western wall would still be shut and the fortress untaken.'

'Really?' the General replied. In the blink of an eye, he dismounted his battlehorse and stood over the cowering prisoner. 'I think not.'

The General leaned towards the warbandman, as if to whisper something, and stabbed Sorimire in the heart, with a curved, black-bladed dagger. 'A Mercian can never be one of us. Especially not traitorous, turncoat scum who will send his fellows to their deaths for the promise of a few gold coins.'

The soldiers dropped Sorimire and scurried backwards, cowering away from the General. Slowly, blood pooled around his chest, seeping into the trampled ground.

Vargal wiped his dagger on Sorimire's shirt. His face devoid of emotion. 'There… your prisoner problem is solved. Do not bother me with such matters again.'

The soldiers exchanged anxious glances, bowed, and quickly moved away from the General.

General Vargal smiled, enjoying their fear, and scanned the moving greyness of the smoke-filled mountainside. The late afternoon sun was hidden by a veil of smoke. He could sense nothing living. Satisfied, Vargal raised his hand, signalling to his servant.

The boy bowed. He ran to hold the heavy black stirrup still as the General mounted his towering battlehorse, then fled back to the safety of the shadows.

Vargal smiled slightly as he felt fear emanate from his servant. He wheeled the horse around and raised his hand in a fist. His troop silently lined up behind him and they galloped back through the mountain pass to rejoin the main Dunmuir force.

SEVEN

Name - Meloc
Location - Welfasten
Allegiance - The Mercian Warbands

Meloc woke with a start as a heavy fist banged against the door of the shack. The forgotten glass in his hand wobbled precariously and tipped into his lap. The cheap golden honey wine hissed slightly as it burnt its way through his clothes. The warlock shrieked and leapt from the armchair. He waved his hand over the smoking stain and muttered several strange sounding words, mingled with a few more common curses under his breath. That was a mistake. His lap exploded in flames. Meloc screamed and ran with remarkable speed to the shack's bathing area – a wash basin and jug situated on the wooden shelf above a cracked chamber pot. Quickly, he threw the dust-laden, grimy water down the front of his faded, tarragon green tunic.

'I know someone's in here,' said a martial voice. 'We have orders to check every building. There's an escaped warlock in the city. Open this door now or we'll break it down!'

Meloc frowned as the water dripped noisily from his tunic onto the wooden floor of the shack. He groaned inwardly, took a deep breath, and whispered '*Alduir*.'

A flash of orange flames danced across the dim interior of the shack. The ageing spell was one of the most excruciatingly painful spells he could cast. Meloc covered his mouth with his hands as he felt every bone in his body break, retract, and then reset. His back collapsed forward as he shrunk, withered by age. His face elongated, his skin sagging from his skull. A trickle of sweat rolled down his forehead, which he wiped away with a clawlike hand. His spiky black hair faded to silver grey, sprouted across his head, and tumbled down his back. A full silver beard hung shaggily around his face as his bright blue magikful eyes faded to grey.

Meloc glanced at his reflection in the mirror and winked at it as he shuffled to the door.

'I'm coming young man. Young people these days have no respect for their elders,' he muttered crossly as he opened the door.

Two burly city militiamen blocked the doorway. They wore matching brown tabards bearing the white sheep seal of Welfasten over their mail coats. The Welfasten militia were known affectionately throughout Mercia as the *Sewelskil* or sheep soldiers.

Meloc stared at the sheep. The guards shifted uncomfortably as they crossed their arms to hide their hated emblems.

'Whoever you are, go away, and leave an old man in peace,' Meloc barked, wiping the front of his faded blue tunic down with a dripping, filthy rag. 'I don't want to talk to anyone. I have no friends, no family I care to talk too, and I don't want to be saved, sold anything, or otherwise interfered with.'

Meloc glared at the guards.

The taller guard looked down at the wet stain on the front of the old man's ragged woollen trousers. He screwed his face up in disgust.

'He's bepissed himself,' the guard said as he turned to his ginger partner. 'Helgods! old people are disgusting.'

The ginger-haired guard shook his head. 'By the grace of the Gods, I hope I never reach that age. I want to die a glorious death in battle. Not sittin' in my own pissin'.'

Meloc thrust his hands down the front of his trousers and began to scratch himself vigorously. 'Don't mind me. It's the crawlers,' he whined, 'they bite and itch like little daemons… Anyway, come on in if you must, and have a seat. I don't get that many visitors. Oh, and don't mind the mess.'

The two guards looked at each other in horror. 'Let's go,' the taller guard muttered, 'I'm not risking catching the crawlers, my wife would kill me.'

The ginger guard nodded in agreement, and they disappeared, ignoring Meloc's outstretched hand. Meloc smiled and waved them goodbye. He shut the door, slid the bolt over, and rested his back against the ancient wood. Then he whispered the dreaded counter spell, and his eyes glowed with amber sparks. Thousands of hot needles pierced his body. His hair and nails felt as if they were retracting back inside his skin. He slumped to the floor and bit his hand to stop him from crying out in pain, as his body realigned to its younger self.

Ten minutes later, the younger warlock crawled his way back to the ancient armchair. He needed to rest. Meloc settled back into the chair. He searched behind the cushion and smiled with relief as he found a small bottle filled with a red liquid. He was not sure how long the bottle had lain there or what it actually contained but he felt no magikal energy emanating from the bottle. Satisfied, he gulped the liquid and felt it burn its way to his stomach.

Somewhere in the distance, the city bells sounded. One long deep strike followed by three higher chimes. It was the thirteenth hour. He had two hours to petition the city chief before he presided over the court sessions in Baldor Tower.

Slowly, his body relaxed, and his eyes closed.

Meloc jolted awake.

He felt the shadow of a frostdrek glide unseen high in the hanging clouds of the afternoon sky across Welfasten. His eyes glowed with reflected fire as they reacted with the galdor trail left by the dragon. Welfasten was in danger from more than just the massing Dunmuir. He needed to warn the city chief to petition the King to unseal the dreaded 'Serpent's Breath,' the most powerful galdor infused weapons in Mercia or the kingdom would stand no chance against such forces.

The city bell stuck and Meloc counted its chimes: one deep chime, followed by a middle lighter chime. 'Oh faen!' he groaned. He had overslept. It was the fifteenth hour, and the court sessions would be starting. He would have to enter Baldor Tower when the Great Hall was filled with the accused, the galdorless, and the city guards. None of which would be keen to see an unmynstered, unsealed warlock walking amongst them.

Meloc stood up and sighed, his tired body unwilling to leave the safety of the galdorhus. However, he had travelled across the moorlands to warn the chief of his visions and could not stop now. Carefully, he covered his face with the hood of his cloak and slipped from the safe house.

The door rune glowed amber as the magikal seals reset and the house quietly faded away into the cityscape.

He hurried along the road which circled around following the interior city walls.

A door swung open, and a dishevelled farmer spilled from an inn, tankard held high in the air, as he tried to avoid spilling the ale as he tumbled over and landed unceremoniously on his bottom in the mud. Meloc side-stepped to avoid the drunk but as he passed by the man grabbed the end of his cloak.

'Y'ere, why don't 'ee stop an 'elp a poor man up? Are you

too good to help the likes of me or what?' The man snarled and tugged hard at the cloak.

Meloc swore and tried to free the cloak from the man's grasp. The man grabbed his leg and pulled. Meloc fell flat on his back and lay there winded and gasping for breath. His right foot throbbed painfully. 'Faen!' Meloc cursed his bad luck.

The man crawled on top of him and grasped Meloc by the cloak collar, lifting his head out of the dirt. The hood dropped from Meloc's face to reveal his pure white skin and cobalt eyes. The farmer stared at his companion's face for a full minute before realisation dawned.

The drunk leapt off Meloc, screaming as he rubbed his hands against his dirty brown trousers, 'Ee touched me, the daemonkin touched me.' He ran back into the public house shouting, 'I've been cursed – there's a daemon lying in the street!'

The public house burst into laughter.

'Pox on you all! I'm not makin' it up!' the farmer yelled.

'He's out there!'

'Calm down, you repugnant drunkard,' a voice growled as heavy footsteps approached the doorway.

Meloc recognised the heavily accented voice of the Wergend officer. Painfully, he crawled to his feet and limped into the alleyway between the inn and a butcher shop; its outside meat hooks hanging empty, its windows boarded shut.

'There is nothing here,' the officer announced.

'But he was, I swear it!' the farmer whined.

There was a loud crack, and the farmer flew past the alleyway, landing face first in the mud. Meloc watched as the Wergend officer put his foot on the back of the struggling man's neck, pushing his face deeper into the mud as he hissed,

'In future, do not waste the time of the Wergend. We are on a holy mission, to interfere with us is to choose a path of darkness and despair.'

The officer released the pressure. The farmer coughed, choking on the swallowed mud, and got shakily to his feet. He bowed his apologies to the officer and walked groaning and coughing down the road.

The Wergend officer was about to go back into the public house when he paused and stared straight into the darkness of the alleyway. Meloc pressed himself against the wooden panels of the butcher's shop.

In the distance, the werhounds howled as they picked up his scent. The howling grew louder and the Wergend officer marched off to meet the hounds.

Meloc breathed a sigh of relief. He pulled the hood down lower over his face, as he limped painfully towards Balder Tower.

The Tower dominated the Welfasten skyline and peered down upon its inhabitants with an air of cerebral contempt. It was four stories high, taller than any other building within the walled city and sparkled white in the midday sun. Each floor was marked by a series of small, shining windows which circled round the tower. A dome created from finely cut squares of glass sat on top of the tower. The sunlight hit the dome causing the rays of light to split, casting rainbows across the city. The old legends stated that whilst the city was protected by the rainbow arches it would never fall.

Balder Tower was the judicial centre of Welfasten and the outlying lands until they reached the foothills of the Witian mountains. Those prisoners fortunate enough to be brought to trial were tried in the Great Hall which occupied the ground floor. For one gold coin the denizens of Welfasten could enter and watch the proceedings. This was also where the magikborne trials were held. Those who were found guilty of crime or the unlawful use of magik were taken through an arched doorway at the back of the Great Room and disappeared.

'Oi serf!' a loud voice sneered at him.

Meloc stopped and peered up at the hall guard from inside the shadows of his hood. His heart raced and his casting hand began to tingle with unchecked galdor energy. Quickly, he thrust it down the front of his trousers.

The guard looked down at him in disgust.

'Can I help you… er…guardsmen,' Meloc asked.

'If you want to get into the Great Hall, you've got to pay the fee. It's one gold coin. Either pay up or get out!'

'Of course!' Meloc nodded, his hood falling further over his face. 'I've got one here somewhere, I'm sure,' he said helpfully as he rummaged around in the front of his trousers.

'Ah! Got it!' Meloc announced. He pulled a coin from his trousers and handed it to the guard. The guard took a step backwards, his arms firmly by his side.

'I'm not touching that!' the guard growled. 'Just put it in the box and piss off.'

Meloc bowed to the city guard and dropped the wooden coin into the box. The coin sounded dull as it hit the pile of metal coins.

The guard's eyes narrowed slightly. He moved towards the warlock.

Quickly, Meloc sidestepped the guard and slipped through the enormous oak doors which opened into the Great Hall.

The hall was a huge stone building with vaulted wooden

ceiling panels painted in green and gold. A row of stone columns ran down the centre of the hall, dividing the room in two. Rows of wooden benches filled each side of the room. The hall bustled with nervous energy as the cityfolk gathered, alarmed by reports of nearby fighting and death, they stood in small groups discussing how they would save the city from the Dunmuir hoarde.

Meloc limped up the left side of the hall, past rows of wooden benches, his eyes firmly fixed on the stone floor, trying to avoid any attention as he made his way to the front.

The front of the hall consisted of a raised wooden platform upon which sat a huge chair. The legs of the chair had been carved with spiral staircase reliefs which twisted around the legs. People ascended the staircase, their arms raised above their heads, mouths and eyes open wide. The chair design was meant to depict the democracy of Welfasten. The concept being that any citizen of the city could ascend to office and power. However, to the majority of the city, it looked as if the citizens were being crushed by the oppressive weight of provincial bureaucracy.

Above the chair, the flag of Welfasten hung limply, a green and white flash against the grey stone walls of the hall.

Meloc reached the front bench. The bench reserved for the well-dressed and worthy of the city.

He pulled down his hood and waited. Beads of sweat glistened across his forehead. His chest felt as if a great weight was crushing down upon him.

A child sitting to the right of the platform whispered to a well-dressed woman in a russet robe and matching cloak. The woman frowned and hushed the child. She patted a long plait of hair twisted with leather cord which framed her head like a golden crown. Her eyes fixed on the grand wooden door to the left of the platform as she waited for Chief Feitar to arrive.

The child shrunk back into the folds of its mother's dress as Meloc crossed his arms and glared at the empty wooden chair.

'It's a daemonkin,' a voice shrieked from across the Great Hall.

The woman screamed in terror and grabbed her child, almost smothering it with her semi-exposed, pale pink breasts. The people sitting on her bench leapt up as one. It overturned, clattering noisily against the stone floor. An elderly corpulent man, sleeping against the end of the bench, collapsed onto the floor, and shouted, 'The Dunmuir are here!'

A hall guard dropped his ceremonial silver topped spear and ran from the hall.

People looked at each other in confusion. Then ran as a herd to the double entrance doors. A little girl in a red gown clutching a ragdoll in her chubby brown fingers and began to cry as her brown eyes widened in terror. There was a loud shout as the sound of marching feet and martial orders cut through the chaos. From the corner of his eye, Meloc saw an elderly lady in grey mourning cloth, fall to the floor beneath the panicking feet.

'Scitte!' he swore as he sprang from his seat.

An unseen force pushed him forward onto his front. The force stood on his back growling in a low deep tone. Its claws digging into Meloc's back.

'Well, well, well, what have we here,' Captain Kasian snarled as he pulled Meloc by the hair, glaring into his face. 'Did you really think you could escape the blessed watch of the Wergend?'

Meloc gasped for breath as his heart pounded through his

ribs. 'You will let me speak to Chief Feitar or I will bring this building down around your feet.' The flames dancing in his eyes seared through the building's shadows as he shouted, '*Eburtu*' and the guards surrounding him flew into the air.

EIGHT

Name - Meloc
Location - Welfasten
Allegiance - The Mercian Warbands

The Wergend soldiers got to their feet and drew their swords.

'Approach the daemonkin with caution, who knows what ungodly spirits he may conjure,' Captain Kasian warned. 'Form the containing ring.'

The men formed a large circle around Meloc who lay panting on the stone floor, his eyes still betraying his magik. Shouts and barked orders mixed with the banging of swords on body armour, as the city militia swarmed into the Great Hall.

'Warlock,' shouted Kasian. 'We command you, in the name of Grand Master Heilagan the Saviour, desist!'

Meloc wrinkled his nose and eased himself slowly into a sitting position.

'I will only desist if I can speak to the chief. It is my right as a citizen of Mercia as decreed by the King,' Meloc stared up at the captain.

'Your rights will be decided upon by the Wergend Court when you are safely restrained,' Kasian growled pronouncing every syllable in the quick soft accent of southern Mercian.

'Well then, you had better step back,' Meloc grinned as he put the palm of his hand on the stone floor and whispered, '*Savtor fyr.*' Instantly, a curtain of black flames surrounded the warlock. A rush of heat radiated across the hall. The ring of Wergend guards gasped and began to shuffle backwards.

'Hold the circle,' Captain Kasian growled. 'Bring me the

chief before this estupido demonio destroys the whole city.'

A young militia messenger bowed and fled.

Moments later the door to the right of the hall opened and two huge city militiamen dressed in identical brown tabards emblazoned with a sheep motif strode through the doorway. Ignoring the Wergend soldiery, they took up position in front of the warlock. Two more guards filled the doorway towering over a grey hooded figure. The figure pulled down the hood of his cloak to reveal a scarlet woollen robe and two terrified deep blue eyes which darted around the room only to settle on the seated warlock.

Meloc nodded stiffly, as his cousin, Chief Feitar, reluctantly neared the raging flames.

The whole room blazed white with a blinding flash of lightning.

The chief screamed in terror. The city militiamen stood firm at their posts, their faces a stern mask of unswerving loyalty and devotion. The black flames evaporated leaving only drifts of black smoke which circled above their heads like thunderous clouds.

The warlock's eyebrows rose, and the corner of his mouth twitched but he continued to look firmly at the floor in front of Feitar's feet. He could feel his cousin's eyes burning into his back, but he said nothing. Feitar possessed a pathological hatred of the daemonkin and had vowed to rid Mercia of its wickedness.

Needless-to-say, Meloc liked to remind him of the many reasons he hated the magikborne every time they met.

'And what is so important you interrupted the Court Sessions and terrorised my people? Why did you not come to me in peace?' Feitar said loudly, two red spots on his insipid face betraying his anger.

'I would have done so, if I had not been thrown in prison and left to rot as soon as I entered the city,' Meloc replied.

'And can you blame me? You yourself have just shown everyone the dangers of magik,' Feitar glared at his cousin.

'I have not come to argue with you cousin, but to warn you. I sense myrkir lurking in the shadows gathering outside the city. Dunmuirlun has unsealed their forbidden magiks and are using them to destroy Mercia. I fear Stonefall Fortress may already have fallen and they look to Welfasten next. You must break the galdor seals and unleash the Serpent's Breath.'

Feitar's eyes flickered for an instant and then his face set in a frozen, angry smile. 'I cannot condone the use of magik in any circumstances. It is forbidden by treaty throughout the five kingdoms.'

A guard whispered to his neighbour.

Feitar's eyes narrowed and glanced at the worried faces of the militiamen. He frowned and shook his head sadly. 'Come into my office cousin and we will discuss your fears over a jug of finest Sunnan wine. You look terrible, by the way, do you know that?'

'And you look most corpulent cousin.' Meloc bowed, the corners of his mouth twitching.

A guard pressed the point of a sword into the small of his back. Meloc breathed a heavy sigh as he crawled to his feet and limped slowly from the Great Hall, surrounded by a guard of Wergend.

The chief swished his cloak around himself. 'Opulent hey? Well, I do like to maintain an appearance fit for one in my position. This cloak was presented to me by King Athelstan himself; finest lamb's wool from the Witian mountain herds,' he said as he caressed the soft material lovingly. Feitar turned to follow his cousin from the hall only stopping to whisper to the captain who was standing impatiently outside the office door.

'Kasian, deal with this. The warlock is obviously quite deranged and suffering from some sort of paranoia caused by the galdor sickness. The use of magik has terrible effects on the mind, don't you know.'

'Yes, Chief Feitar,' Kasian put his fist to his chest and bowed. Feitar waved his hand at the Wergend officer and walked majestically back to his office.

'The prisoner must be cured of his magikal infliction. Prepare a protected cart to transfer the prisoner to Eldingar Tower for his unmynistering,' Captain Kasian ordered the Wergend guard standing next to him, then slipped silently into the Chief's Office.

The Chief's Office was only slightly smaller than the Great Hall. At the far end of the room stood a solitary oaken table, its legs carved into tree trunks which sprouted branches that wrapped around each leg and twisted around the edges of the table. The top of the table had been polished so brightly that it caught the sun rays as they shone through the narrow windows and cast dancing shadows across the room. Above the table hung a series of unlit red pottery lamps with serpentine faces and hollowed eyes.

Meloc shivered as he felt the eyes follow him across the room.

A guard hit the backs of Meloc's knees with a heavy iron sword, caught off-guard he fell forward onto the floor matting. A heavy boot pressed against his back, pinning him to the floor.

'Hold the daemonkin firm!' Kasian ordered. He took a large wooden seal and small glass vial from the shoulder bag he carried hidden beneath his cloak. He poured the liquid into the seal and said the First Wergend Evocation: The Call to Protect. The liquid bubbled as it sunk into the seal and the citrus smell of willowing flowers seeped across the room. The Wergend officer knelt next to the prostrate warlock and grabbed hold of his sweaty black hair, lifting his face from the matting.

'Get away from me!' Meloc shouted and tried to kick at the guards, but his legs were held firm. Kasian pressed the seal into the warlock's forehead. There was a sizzling sound as the seal burnt into his forehead. Meloc screamed in pain and struggled as he felt his galdor connection fade. His energy dissipated and his body became unresponsive to his commands.

Kasian felt the warlock go floppy under his grip and dropped him onto the floor matting.

NINE

Name - Kasian, Captain in the Order of the Wergend
Location - The Office of the Chief, Welfasten
Allegiance - The Mercian Warbands

A loud knock at the door startled the warlock awake. He turned his head slightly. Kasian nodded. Two Wergend guards moved towards the warlock. One grabbed Meloc's shoulders and pulled him upwards onto his knees, while the other tied his hands tightly behind his back. The warlock swayed as the effects of the First Evocation dulled his senses.

A heavy knock on the office door broke the silence. The Wergend guardsmen looked towards the sound, as their bodies stiffened like coiled springs ready to attack. Kasian's hand moved towards his sword. His brown eyes narrowed. No amber halo illuminated the door. He shook his head and the guards relaxed. Chief Feitar, who had been moving stealthily towards the safety of his desk, breathed a sigh of relief. He rearranged the tapestry hanging behind his desk and then sat down, busily unrolling a scroll, and pretending to read it.

Kasian looked across at the chief, his expression betraying a mixture of distaste and disappointment. Feitar looked up from his desk and glared at the Wergend officer. Kasian stumbled backwards, caught by the force of his glare, and frowned.

The office door flew open as the Lord of the Eastern Warband strode into the room. Kasian saluted, banging his right fist against the left side of his mail coat as the battle-scarred warlord marched past him.

'Ah, Haukar you have arrived at last… I was worried that

your convoy might have been attacked and you had been left for dead somewhere. The Dunmuir advanced forces seem to have crossed through the mountain border yet again. They are as ticks on sheep's wool, an annoyance which interferes with city trade,' Feitar declared angrily.

The warlord bowed before the chief. The clouds of smoke and ash which were circulating around the Great Hall, had speckled his iron mail coat with tiny grey flecks, and he brushed them off onto the office floor. Feitar watched in horror as the flakes fell across the fresh matting. His smile became fixed, and his right eye began to twitch.

Haukar's hazel eyes narrowed. 'We experienced a slight problem with some Dunmuir foot soldiers, Feitar. However, they hindered us little and fell to the might of the Eastern blades.'

Haukar turned his sharp features to Meloc, his domed iron helmet accentuating his hawkish features. 'Talking of rabble, what have we here?'

He grabbed the kneeling warlock by the chin and lifted his face upwards, squinting at his features.

'Meloc, still wandering around unmynistered, I see?' Haukar turned to Captain Kasian. 'I thought the Wergend picked up the last of the free magikal creatures in your summer sweep? How did this one escape?'

Captain Kasian blushed red under his dented helmet. 'He was caught and transported to Eldingar Tower with the rest of the Witian Mountain magikborne for his unmynistering. I can only assume it failed.' He glared down at Meloc.

'What can I say, my Lords? I must be protected by the Gods,' the warlock interjected.

Kasian's hand curled into a fist, and he fought to contain

the urge to punch the smirking, blasphemous warlock in the face.

There was another knock at the door.

'Come in, come in!' the chief answered.

Meloc yawned loudly and shifted his weight. His eyes caught Kasian's for a second. The officer gasped. The seal on the warlock's forehead was already failing and Kasian could see a faint galdor glow return to the warlock's form.

The chamber door opened, and Councillor Hundar entered, his cloak brushing against the grime-ridden floor, causing more dust clouds to rear up and linger menacingly in the airless room. Behind him, Azrael, the appointed Warlock Envoy to the King's Council slipped in, his cobalt eyes darting from Meloc to the surrounding officials. They bowed to the chief, and Lord Haukar but ignored the Wergend. It was a deliberate smite on the Wergend order, but Kasian was used to such things, fighting an unseen holy war brought the order few friends.

A shower of disturbed ash fell on Meloc. He sneezed loudly and wiped his nose on a dirty-looking sleeve.

'Welcome Councillor Hundar. What news from the Star Council?' Feitar asked, settling himself into an enormous oak chair, its back carved with branches bursting with leaves, twisting around his face. It did not look like a particularly comfortable chair. Kasian and the other advisers sat on the lower chairs simply made from two diagonal planks of unpolished wood bisecting each other.

Hundar cleared his throat. 'I have no good news to report, I'm afraid. Stonefall Fortress fell two nights hence. The Dunmuir soldiers are pouring through the mountain passes. The Northeasternlands are all but lost.'

'I told you so,' Meloc interjected.

Every eye in the room turned to the kneeling warlock.

'And there's a dragon too,' Meloc announced.

'Silence warlock!' Haukar ordered and struck him across the face. Meloc fell forward but the Wergend guards pulled him back onto the heels of his worn boots. A trail of blood trickled from a cut in the corner of his lip.

Azrael shifted his feet uneasily and glanced towards Hundar. The councillor shook his head.

'This warlock is the prisoner and property of the Wergend Order. You will not touch him again.' Kasian's quiet voice betrayed his anger.

'Yes, and the Wergend Order are doing so well. I see you have managed to capture one of the magikborne when the whole country is being invaded by thousands of magikally enhanced monsters. Go back to your temple and leave this war to real soldiers,' Haukar hissed.

'Do not underestimate the power of the Wergend,' Kasian growled, his hand reaching for his sword.

'Oh silence, both of you!' Chief Feitar commanded. 'We do not have time for your petty squabbles. If the Northeast has fallen, we have lost the mountain trade routes, it will ruin Welfasten.'

A heavy silence descended on the room. Haukar and Kasian stood glaring at each other, while Feitar took out a leather backed ledger and began to make a series of calculations.

'Ahem…' Hundar cleared his throat. 'Can we get back to the King's orders, please.'

'Of course,' said Feitar, not looking up from his ledger.

'The King has sent out messengers to summon the combined Mercian forces to Fastness Fortress, but the messengers are being attacked and the call is slow at crossing Mercia. The East under Lord Haukar,' he bowed slightly to the warlord, 'have been charged with disrupting the enemy's march across Mercia to provide time for the refugees to flee the fighting and the defences to form. Lord Vestar of the Westhelm is still confined to his sickbed and the Western warband is in disarray and will not be gathered at marching strength until the week's end. The remains of the Northern band are trickling down from the mountainside to join with the Southern in forming a defensive line south of the Vimur river.' He gestured towards Haukar.

'We rode past the Southern not three days ago. They are gathered on the banks of the Vimur and building wooden defences ready to defend Fastness,' Haukar nodded.

'But Welfasten is north of the Vimur. And what are we to do, just sit here and burn?' Chief Feitar exploded as he thumped the desk with his fist. His silver inkpot, soldered into the globe with a topper carved into the shape of a flying Stryx, overturned. Ink ran across his desk and trickled down the decorative carvings on its legs. It was a warning from the Gods. Blood would run free, and everyone gathered in the office would be affected. Kasian and Meloc's eyes met.

Quickly, Kasian turned away from the warlock's gaze.

Councillor Hundar took a step backwards. 'The defensive line is only a temporary strategic measure, while we regroup and plan our offensive. We, of the Star Council, are confident the Dunmuir will never drive that far south. They will be stopped at Dreagur Tower, as they will be unable to navigate the Grey Marsh, now all the stone bridges have been removed.'

'Well, that should stop their dreks turning the city to ash

then,' Meloc commented.

'You idiot,' Feitar screamed in Hundar's face and hurled the wine jug at the councillor.

The councillor sidestepped the bottle with remarkable speed and edged towards the office door.

TEN

Name - Chief Feitar
Location - Welfasten
Allegiance - The Mercian Warbands

Chief Feitar looked at the cowering councillor and swore again as he flopped back into his chair and drained the last dregs of his wine. It had taken him over a decade to reach the chiefdom of even this forgotten backwater, when by right and ability, he should have ascended to the Star Council at Fastness and become a councillor to the King. His whole career had been blighted by the curse of having a daemonkin in the family. He glared at the dirty bloody warlock sitting on the floor in front of him and shook his head. For the hundredth time he wondered how he could possibly be related to such a monster.

The warlock looked up at Feitar and winked.

The chief felt a silent rage roar through his body as a red mist rushed across his thoughts. He was the most important man in the Midheim, he controlled the trade route from the Northlands to Fastness Fortress and the people of Welfasten idolised him. Obviously, the King felt threatened by his popularity and power. This was why the King had left Welfasten to the Dunmuir. Athelstan wanted Welfasten destroyed, and his rival murdered.

Feitar frowned and twisted the emerald ring dominating his right hand as he quickly assessed his options. To leave Welfasten with the gold he had acquired, as an additional supplement for his work overseeing the collection of taxes, would be impossible. He smiled slightly. Hidden at the back of the ale cellar of the Great Hall were six sealed barrels of finest Sunnan wine, each filled to the brim with gold coins. It would take a team of horses to move them south to the safety of Fastness Fortress and that would raise questions which he did not wish to answer. The King had spies everywhere and his enemies regularly spread malicious rumours at court about the entrepreneurial nature of his business dealings.

However, the roads to the north and east were deadly. When the wind turned southerly the thunderdrums of the Dunmuir forces, which were massing on the Witian lowlands, could be heard within the city walls. If he fled Welfasten, he risked meeting the roving Dunmuir forces and could be killed. While moving to the safety of the West would risk him being labelled a coward by his enemies at court and have his land and coin confiscated by the serpents of the Star Council.

No, he was safer behind the strong stone walls of Welfasten.

Feitar stared at Meloc, who was now sitting nonchalantly with his legs stretched in front of him, a bored expression on his unnaturally attractive face. Feitar was sure he had spelled himself to look prettier than he should have been.

Slowly, the beginnings of a plan began to formulate in the cunning, animalistic recesses of his mind. Feitar signalled for his maidservant to fill his glass once more and silently congratulated himself on his cunning.

He knew how to get rid of all his problems in one move.

The thunderdrums began to sound in the distance. This time they seemed louder; the horde was coming nearer. He had to act now before it was too late.

Councillor Hundar jumped and looked towards the narrow office window in horror.

'You!' Feitar said pointing to the councillor, 'Get out now!

You've delivered your message.'

'But chief, the King wants an update on your munitions and provisions,' the councillor frowned, his eyes darting about the office hoping for support from his fellows.

'Helgods! Just get out of my sight, you whimpering dog!' Feitar screamed and thumped his fist on the desk. A mountain of scrolls slid from the desktop and fell onto the stone floor.

Hundar bowed and ran from the room. Azrael hesitated for a moment and quickly followed his master.

'That's right, run away! Fastness scum!' Feitar shouted after them.

'Well don't just stand, there pick up my scrolls, you idiot!' he shouted at his maidservant. She bowed and fell to her knees trying to catch the scrolls as they scattered across the floor.

'The King has been ill-advised. If Welfasten falls the whole of the Nordheim will fall too and his southern defences will collapse under the might of the Dunmuir onslaught,' Feitar growled.

Lord Haukar shifted his feet uneasily.

'I will not stand by while Mercia is in danger. The Welfasten militia will defend Mercia and the King, and we will fight for our survival with fire, iron, and blood,' Feitar said as he stood and signalled his servant to strap a sword belt around his enormous girth.

Haukar stiffened. 'The men of the East have never run from any battle, Feitar.'

'I see,' said Feitar drawing his sword and waving it wildly around the office. The maidservant scurried behind his desk. 'So, what say you? Will the men of the East join with the city militia on a mission of almost certain death to protect Mercia?'

'The men of the East fear no death,' Haukar growled, his

sword hand resting on the hilt of his sword.

Feitar smiled. 'I knew I could rely on you Haukar. We must combine our forces and take the fight to the Dunmuir.'

'But what of the King's orders?' Haukar queried. 'My orders are to harry and disrupt their supply lines, to create chaos among the Dunmuir ranks, until the Mercian offensive begins.'

'The King is still asking for munition numbers and planning the defence of Fastness. By the time the offense of Mercia has been planned, there will be no Mercia left to defend. We must attack the Dunmuir now and grant the King time to organise the Mercian defences. You, yourself heard Hundar, the King needs time to organise and mobilize his troops.'

'Hmm,' said the elderly warlord stroking his plaited grey beard. 'It is true. The call to arms proceeds too slowly.'

'Precisely,' said Feitar triumphantly. 'And it is the Eastern warband's duty to harry and hinder the enemy. Surely an attack on the Dunmuir forces will do so?'

'That is true, but I only have a quarter of the warband here. Half my men are at Steinnhelm Fortress lest the Dunmuir turn their attention eastwards. While the other quarter have entered the Hall of the exalted fallen,' Haukar said shaking his head sadly. 'My eldest son, Hauk the Restless, fell at the attack on our Northern Outpost not one week hence.'

'I am so sorry, my Lord. I did not know. May he find peace with his exalted ancestors in the Valholl. Let us join together and avenge his death or join him in eternal glory.'

Haukar nodded. 'You have the support of the East, Feitar,' he vowed.

Meloc tutted loudly and muttered something under his breath.

'However, if we are to meet them in the field, we must first weaken their forces. We must cut their galdor supply lines. Without access to the magik of galdor crystals, their forces will weaken and then we can meet them as equals on the battlefield. As I stated at the last city meeting in Fastness, if the Dunmuir enter the Kristal Cave and retrieve the Serpent's Breath, our hidden galdor munitions, we are all doomed,' Haukar stated.

'The King has surrounded himself with cowardly fools. Your council was correct. Us men of war must band together and battle to save the kingdom even if we are greatly outnumbered and our death is almost certain. But I have a plan to save Mercia and it is brilliant,' Feitar announced.

'But this is treason,' Kasian stated as he stared suspiciously at the chief.

'This is stupid, even by your standards,' Meloc said, shaking his head.

Feitar's eyes flickered towards the militiamen guarding the office and nodded slightly. The militia edged around the chamber wall towards the Wergend guards.

'Lest you forget, the Wergend answer to a higher power. Do not lay a finger on my men,' Kasian said in a low, threatening voice. There was a flash of metal. Kasian gulped as the cold point of an iron sword pressed against his throat. A trickle of blood ran down his neck.

'Yes, we all know where the Wergend loyalties lie,' Feitar hissed. 'Disarm them. Lock those two in the cells,' he said pointing to the Wergend guards. 'We will take the captain with us.'

Kasian's hands were tied behind his back, and he was forced to kneel in front of the chief.

'Wergennis will punish you,' he growled.

'I doubt it. The gods will reward me for my loyalty to the King and Mercia. You hide behind the veil of your religious vows like cowards,' Feitar said.

'I have never seen the Wergend in battle,' Haukar nodded.

'We fight for…' Kasian was cut short as the chief kicked him in the stomach and he fell forward onto the floor.

Feitar's mouth twitched in delight and then instantly transformed into a frown. He stepped over Kasian and put his hand on Haukar's shoulder. 'Together we will turn this city into an impregnable fortress. A base upon which to destroy the Dunmuir supply lines and stop their advance. Welfasten will become a beacon of hope in the fight against the Dunmuir.'

'But what of the Northlands and the refugees?' Haukar queried.

'They will not be forgotten, my Lord. While most of the Dunmuir army is kept busy here, we will send a small elite force into the very heartlands of their kingdom. If they can destroy the Spring of Rapture, the flow of galdor into Dunmuir will cease. Without magik their society will crumble and may even dissolve into war, while our combined forces can meet them in glorious battle as mere mortal men and rout their humbled forces.'

Meloc raised one fine black eyebrow in surprise.

The mountain border was virtually impregnable and the Dunmuir reserve that lurked in the shadows thrown up by the mountains were rumoured to be many thousands strong.

'And that would be a suicide mission,' Meloc almost laughed at the ridiculousness of the plan.

'No, it's a fine plan,' Haukar commented. 'And if we have the honour of dying in battle, so be it.'

'Speak for yourself,' Meloc remarked.

'Oh, you'll be fine,' Feitar smiled down at him.

The warlock stared back at him; his jaw hung loosely in shock. 'Regrettably, I was never chosen to enter the Tower of Fregna and be trained as a Sealed Warlock. I do not have the skill. Send Azrael instead.'

'Do not worry,' Feitar smirked. 'I have taken your lack of ability into consideration. We will enter the Kristal Cave and unseal the Serpent's Breath but if you fail, Azrael will be your replacement.' He turned to the two militiamen guarding the office door. 'Confine our Fastness guests to quarters.'

The two guards bowed and disappeared from the room.

'But Chief Feitar, this is blasphemy, you will condemn our souls to hel,' Captain Kasian hissed.

'Oh... don't worry captain, I will leave the religious penance to your expertise. You will go with him and keep the monster in check, so to speak. No offense, cousin.'

'But the Galdor Weapons were hidden with ancient magik,' Meloc growled. 'Sealed with the greatest spell ever created by the Grand Warlock Gaderel himself, just before his disappearance. If you cast the spell wrong, it will trigger the curse of the mountain upon you.'

'Do not speak the name of that abomination in my presence. When he created the Star of Mercia and banished the blackness from the night sky, he tainted the work of the gods,' Kasian glared at Meloc.

'Don't look at me!' Meloc replied. 'I wasn't even born then!'

'Enough!' shouted Feitar. 'Regrettably, we must fight magik with magik, unsealing the Serpent's Breath is our only chance to defend Welfasten and defeat the Dunmuir.' Feitar stared down at the Wergend officer. He had no interest in the unsealing of the weapons but if he could get Lord Haukar, the dregs of the Eastern warband, the interfering Wergend unit, and his accursed cousin away from his city, he was positive that with his charm and position he could create an accord with the Dunmuir. He would be willing to pay one or maybe two barrels of gold for the privilege.

'So, can I go back to prison now?' Meloc asked as he and Kasian were hauled onto their feet.

ELEVEN

Name - Meloc

Location - Kristal Cave, Kristal Mountain, Southern Witian Mountains

Allegiance - The Mercian Warbands

The sides of the rocky chasm rose vertically, their tops lost in the greyness of the hanging clouds. Through the millennia the quiet currents of the Witian river had carved its way through the soft stone delving ever deeper into the under earth, becoming faster and more treacherous.

Over time, a rough zig-zag path had been etched onto the rocky sides of the cliff by generations of pilgrims seeking the blessing of the Witian river spirit and a cure for their various ailments or failing luck. The path was lined with miniature terracotta figurines each depicting a pilgrim's sorrow. Some had delicately carved daggers sticking out from various parts of their bodies; a realistic representation of the pain from injuries or disease. Other figurines represented wishes. A woman cradling a new-born baby in her arms or a man holding an empty bowl, begging the river spirit to fill it.

Occasionally, a falling boulder or collapsing rock disrupted the path or left only a toe width's worth of ledge. This was a pilgrimage only undertaken by the dying and the desperate.

Meloc reached the bottom of the path and wiped the dust covered sweat from his forehead. His black hair sticking upwards in latent terror. Quickly, he blinked the flames from his eyes and the amber aura that surrounded his hands and feet disappeared.

'You climb well for a civilian,' Kasian commented as he

jumped the last few feet of the path and landed nimbly next to Meloc.

'It's a gift,' Meloc replied, the corner of his mouth twitching.

There was a flash of brilliant white light, followed by a rush of wind which stirred the settled dust, as Azrael and Chief Feitar appeared. Meloc coughed and took a step backwards covering his eyes with his arm as the dust bit into his face.

'Have a care!' Kasian yelled, seizing the warlock by the tunic collar, and pulling him back onto the path.

Meloc looked down at the rushing blue river and shivered as he sensed something malevolent lurking in the shadows, hungrily watching the convoy.

'Secure the prisoners,' Chief Feitar ordered.

Meloc and Kasian were thrown against the rockface, and their hands bound.

'How are we expected to tread such a path without the use of our hands?' Kasian growled.

'Oh, I'm sure you will be just fine,' Feitar half-smiled. 'Azrael keep to my side, in case there is any danger, or I need to return to Welfasten on urgent business.'

Rough hands pushed the prisoners along the rocky path which twisted around the river's edge. Meloc fell forward onto his knees.

'Helgods!' he swore as he was dragged to feet and looked down to see a blood-rimmed hole had appeared in his ancient grey woollen trousers.

'Do not call upon the daemon gods,' Kasian warned, 'in case they find you and bring bad luck down upon you.'

'Really?' Meloc replied raising an eyebrow, 'I think they already have.'

'You should not take religious matters so lightly daemonkin, repent now and there may be time to save your soul,' Kasian said. The sound of a whip cracked through the air and Kasian collapsed onto the path.

'Silence traitors!' the heavyset guard ordered, his whip dangling from his hand. He raised it again.

The Wergend officer had been stripped of his armour and weaponry. The whip had cut straight through his light blue tunic and into his back. Kasian staggered to his feet. His face was flushed red and sweaty, but he said nothing as he followed the line of soldiers.

Meloc shook his head. Those called to the Order of the Wergend were chosen by the gods and it was not wise to injure them.

A blinding white light flashed through his brain. The pathway before him darkened and filled with the frightened faces of the convoy's soldiers screaming in terror as rocks reigned down upon them. Meloc stumbled blindly forwards. His vision cleared and sweat poured down his brow and stuck his undershirt to his back, as he realised this was a premonition. The expedition to the Kristal Cave would end in bloodshed. It had been doomed before it had even begun…

Before dawn, Chief Feitar had hobbled into the Tower courtyard in his woollen dressing gown and announced that he would be unable to ride with the expedition. However, Haukar had insisted that the chief accompany them to the Kristal Cave. Feitar had paled and twisted under the elderly warlord's gaze but his prostrations of a bad case of gout had fallen on unsympathetic ears. The expedition would only proceed if jointly led by the two militia leaders. Reluctantly, the injured chief had agreed to come, provided he was accompanied by the court warlock.

Lord Haukar did not trust the chief enough to leave him behind.

Further along the riverbank the nature of the river changed. The cliffs drew closer, frowning down upon the straggling convoy as they stood for a moment, watching in awe, as the frothing water thundered angrily through its cage. The very air felt heavy. The blue sky covered by a permanent veil of greying mist.

In places, the opulent blueness of the raging river was marred by darker shadows; a suggestion of the menace that lay in its uncharted depths.

Hidden within the dark chasm shadows, granite boulders sat at the river's edge like faceless monsters patiently watching and waiting. Occasionally, the dark shadows were banished as pale angular rocks obtruded from the chasm wall, sparkling seductively with the iridescent lights of galdor crystals. Meloc felt the heat radiating from the shimmering stones and sensed their power. He glanced over his shoulder at the line of grim-faced Wergend guards behind him and quickly pulled away from the inviting stones. He had no doubt any unauthorised absorption of galdor would be dealt with severely.

Captivated by their beauty, Azrael reached out to touch one of the galdor intrusions streaking through the rocky wall. Meloc shook his head and hissed a warning at the entranced warlock. Azrael stared vacantly into the opalescence. Slowly, he raised one hand and touched the enticing stone. The cobalt tones in his eyes turned amber, throwing burnished shadows against the grey as the galdor energy coursed through his body.

The flat blade of a heavy sword thudded against his outstretched arm. Azrael broke from his trance and yelped in pain.

'There will be no daemonry here, warlock. You may be protected…' Lord Haukar eyed Councillor Hundar with distaste as he whispered, 'but use magik without my leave and I will see you dead.'

Azrael clutched his arm and cast a furtive glance towards the councillor who seemed oblivious to the incident.

Meloc shuffled onwards following the river's path. No fish or waterfowl inhabited these waters. The river had been corrupted. He shivered in the biting wind as he sensed the river's darkness; its rage and hatred slowly infecting the little convoy.

The river's path ended in a wall of shining rock.

The expedition stopped to watch the river as it disappeared, falling through a huge limestone fissure in the chasm floor.

The ground started to groan.

The convoy grabbed handholds in the rocky walls as the mountain floor shuddered. Loose rocks tumbled down the vertical chasm sides, crashing against the hardstone floor, sending clouds of stone powder into the damp air. A jagged shard of opalescent galdor hit Feitar. He stumbled forward.

'Help me! I'm dying!' Feitar screamed as he clutched the back of his head, blood oozing through his fingers. He collapsed onto a lichen covered mossy boulder, while his harassed maidservant raced up and wrapped his head tightly in a cream bandage ripped from her underskirts.

Meloc watched as the drips of blood mixed with the falling ice-tinged spray and was taken by the raging waters.

It was the second ominous sign.

The violent shaking increased. An angry rumbling came from beneath the riverbed as the trapped river exploded though a gaping black cave carved from the mountainside. The arc of water fell onto the lower course of the river which circled the foot of the Kristal Mountain. A storm of icy droplets fell across the convoy.

The expedition seized their opportunity and raced through the dripping air towards a little cave, hidden within a crack in the chasm walls.

'This was a bad idea. We should not enter the underground passages. The river is angry. I can feel it. It doesn't want us here,' Meloc whispered as he backed away from the cave.

Feitar glared at the anxious warlock. 'How dare you council me! I am a city chief, and you will do well to remember it!'

Lord Haukar smiled slightly and turned to his men. 'Men… help the warlock into the cave!'

Two sour-faced warbandmen grabbed Meloc and threw him into the small cave. The warlock landed heavily against the damp floor. Azrael rolled his eyes and tutted as he quietly helped the warlock to his feet using his good arm.

Meloc grabbed his shoulder. 'You know this place seeks blood.'

Azrael shook his head, worried cobalt eyes staring straight at Meloc. 'For once in your life just do as you are told, or you will have us both killed.'

Meloc sighed and nodded reluctantly as he looked around the cave. Lord Haukar stood, arms folded, watching them from the mouth of the cave. Even being seen talking to a fellow warlock could bring claims of conspiracy and treason. Meloc was in no doubt that such judgement would be swift and deadly.

They marched through the cave and into a chamber cut from the very mountain itself. The chamber pulsated with the shimmering opalescence of galdor crystals. The presence of primordial magik was so strong, it was overpowering, almost tangible. Meloc shivered as an unknown shadow walked across his soul and galdor pulsed through his body. The voice of his old potion master's spoke clearly through his thoughts.

'Well, well, young master Meloc, reading again? Do not study your forbidden texts too hard,' the Master smiled. 'Yes, I was young and eager once, but to follow the path of spellkraft will only lead to death, for magik will always require a sacrifice.'

Meloc sighed to himself; back in the days of his apprenticeship, he had not realised that he would be the sacrifice.

He was rudely jolted back to the present as two damp warbandmen dragged him to the back of the cave, towards a rough limestone sarcophagus, which glowed in tones of amber through the darkness. An image of an ancient man with a long beard dangling to his waist and wild, wavy hair which had been cropped at his shoulders was carved onto the tomb. Two troubled, deeply lined eyes stared up at Meloc from beneath a frowning forehead.

'This sarcophagus hides the Serpent's Breath, the mighty Galdor Weapons of Mercia. Only five of the most important members of the Star Council know of its location,' Feitar announced resting a mutton-like thigh against the corner of the stone.

'So, who told you about it?' Meloc asked.

'Silence!' Feitar snapped. 'Just because I am not an official member of the Star Council, it does not mean I am not one of the King's closest advisers.

'Er… actually, I think it does,' Councillor Hundar replied. 'Are you sure this is wise?'

Meloc glanced at Azrael who shook his head and silently backed away from the effigy.

'Why is there an image of the Grand Master upon this tomb?' Meloc frowned. 'I thought his body has yet to be found?'

'Does that really matter?' the chief replied. He turned to the heavyset guard, 'Prepare our guests for entry into the passages to receive the weapons.'

The guards seized Meloc, Azrael, and Kasian and forced them to kneel, facing the chief.

'Unhand me!' Azrael hissed, 'I am Warlock to the Royal Court. You have no right to do this. I will report you to…'

'Silence magik-scum!' the guard ordered, his hand reaching for his whip. Azrael bit his lip and stared at the rocky floor.

'So, which warlock are we to use, chief?' Haukar enquired.

A slow smile spread across Feitar's wide face. He paused and smoothed his straggling chin hairs with a grey gloved hand. 'It pains me greatly but Azrael, as a Sealed Warlock, will possess greater spellkraft to protect the kingdom. Whereas my beloved cousin, even though similarly cursed, is ungifted with magik. For the good of Mercia, I will have to send my own flesh.'

'What!' Meloc shouted his voice echoing through the caves. 'I am not ungifted, and I came to you to try to protect the country.'

'Yes, and Mercia thanks you for your service,' Feitar replied and signalled to the city militiamen standing by the sarcophagus. They pushed at the lid. It slid from the coffin and crashed onto the floor. Two city militiamen peered into the tomb.

'My chief, there are steps within,' the elder militiaman stated, sweeping a flaming torch across the entrance.

There was a whoosh as trapped foul air escaped its tomb and filled the cave with a clawing sulphur-tinged gas. A loud crack echoed around the cave as a jagged, black tear ran across the slab.

The effigy broke in two.

The warlocks gasped in horror at the effigy as its eyelids opened to reveal eyes inlaid with sapphire gemstone eyes, which cast tinted blue shadows across the cave.

'Oh… and Captain Kasian, you had better join him. Obviously, you do not wish him to access the greatest magikal weapons in Mercian history without Wergend supervision,' the chief announced.

Kasian glanced towards Feitar in surprise. 'I will not help you. These are forbidden weapons. They are cursed with magik.'

'This is not a good idea cousin,' Meloc hissed. 'A curse has been triggered. I can feel it. We will be entering our doom.'

'Meloc… always so dramatic,' the chief stated. He turned to the guards, 'Untie their hands and here… you might need this to put the Galdor Weapons in.' He threw Kasian his shoulder bag.

The Wergend officer slipped the bag over his shoulder, 'And what about my sword and shield. Who knows what beasts dwell down there?'

'I am not an unreasonable man. Give him his shield,' Feitar ordered. 'And you girl!' he said pointing to his maidservant, 'bring me my seat and blankets… lots of blankets. It's damn chilly in here.'

Sergeant Slater, a tall, dirt-stained militiaman tossed Kasian his shield and pulled his tabard back to reveal Kasian's sword hanging from his belt.

'Give me my sword back!' Kasian shouted and leapt at the man but was restrained by four grinning guardsmen.

The two militiamen standing nearest to the sarcophagus began to cough, their faces turned ashen grey as a blackness spread through their veins. They clawed at their throats trying to scream, however their gurgling sounds brought no aid, and a trail of blackened blood began to pour from their eyes and mouths.

The surrounding men hurriedly ran to the edges of the cave, tying their scarves around their noses for protection from the escaping poison.

'Quick! Throw them down the hole and seal the tomb… it's poisoned!' Haukar ordered, rushing forward with his men as they tried to reposition the broken lid.

'Unhand me. I follow no orders but those of my god. You will be punished for touching the Wergend!' Kasian shouted as two warbandmen dragged him towards the sarcophagus and threw him headfirst down the broken steps and into the darkness. Seconds later there was a heavy thump as his body landed on the passage floor. A low growl echoed from deep within the rock but was lost amid the chaos as the cave began to shake. Fault cracks ran across its roof and walls as black dust began to fall on the company.

Feitar looked up at the roof of the cave in alarm.

'It's the curse. I warned you,' Meloc whispered.

Feitar shrugged off his blanket and grabbed Meloc by the

face, squeezing his flesh under his fingers, 'Well, you had better be quick then cousin, when you have the weapons, we will lower a rope. Once we have the Serpent's Breath, we will get you both out, you have my word,' Feitar smiled.

'This is a mistake! Get away from me!' Meloc screamed as the warbandmen approached him.

A heavy force hit him from behind and he tumbled into the sarcophagus. Meloc's last image before the lid was replaced was of his cousin's flushed face staring down at him.

TWELVE

Name - Meloc

Location - Beneath the Kristal Cave, Kristal Mountain

Allegiance - The Mercian Warbands

'Get off me, daemonkin,' Kasian growled. His bruised face touched by the last flickers of light filtering through the broken sarcophagus.

Meloc half-smiled, his landing had been softer than he had expected. Perhaps the Wergend were not as useless as the tavern graffiti stated. He rolled off the officer and stretched, testing his limbs for signs of damage.

'Let us find the galdor weapons and leave this cursed place,' Kasian said as he squinted through the darkness.

'You don't really think that heap of cow dung, Feitar, is going to let us walk free once we give him the weapons, do you? We need to find a way out of here and leave. Welfasten City is lost,' Meloc stood, his hands on his hips, staring defiantly at the officer.

Kasian shook his head.

'Chief Feitar gave us his word. He is appointed by the King. I trust him over the serpent's tongue of a daemonkin. Save your words, warlock, we will complete this mission and then report back to Fastness. You will be presented before the Domur Court. If you perform well, I will speak on your behalf.

'Thanks!' Meloc retorted. 'I'm sure that will persuade the Domur, not to send me to Eldingar to be unmynstered again.

'Wergennis' will, will prevail in all things,' Kasian stated.

Meloc rolled his eyes.

'It is best not to make light of the judgement of the gods,'

Kasian said, shaking his head. He rummaged through his leather satchel and produced a metal box sealed with the knotted cross of the Order of the Wergend.

Meloc watched the officer suspiciously.

'There is a passage ahead of us,' Kasian pointed into the darkness, 'but I do not know if any traps were laid to protect the weapons.' He opened the box and took out a white candle. The candle was bigger than his forefinger and infused with galdor dust. He placed the candle in the metal ring inside the box.

'Don't light it,' Meloc whispered. 'It will attract that which hides in the shadows and seeks out the light.'

'I do not take orders from daemons,' Kasian growled and passed his hand over the candle. A brilliant ball of white light radiated from the candle to reveal a narrow passageway hewn through the sandstone. The sides of the tunnel were pale cream and crisscrossed with deep gouges. The floor was greyer and comprised of a layer of compressed powdered stone which rippled like the seabed as it receded into the darkness.

The underground passage began to glow as the galdor crystals reacted to the candlelight. A three-pointed archway appeared across the passageway. Runic writing inlaid with gold was carved into the stones above the arch.

'What does it…?' Kasian's question was left unfinished as he stood open-mouthed; mesmerised by the beauty of the crystals which floated out from the sandstone walls. The air became charged and crackled with galdor energy. The crystals seemed to take on a corporeal form, creating amber spheres which danced around the chamber.

The spheres drew together into one giant shimmering orb

which raced through the passageway towards Meloc and Kasian. Instinctively, Kasian pushed Meloc against the wall as the orb rushed up the stairs and exploded producing a series of concentric shock waves. The ceiling of the passage cracked. The righthand side dropped, falling diagonally just above their heads. A cloud of choking debris billowed down the staircase. There was a moments silence and then a series of high-pitched screams came from above, echoing through the tomb.

'Run,' Kasian shouted, as they both dived under the archway. A second later the dislodged ceiling collapsed into the chamber.

THIRTEEN

Name - Meloc
Location - Beneath the Kristal Cave, Kristal Mountain
Allegiance - The Mercian Warbands

Meloc stirred and coughed as the dust fall began to settle on the tunnel. He squinted through the eerie greyness. Kasian lay face down, his back covered in pieces of stone. The candle box lay on its side inches from his outstretched arm, its candle still burning dimly through the falling dust. There was a tremor as the ground shivered and huge black lines ripped through the walls of the tunnel.

'*Eldur*,' Meloc whispered as he staggered to his feet.

The torches mounted in the iron brackets on both sides of the passageway exploded into flames, casting elongated red tinged shadows upon the sandstone. Meloc touched the walls. They felt cold and slightly damp as if their pores were filled with river water. Patches of green algae grew from the larger joints in the sandstone, a splash of colour in the stark whiteness of the passage.

'Captain Kasian are you still alive?' Meloc said, looking down at the body of the officer.

'Yes, I am. Praise the goddess Wergennis,' Kasian answered as he struggled to his feet, wiping the dust from his uniform.

A black shadow passed through the flickering torchlight. Meloc spun round. The hairs at the back of his neck rose as he felt a presence watching him in darkness.

'Did you see that? Does anything guard the weapons?' Meloc whispered uneasily.

'It's just the fire wavering, keep moving. The weapons have been hidden here since the Treaty of Yus, in the age of my great-grandfather, Alvaro the Arquero, High Councillor to King Torvald. I can assure you no one is down here,' Kasian stated.

'No one mortal that is,' Meloc muttered, as he squinted into the darkness.

'If you concentrate on our mission and embrace the goddess, you will have less time for such imaginings,' the Wergend officer declared, striding through the shadows. He stopped as a howling roar sounded from deep within the darkness of the void. Kasian frowned. His right hand went instinctively to his missing sword, and he cursed.

'Get behind me warlock!' he ordered, dragging Meloc into his shadow as he raised his shield.

'Oh, a wooden shield, that will definitely help us defeat a dragon,' Meloc replied, snatching his elbow away from the officer's grip and backing against the passage wall. A low wind began to blow. It picked up the layers of dust and fallen flecks of stone and spun them across the passage in a series of wavering vortexes.

The floor of the passageway began to ripple.

'Find a handhold quick!' Meloc screamed as he grabbed hold of a rough sandstone outcrop. Kasian took hold of the iron torch bracket with one hand, his shield in the other, 'What daemonry is this?' he demanded.

'Don't look at me!' Meloc said indignantly, 'I didn't do anything, but I think our coming here has awoken the spirit which has been entombed in here to watch over the galdor weapons.'

'Umm…' Kasian frowned and cast a suspicious glance

back towards the archway and the destroyed staircase.

The middle of the pale floor began to sag, forming a depression in the stone. The sandstone crumbling into grains of sand which trickled downwards towards its centre. A small black hole appeared. More and more sand poured into the hole as its edges grew wider, spreading across the passageway.

A faint white glow appeared in the depths and stretched upwards through the hole until it touched the roof of the passage. The light began to turn, slowly at first, and then progressively faster, whipping through the empty air, tearing Meloc from his feet and throwing him against the remains of the staircase. The noise was deafening. Kasian tried to reach out towards Meloc but found himself pinned against the wall.

'Something's coming!' Meloc screamed over the thundering wind.

Spirals shimmered within the whiteness. Then the white column collapsed to reveal a pile of shiny, green coils which filled the tunnel before them. Slowly, the coils begun to unwrap. Two huge green feet appeared from the base possessing talons the size of Meloc's arms. The talons dug into the remains of the soft sandstone as the face of the river spirit unwound from the bottom coil. Its head rose menacingly above the intruders.

The river spirit glared down at the cowering warlock and hissed, 'I am Fafnair, Lord of the Witian river, Guardian of the Serpent's Breath. You will pay dearly for entering my kingdom uninvited.'

Meloc opened his mouth to speak but no words came, for the first time in his life the warlock had nothing to say.

The creature tossed its silvery head, water trickling from its long whiskers and splashing onto Meloc's face. Fafnair opened its mouth wide to reveal two rows of sharpened white fangs, its black forked tongue licking the air, tasting the two intruders' scent as it filled the darkness. Startled from his reverie, Meloc screamed and tripped over a pile of fallen rocks, tumbling backwards onto the floor.

The river spirit bent down and sniffed the little warlock, its whiskers quivering inches from his face. Meloc stiffened with terror as he felt the heat from the serpent's breath on his face.

He cast a furtive glance at the monster before him.

Fafnair had the serpentine green shape of a river spirit, but its body was supported by four short legs each ending in five razor sharp green claws. This was no river spirit Meloc realised in mounting horror. This was a living, breathing, and rather angry waterdrek. He would have little interest in helping to restore peace to the living lands. Dragons, like most of the magikind were capricious, unpredictable, self-serving creatures, notable only for their insatiable hunger.

'Err… um, forgive me, my Lord,' Meloc gulped and bowed deeply to the glaring dragon.

Kasian pushed past Meloc and thumped his right fist against his chest as he bowed to the dragon. 'I am Captain Kasian, commander of the Southern Wergend Legion. You must be the keeper of the Serpent's Breath, the great galdor weapons of Mercia. I have been sent to relieve you of your charge.'

Meloc pressed himself against the clammy wall, expecting to be burnt alive with one angry roar.

The dragon threw back its head and roared, 'How dare you try to steal the galdor weapons from me. I am their keeper and their end. You will never take my treasure.' The dragon lifted its head towards the roof of the passage. Kasian and Meloc stepped backwards as the dark green scales on its abdomen began to fade to white, glowing in moving shadows as waves of intense heat pulsated through the tunnel.

The dragon took a large breath, its nostrils quivering.

'Run!' shouted Kasian and they fled towards a tunnel leading off from the main passageway, as the dragon unfurled its wings and with one whoosh flew upwards, its head almost touching the passage roof.

Kasian slipped the shield from his back and held it up protecting his head. 'By Wergennis' Grace, I hate fighting the magikborne. They never fight with honour,' Kasian swore. 'Get to the ground and fight me with honour, man to beast.'

The dragon's green eyes glowed amber as it blew a trail of fire across the sandstone floor which super-heated and rippled, its paleness tinged yellow. A white crust formed on the ridges of the floor and clouds of powder rose in a choking white cloud, which hung across the middle of the passage.

The powder irritated their lungs and made their eyes stream with burning tears. Meloc sunk to the floor, covering his mouth and nose with his sleeve. 'I don't think he follows orders,' Meloc rasped. 'And I don't think trying to outrun a dragon is going to work either.'

'Get up!' Kasian ordered. He ran over and pulled the choking warlock to his feet.

A gust of scorching wind raced through the white powder, which swirled around them. Kasian braced himself and stood in front of the warlock as he raised his shield.

A stream of fire burnt through the clouds of powder which fell across the floor as flecks of ash. One second later the full torrent of fire smashed into Kasian's shield. His legs buckled and he fell against Meloc. The shield began to glow in the semi-darkness radiating furnace-like heat, burning Kasian's shield arm. The leather shield straps began to smoke and wither.

'I can't hold him off for much longer. Do something warlock!' Kasian shouted over the flaming wind.

'What? So, now I'm useful after all…?' Meloc muttered as he covered his head with his cloak.

'Do some magik!' Kasian ordered, as the fire stream evaporated while the dragon paused for breath.

'Well,' Meloc said as a smirk spread across his soot-blacked face, 'This is the first time a Wergend dog has ever begged me for magik.'

'May the goddess protect us!' Kasian prayed as he drew the small dagger which had been hidden inside the lining of his boot. His naturally tanned face turned scarlet as the perspiration dripped down his forehead matting the strands of his dark brown hair to his sweat-stained face.

'Now would be a good time warlock unless of course you cannot, and you are in fact just a trickster and not really magikborne.'

Meloc stared at the officer for a second. If he cast an invisibility spell, he could make it to the tunnel and escape while the dragon was busy toasting the captain. It was a tempting thought.

The air crackled as the dragon drew another deep breath and blew a stream of red fire down upon his victims. The black writing inscribed on the blade of Kasian's dagger glowed white. Kasian raised the blade above his head and shouted, 'Oh most holy mother Wergennis, protect the keeper of your word.'

The milky moonstone set in hilt of his dagger sparkled blue

as a shimmering orb exploded covering Kasian and Meloc in its arc. The orb cleaved the dragonfyre in two as it rained upon them, spilling across the passage floor, which instantly blackened and smoked.

'The power of my lady will not hold off the dragonfyre for long,' Kasian warned.

Meloc touched the wall of the orb. Instantly, galdor energy surged through his body and his eyes filled with amber flames. He stared up at Kasian in fascination.

The rumours were correct. The warlock keepers wielded the very magikal energy they were sworn to destroy. However, Kasian did not possess the features of a magikborne. Somehow, he must have been infused with galdor. Probably in one of those weird, highly secretive, Wergend initiation ceremonies at Heilagar Fortress, Meloc decided.

'Anytime now would be good warlock! If it is not too much trouble!' Kasian shouted. The orb surrounding them began to flicker.

'Faen!' Meloc swore as the orb exploded into a cloud of amber galdor shards, which fell against the sandstone floor and shattered into dust.

The dragon roared and flew towards them. Kasian picked up his smoking shield as he dragged Meloc to his feet and pulled him further down the tunnel, his arm raised as he braced himself for the next attack.

Talons the size of a man's arm smashed against the shield. The sound of claw on metal and wood reverberated through the passage. Kasian screamed in pain as his shoulder was pulled from its socket as the shield was ripped from his arm and smashed against the wall. The dragon's green plated tail ripped round cracking through the heated air and smashed into the captain's body. The force tossed his body against the roof, and he fell heavily to the floor.

Fafnair raised its head and roared loudly. Then opened its long serpentine snout as saliva dripped from the ends of its tongue. It sniffed the blood pouring from a deep, diagonal cut which crossed Kasian's face.

'Oh helgods,' Meloc muttered as he watched from across the passage.

He scratched his forehead willing a spell to appear. Unfortunately, the dragon did not seem in need of a love potion or hair restorative tonic. This situation required real magik. The magik hidden from all magikborne who had not passed the exams and entered the elite corridors of the Tower of Fregna. It was a life he had lived for three months, until the unfortunate incident with the Master of Primal Forces' cat and the *Leir* spell. The Master had had to dive into the sinking mud where the eastern corridor had been, fully clothed, to rescue his mewing cat.

It had been a complete accident, but no one had believed him. Meloc had been labelled as 'untrustworthy to receive the gift of magik learning,' and asked to leave the Tower.

Meloc grinned.

Apart from getting him expelled, it had been a highly successful spell.

'*Leir-nuna*,' he whispered as he placed his right hand on the tunnel floor. Instantly, the soot-blackened floor began to melt and sink slightly as it turned to mud.

The dragon's feet began to disappear into the mud. He turned his head towards Meloc and unleashed a stream of fire.

Meloc dived from the mouth of the tunnel. The fire caught the ends of his cloak. He swore and threw the cloak away to reveal his thin grey under tunic.

Kasian began feeling his way along the passage wall. He stopped for a second and ripped a large piece of linen from his undershirt and tore it in two as he mopped the blood from his face. The rest he folded into a rough bandage and tied it around his forehead.

'Take my hand!' Meloc whispered.

A look of horror crossed Kasian's face.

'All is good, I don't bite, and I even wash occasionally,' Meloc said, grabbing the captain by the hand and pulling him along the passageway. Instantly, the two sources of galdor energies reacted. Blue electricity crackled and exploded flinging them against the different sides of the tunnel.

'I've never touched a magikborne without my gauntlets before. Now I understand why,' Kasian muttered as he picked himself up from the floor. 'It does not feel pleasant.'

'You don't say!' Meloc groaned as he sat on the floor and rubbed his tingling arm.

The dragon sunk lower and roared. Smoke poured from its nostrils and rolled down the tunnel. Meloc and Kasian began to choke, as soot-stained tears rolled down their faces.

Fafnair stretched its neck upwards revealing its cooling chest in iridescent shades of blue and green as it unfurled its huge wings. With two huge flaps the dragon freed its feet from the sticky ooze and flew to the roof of the passageway. The wind from its wings dragging the soot and fallen rocks into the dense smoky air, creating a deadly vortex.

Ahead of them the passageway divided in two as a narrow passage led off from the right, Meloc crawled to his feet, took hold of Kasian's sleeve, and helped him into the smaller tunnel.

Fafnair's neck darted below its body as it searched for its prey beneath the cloud of grey. He sniffed the opening of the passage. Then dived, its long snout reaching inside, snapping inches away from Meloc and Kasian, who ran stumbling through the passage.

They felt the air being sucked backwards.

'Quick! Get round the corner it's going to blow!' Kasian said.

The dragon's belly rumbled, and a river of yellow-red flames poured through the passage.

Kasian fell around the corner and bumped into Meloc.

'Don't move!' Meloc whispered. His overlarge pupils seeing through the semi-darkness. He pointed to the roof of the tunnel.

The roof was a roughly carved series of axe marks covered in shadows which quickly moved away from the light of the torch.

'I can't see anything,' Kasian replied, squinting up at the roof.

Meloc rolled his eyes and pointed to a black circular hollow hidden by the crossing shadows.

'May the Gods protect us!' Kasian replied grimly. He bent down and picked up a fallen rock then threw it into the hollow. There was a grinding of gears and a loud click. Then a large wooden spear catapulted from the hollow, its sharpened tip drove several inches into the ground.

'Head slammers, I was not informed the way was boobytrapped.' Kasian wrestled the spear free from its hole and poked several hollows in the ceiling with the spear point.

'Just spring one trap at a time!' Meloc shouted. 'They may all be linked.'

Kasian removed the spear tip from a hole and listened. The whole passageway reverberated with the sounds of rolling gears.

'I think you are correct,' he said as small shower of dust fell from the ceiling, sparkling white in the torchlight.

There was a whoosh. A spear thudded into the ground between his feet. Kasian's eyes opened wide in surprise, then he sprinted through the passage.

'Idiot!' Meloc muttered under his breath dodging from side to side as the spears smashed into the passageway one after the other. He jumped over a dust ridden skeleton, still wearing the helmet of a Mercian raider. There was a large hole in the back of its chainmail shirt where it had been harpooned by a falling spear.

'It appears we were not the first ones to be sent to retrieve the galdor weapons,' Meloc panted as he rounded the corner into another long passageway.

There was a scratching sound and several rocks fell from the roof and smashed into the floor in front of them.

'What was that?' Meloc asked staring up at the roof in alarm.

There was more scraping, and the rocky path underfoot wobbled slightly. A gust of wind blew through the cave disarranging the choking dust and hanging smoke. Kasian covered his face with his sleeve, 'It appears Fafnair is trying to dig us out. I think we should move more quickly.'

'Let me spell the tunnel first, we don't want to walk into another trap,' Meloc argued.

Kasian shook his head. 'The Wergend have no use for spells.' He walked through the passage blinking up at the ceiling, checking for holes.

‘Oh hel!’ Meloc groaned as he hurried after the officer.

99

FOURTEEN

Name - Azrael, Warlock Envoy to the King's Council
Location - The Kristal Cave, Kristal Mountain
Allegiance - The Mercian Warbands

Azrael stood watching helplessly as the Kristal Cave disintegrated around him, its destruction caught as time slowed.

The granite sarcophagus exploded but the fragments of grey rock were left suspended in the air. Clouds of dust stood motionless as they mushroomed around the tomb, enveloping the rocky chamber in a veil of grey.

The court warlock whispered under his breath and was instantly surrounded by a faint orange aura.

Chief Feitar sat cowering behind a piece of broken granite, his mouth gaping open. His normally ruddy face, ashen as destructive amber coils of galdor arced through the air.

Sergeant Slater ran screaming through the chamber heading towards the waterfall, chased by an amber arc. He swerved as it struck the ground behind him. Instantly, the puddles of dark water which covered the chamber vapourised to reveal a smoking black hollow in the rock.

Councillor Hundar cowered lower behind the heavy shield of a fallen warbandman.

Lord Haukar's worn leather boots stuck out from underneath a pile of rocks in the corner of the cave. A small red stain was spreading out from beneath the rocks.

'Fall back to the waterfall,' Slater shouted to the city militiamen, 'the chamber is about to explode!'

Groups of dust-covered men rose from the semi-darkness

and ran towards the waterfall.

'Save me first!' Fcitar screamed as his ring-covered hand waved from behind the granite slab.

Two amber energy arcs combined, twisting around themselves, as they followed the fleeing sergeant. Slater stopped in front of the waterfall and reached out to touch the water, then froze. Something was not right. The waterfall was covered in dust. Jagged rock shards protruded from its waters which had stopped falling and the water itself pulsed with a galdor undercurrent.

'Faen!' Slater swore. 'Get back! The waterfall is part of the curse. It's a trap!'

The twisted arcs smashed straight through his midriff, leaving a large black hole in his brown tabard. Slater stared down at his stomach, a look of surprise on his face. His hands moved towards his stomach. His legs collapsed, he fell onto his knees, and then tumbled headfirst into the waterfall.

Everything accelerated forward into normal time.

Rocks rained down from the chamber roof, splintering against the stone walls, and smashing against the wet, slippery floor. Cries of injured men trapped beneath the fallen rocks filled the cave, which cracked and sizzled with galdor energy. Several militiamen made for the waterfall, some hid at the side of the chamber, whilst others screaming in terror, jumped down into the jagged hole left by the sarcophagus.

The acrid smell of burning began to fill the cavern. Black-tinged water began to trickle down the cave walls and fill the gaping hole in the ground, where the sarcophagus had lain.

The surviving soldiers ran through the collapsing cave searching for their lost leader. Haukar's leg twitched under the rubble and a mountainous warband corporal ran over. The sleeve of his tunic hanging from his wrist to reveal a large red cut covering the length of his arm.

'Help me!' he shouted across the cave to Azrael. The warlock ran lightly over the stone debris and helped the corporal throw the smaller stones from his leader's body.

Sergeant Dygg wedged his shield beneath the largest stone, and roared as adrenaline surged through his body as he pushed down upon the shield. The rock moved upwards. Quickly, Azrael pulled the elderly warlord out from underneath the rubble. Haukar groaned in pain, his eyes closed, as a thin stream of blood trickled from the corner of his mouth.

The last of the sarcophagus' debris clattered against the cave floor, which began to buckle as a wave of black water surged through the sinking chamber.

'You have to get me out of here!' The chief screamed above the deafening noise.

'Do something!' The corporal ordered Azrael, 'you must save the city chief!'

'But where is Councillor Hundar? I cannot leave without him.' Azrael's cobalt eyes searched desperately for Hundar among the collapsing chaos of the cave, but the councillor was nowhere to be seen.

'Get me out of here!' Feitar screamed and lunged towards the Court Warlock.

There was a flash of iron and the point of a sword pressed against Azrael's throat. 'You will save the chief,' Dygg growled.

'But of course,' Azrael croaked and pushed the blade from his throat. He raised the palms of his hands out in front of him and whispered a vocation to the god, Eir. An amber glow radiated from his hands. Carefully, he placed one on Feitar's arm and the other on his forgotten maidservant's and shouted, '*Leika- nuu*!'

Lord Haukar jolted awake. His eyes darting from side to side. 'What happened?' he demanded as he struggled to his feet.

'Have a care, my Lord,' Dygg went to support the wounded warlord. Haukar shook his hand from his shoulder. 'I can stand unaided.'

'The sarcophagus was cursed. It exploded, my Lord,' Sergeant Dygg answered.

'How many casualties?' Haukar demanded as he watched a group of warbandmen drag their wounded comrades from the chamber, through the roaring waters of the reanimated waterfall, and collapse exhausted on the mountainside.

'Five warbandmen dead, seven injured, my Lord, and the city militia are all but gone,' Dygg answered, shaking his head sadly.

Haukar signalled two warbandmen carrying a corpse shrouded in its own cloak from the cave. He walked over and removed the cloth from the face. The battered face of a young warband messenger peered from the wrapping. The left half of his face swollen purple.

'Freydis Eiríkson, he was from my fortress. He died without seeing his first battle. He will not enter Valholl, the hall of the fallen. Let us pray to the goddess Domari that in her wisdom she will look kindly on his young soul and judge him worthy.' He took some blue powder from a pouch hanging from his leather belt and drew a triangle on Freydis' forehead.

'Domari, receive this son of the Easthelm. He died on duty with honour,' the warlord prayed thumping his fist to his heart.

'Domari, hear our prayers,' the warbandmen responded and

bowed to their lord.

'We should never have come here,' Haukar shook his head as he watched the dead cadet being carried from the cave. 'Magik corrupts everything it touches. It can never be contained. It must be driven from our land once and for all.'

'Stop chatting and save me! That useless warlock has misspelled!' Feitar screamed over the rushing waters of the flooding river.

'Help the chief from the boulder before we all drown,' Haukar ordered and marched down the path followed by a squad of Eastern warbandmen.

Sergeant Dygg waded through the water towards the chief, who was standing with his maidservant on a rocky outlet which rose island-like amid the swirling waters. Dygg held out a hand to help the woman from the rock. Feitar pushed her out of the way and grabbed his hand. The maidservant screamed and splashed into the dark water.

'Get me away from this cursed place,' Feitar screamed. 'I'm too young to die!'

Dygg linked his arm around Feitar's elbow and pulled the maidservant from the water with the other.

She stood, her long brown hair had been loosened from its coils and fell, plastered against her plain robe.

'Thank you for rescuing me, Syr,' she gasped as she held onto the corporal's calloused hand tightly as he waded through the waist high waters pulling his charges behind him.

Azrael could see the corners of the big corporal's mouth twitch as he squeezed the maid's sturdy waist.

'Did you have to drop them in the river?' Hundar whispered.

'A pure accident,' the sealed warlock winked, and the

councillor raised a fine blond eyebrow as they followed the amorous Dygg and the remains of the convoy down the mountainside.

FIFTEEN

Name - Meloc

Location - Somewhere in the underground passages, Kristal
Mountain

Allegiance - The Mercian Warbands

The scraping of the dragon's talons on the outside of the tunnel echoed down the smaller passage. Fafnair roared in frustration, the heat of its breath burning the air.

Kasian wiped the sweat from his forehead as he tapped the roof of the passage with the spear. 'See, there is nothing to worry about. No one would be expected to survive the Head Slammers. We have passed all the traps. Praise the goddess!'

Meloc tutted. 'Well, let's just hope we are going the right way then.'

'Umm…' Kasian replied. He stopped prodding at the roof and propped the spear against a wall torch stand as he rummaged through his leather satchel.

Meloc leant against the side of the cave, seemingly uninterested.

'Ah! Here it is!' Kasian smiled with relief as he pulled out a golden ellipsoid object.

Meloc sighed dramatically and glanced at the Wergend officer. The golden egg glowed slightly amber in the dark. Meloc frowned through the semi-darkness, as he felt the galdor energy transmitted from the object. The blackness of his pupils enlarged to cover most of his iris, giving him near perfect night vision.

Kasian pressed a small button on the side of the egg. The springs inside churned and the lid sprung open to reveal a compass. Meloc moved closer. The face of the compass had no directional headings only runes written in an ancient language he could not understand. In front of the face of the compass was a silver rotary dial containing one smaller ring. A silver arrow arose from the compass and hovered an inch from the dial. Kasian squinted at the compass through the darkness and moved the dial until the rune shaped like a twisted diamond was within the circle.

'This is a *Leitandi*, a seeking compass,' Kasian explained in a low voice, 'It locates things you cannot see.' He checked the dial. 'I have set it to the corrupted diamond… it seeks out sources of galdor and will locate the weapons for us.'

The arrow turned slowly towards Meloc.

'Umm…' Kasian said, shaking the *Leitandi*. Its arrow swept around the dial once more and then pointed directly at Meloc.

'It appears you do indeed possess galdor and are magikborne,' Kasian said with the slightest traces of a smile on his lips.

'Really?' Meloc said. 'Well, that is a shock. Does it say anything useful, like the location of a chest full of ancient galdor weapons?'

'Er no,' Kasian replied circling the cave with the *Leitandi* in his outstretched hand. The silver arrow remained firmly fixed in the direction of Meloc. He shook his head and sighed, 'Your energy field must be blocking out all other sources of galdor energy.' He snapped the *Leitandi* shut and put it back into his shoulder bag.

'What can I say? I'm just irresistible,' Meloc winked as he shrugged his shoulders.

There was a moments silence.

'Well, at least Fafnair has stopped trying to dig us out. We will not be dragon dinner today,' Kasian said relieved.

'I don't think that is necessarily a good omen, 'Meloc replied.

A low roar echoed through the passage. The air turned colder, and a breath of ice crystals sparkled across the stone walls. Meloc shivered and pulled his threadbare cloak across his body.

'By Wergennis' grace, what demonry is this?' Kasian whispered. 'A dragon cannot use nature magik.'

'I think you better tell Fafnair that,' Meloc shouted. The roaring became deafening, as a torrent of icy water thundered through the tunnel.

'Run!' screamed Kasian.

The water thundered past their knees, almost knocking them from their feet, as they waded through the rising waters and followed the tunnel as it swung around to the right. Then they stopped. The tunnel ended in a wall of sheer rock.

'Helgods!' Meloc cursed. 'Can our luck get any worse?'

A wave of freezing water poured through the passage reaching their waists, trying to pull them into its depths as dark shadows darted beneath the water's surface.

'You had to challenge the gods, didn't you warlock?' Kasian growled, as he watched a tiny ripple of silver move across the swirling waters.

'Ow!' squealed Meloc. 'Something just bit me!' He rubbed his leg, his gaze following the silver ripple.

'Demonios! Me too!' Kasian exclaimed and grabbed at his leg. Then he lunged at the water with his spear. 'Got it!' he smiled and lifted the spear from the water, caught on its tip was a shining russet, wriggling, eel-like creature with big black eyes surrounded by a smudge of red.

'Watch out!' said Meloc grimly, 'that's a fangfiskar. Pesky little flesh creatures from the Westernlands. They must have been dropped in here to guard the weapons. On their own, they're relatively harmless but in a mob, they will strip the flesh from your bare bones in less than a minute.'

The fangfiskar slid off the tip of the spear, twisted around the spearhead, and leapt at Kasian. Its jaws opened to reveal a carnivorous mouth lined with rows of serrated, white teeth. Kasian stepped backwards, holding the spear at arm's length as he quickly pulled his dagger from his boot and lunged at the creature. The dagger caught the fangfiskar in mid-strike, splitting it in two. It plopped back into the rising water, as a halo of blood leaked around it.

'Well, that should attract the rest of the pack,' Meloc tutted.

'It attacked me,' Kasian said grimly as he wiped the blood from his blade on his dripping undershirt. His face flushed darker as he began to sweat profusely as he rummaged beneath his shirt.

'Er… are you alright?' Meloc frowned as he waded towards the rocky wall.

'It is nothing,' Kasian growled as he fished a small fangfiskar from inside his trousers and hurled it against the wall. The creature flew through the damp air, wrapped itself tightly around a rocky outcrop, and watched the Wergend officer hungrily.

'You will probably need to put some cream on that,' Meloc grinned and then toppled backwards into the rocky wall as a wave of water swept over his head.

'That is none of your concern, warlock,' said Kasian as he wiped the sweat from his forehead and limped painfully towards Meloc.

'Anyway, it's not as if there's anything down there you actually use,' Meloc giggled.

There was a flash of silver and the point of Kasian's dagger pressed underneath Meloc's chin.

'Have a care,' Kasian growled. 'Make fun of the Order of the Wergend at your peril.'

Meloc pushed the blade away from his neck, 'Please accept my apologies. I'm sure there's nothing at all fun about the Order of the Wergend.'

His eyes glowed with amber flames.

Kasian stepped backwards in confusion, clutching the amulet around his neck. 'What daemonry is this?' he demanded.

Three fangfiskar rose wriggling from the swirling waters and were instantly evaporated.

'You're welcome!' Meloc laughed.

Kasian glared at the grinning warlock and released his grip on the amulet.

A circle of white glowed from beneath the darkness of the waters. Kasian prodded the circle with his spear. The circle crinkled and glowed once more. The officer smiled. 'The Mother Goddess has been merciful!' he pointed to the roof of the passage. High above them was a tiny circle of light.

'Quick! Up there… there's a vent. It must lead to the surface!' Kasian shouted as he grabbed hold of a protruding rock.

Another wave of cold water smashed against the rock wall. Then there was a loud, low roar as the sound of dragon breath filled the passageway. The tops of the waves sparkled white and turned to ice.

'Help me!' Meloc shouted up at the Wergend officer as the water around him froze, trapping him in the ice.

Kasian hesitated for a moment and sighed, then with his free arm pulled Meloc from the waters grasp and hoisted him up onto the rocky wall.

'For a moment, I thought you were g-going to leave me,' Meloc stuttered, his white face pinched blue with cold.

'So did I,' Kasian agreed, 'but I do not have the right to leave you to die.'

'W-well, thanks… I g-guess!' Meloc said shivering as he clutched hold of the wall. His handhold began to crumble beneath his fingertips as the magikal ice ate through the rockface and sheered rock from rock. There was a loud splash as a sheet of rock fell into the grasping waters below.

'We have to climb out of here and quickly!' Kasian shouted as he stretched his leg upwards and pushed the toe of his boot into a tiny gap in the rockface. The gap enlarged forming a fissure in the rock and Kasian's toe hole vanished, and he was left hanging by his fingertips.

'*Stayay*,' Meloch screamed as he slipped further down the wall, his boots dangling into the water.

A flash of amber illuminated the shaft and Kasian watched open-mouthed as the rockface began to alter; moving in and out as if it were a breathing creature. Short rock ledges jutted out from the wall, slowly winding their way up the shaft, in a spiral of ascending stepping stones.

'For an unsealed warlock you certainly seem to know a great many spells,' Kasian commented as he began to leap from step to step.

Two red circles appeared on Meloc's cheeks as he looked up at the Wergend officer. He muttered under his breath and a large ice-tinged wave thundered against the rockface drenching the officer.

'May my lady protect us,' Kasian prayed as he tried to shake some of the water from his freezing clothes.

Something knocked against the cave wall, the sound echoing up through the shaft.

'What's that?' Meloc stared suspiciously into the swirling waters, searching for signs of unwelcome creatures.

Kasian pointed to several broken pieces of wood floating on the waving waters. He stared at the wood and smiled. On one of the broken pieces of wood was the remains of writing and an image of a golden snake.

'The property of King Awain,' Kasian read. 'These must be the chests containing the Serpent's Breath, but I cannot see any weapons,' he said glancing towards Meloc.

Meloc tutted and raised his arms across the waters, his palms facing downwards as he closed his eyes. He felt the slightest touch of latent galdor energy rising from the broken chests.

'No galdor weapons have touched that box for at least the past five years,' he replied.

'Perhaps they have been removed by the King for safe keeping at Fastness Fortress?' Kasian frowned, rubbing the dark stubble on his chin.

'I wouldn't count on it,' Meloc replied.

'Come on,' said the captain grimly. 'Climb faster! We need to report this to the chief at once.'

'Another great idea,' said Meloc rolling his eyes as he watched Kasian climb.

SIXTEEN

Name - Lord Haukar, Lord of the Eastern Warband
Location - The Stone Circle, Kristal Mountain
Allegiance - The Mercian Warbands

The remains of the Mercian party stumbled through the waterfall of the Kristal Cave, blinking in the sunlight reflected from the rushing river which cast dancing sunspots across the chasm. Black waters tumbled from the cave and became a surging current as it followed the narrow path around the mountainside to rejoin Hiwan, the mother river.

Haukar and Dygg stood outside the cave as they watched the current rip bushes and small boulders from their resting places and carry them away down the mountainside. A loud crash sounded through the chasm as part of the path fell away and tumbled down into the raging river below.

'Faen!' swore Dygg, rubbing his beard. 'The path is gone.'
'Then we need to find a new one.' Haukar took a piece of wet parchment from his jacket pocket. He unrolled it carefully and held it against a sandstone boulder glittering with galdor. The boulder glowed amber and the map dried. The warlord picked up the map and after staring at it for a minute smiled. 'We have been blessed, there is another way down the mountain.'

'Fall in everyone. We are leaving, make sure the wounded are given aid,' Haukar shouted and raised his hand. The convoy formed a rough line behind the warlord, the wounded carried between the able bodied. Feitar puffed and panted, leaning heavily on his maidservant and a walking stick she had fashioned from the broken branch of a dwarf aspen tree, even though he was uninjured.

Haukar looked at the chief and shook his head in disgust. 'Move out men! And have a care; we will avoid the main path, but every path from this mountain may have claws.' He signalled the remains of the company to follow him and disappeared down an overgrown track, which veered to the right of the chasm, scrambling over vaulted rocks which sparkled with galdor minerals.

Occasionally, the shattered grey stone landscape was broken by strands of green as thick-leaved creeper bushes burst through cracks between the stones. The wind whistled through the convoy, their wet clothes sticking to their bodies as they moved. They climbed further downwards until the falling sun's shadows began to stretch across the mountainside and the air grew colder. Eventually, they reached a clearing on the gentler incline of the lower plains of the Kristal Mountain.

A circle of weathered towering torstones, had been erected in the clearing. Some had collapsed, whilst others remained standing, their upright supports framing the fading sun. In the centre of the stone circle, was a smaller circle of rocks arranged around a deep opening in the ground. The stones were overgrown with spiking fernlings and white creeping trumpet flowers.

'We will rest here. Men of the warband and militia, search the ruins, be alert for danger. This ruin is on no map of Mercia. Officially it does not exist and that is always an ominous sign.' Lord Haukar waved his hand and the men set out in groups, wandering hesitantly through the ruins. Their wide eyes betraying their fear.

'Make haste!' Haukar shouted. 'I want the area secured and the fires lit.'

A chorus of 'Yes, my Lord!' echoed through the ruins as

the men renewed their search with greater confidence.

Lord Haukar squatted next to the hole, his arthritic knees creaked and complained about the unwelcome movement. Haukar ignored the pain and stared into the darkness.

The hole was an old well, set into the ground. The walls surrounding the well had fallen away and lay crumbling among the long grasses which were slowly reclaiming the cleared land. The foul odour of fetid water rose from the hole. Haukar drew back, covering his nose with his hand. The water had been poisoned. Either an unfortunate animal had fallen to its watery doom, or the water had been touched by violence and cursed. He looked at the exhausted, bloodied men and shook his head. If they travelled through the night, the spirit of the black sickness would take the most seriously wounded of the convoy and the exertion would further weaken the remaining men. Their only choice was to stay and rest among the ruins, which offered at least some protection against Dunmuir arrows. Hopefully, the campfires would keep the wild animals and cursed spirits away and maybe some of the company would survive the night.

'We should be safe here. Just do not venture too near the well, there may be something lurking in the darkness that we do not wish to disturb,' Haukar announced as he stood and surveyed what was left of the company.

'You... warlock!' Lord Haukar pointed to Azrael. 'See to the wounded, as for the rest of you – Welfasten militia tend to the fires. Men of the East, divide in halves, you are on guard duty, with change of guards every five hours.'

He turned to Sergeant Dygg. 'Position men around the camp's perimeter.'

'Yes, my Lord,' the sergeant replied as he carried Feitar

into the stone circle.

'Over there! Put me down on that large rock,' the chief ordered.

'Yes, my chief,' Dygg nodded as he helped Feitar onto a collapsed torstone which lay sideways in the grass.

'I need water and get that bloody warlock here. I am dying here if anyone cared to notice!' Feitar sat on the stone his legs outstretched as he turned his face towards the sun. He reminded Azrael of a fat-bellied lizardling.

'I am coming, my chief,' Azrael replied. Quickly, he finished rubbing a green-tinged ointment onto the blackened arm of a warbandman. Instantly, the bruise faded to grey. The warbandman stretched the fingers of his broken arm, smiled, and thumped the slight warlock on the back.

'I don't know the magik of your potion, but it has cured by bow arm, even the pulling pains have gone from my shoulder, and I've had them since I was recruit. Thank you, warlock,' the warbandman grinned.

'For the love of Nijord, may he bestow much gold to my city, will you hurry up, warlock!' Feitar screeched. Azrael bowed to the bowman and ran over to the chief.
'Here at last I see.' Feitar glared at the warlock. 'Mend my head and you had better not leave a scar.'

Azrael reached inside his ornately pattered shoulder bag and took out a small brown vial. He poured two yellow drops onto the bandage covering the chief's head and a smell of oranges filtered through the encampment. Instantly, the dark red stain on the coverings vanished.

Azrael nodded at the maidservant who began to unwrap the bandage.

'Ow… the pain…get away from me, you clumsy whore,'

Feitar shouted.

The servant bowed and quickly moved away.

'You do it, and you'd better be careful, or I will have you whipped, warlock,' Feitar growled.

Azrael gently unwrapped the bandage, his hands shaking, as the chief groaned and winced in pain.

'There you are, my chief,' Azrael let out a sigh. 'All done. You see, the cut has completely vanished.'

The chief beckoned to his servant, and she arrived carrying a small, looking glass. She held the mirror up in front of his face as he carefully examined his forehead. Satisfied, he dismissed her.

'What is this bloody place anyway?' Feitar demanded as he stared at the glistening torstones.

SEVENTEEN

Name - Councillor Hundar, Member of the King's Council
Location - The Stone Circle, Kristal Mountain
Allegiance - The Mercian Warbands

Chief Feitar's eyes narrowed suspiciously as he stared at the ruined circles.

'It appears to be a...' Azrael stopped in mid-sentence as Councillor Hundar, who had quietly crept behind him, shook his head. 'From my studies of the old records, I believe it is a simplistic form of dwelling. Probably the remains of an ancient Eldor Age village.'

'I thought everything from the days of the old religion was destroyed in the reign of King Torvald after the Recantation of Magik,' Feitar said as he stared at the torstones suspiciously.

'It does indeed look most destroyed, my chief,' Hundar bowed.

'Oh... I see,' replied the Chief. 'And a good thing too. All those child sacrifices and mass executions to appease mere daemons dressed up as gods. It was positively barbaric.'

'There were no... ow!' Azrael protested but was cut off by Hundar stamping on his foot.

Chief Feitar ignored Azrael and continued, 'Did you know one of my ancestors, Gorm the Hammer, destroyed a whole dragon temple in the Sunderfell, it is said there was not a temple stone left standing when he had finished.'

'Yes indeed,' said Hundar softly, the slight narrowing of his hazel eyes betraying his disdain. 'I have heard the tragedy of Gorm the Hammer in the *Book of Legends,* but I did not realise your lines were aligned, especially with your recent ties to the magikborne.'

'What bloody magikborne ties? That meddling warlock is no relation of mine! He's a bloody half-cousin on his mother's side. The feminine line is weak and does not count. My veins are filled with the manly blood of Gorm the Hammer,' Feitar exclaimed angrily rising from the rolled-up cloak which cushioned him from his hard torstone seat.

'Yes, of course you are.' Hundar smiled and bowed as he walked backwards away from the irate chief, dragging Azrael with him.

Feitar glared at them, his face ruby red with indignation. He fell back against his cushion which was perched precariously on the side of the stone. There was a scream and a thump as both landed on the rock-strewn floor.

Hundar smiled slightly and turned as he walked away without a backward glance. Several militiamen ran past him as they dashed to save their master. Satisfied the noises coming from the toppled chief had caught much of the camps attention, Hundar grabbed Azrael by the elbow and dragged him behind an upright torstone.

'Go and wait for us at the bottom of the mountain. We'll meet you on the Southern Road,' Hundar whispered.

'I cannot. There are more wounded to attend to,' Azrael whispered, his cobalt eyes scanning the lengthening afternoon shadows.

'No magikind shall suffer to be part of the old religion, the penalty for disobedience is still immediate execution...' Hundar recited. 'If Feitar or Haukar realise this is actually a temple, they will have you killed, whether you are tending to the injured or not.'

'I know Hundar, but you worry too much. Look around

you. I doubt whether anyone here will be able to read the runes or decipher the pictograms,' Azrael nodded at a muddy militiaman who was sitting by a pile of twigs, as he tried to light them over and over again, by scratching down the side of his flint firestone with a knife. 'They don't seem the brightest even for soldiers.'

Hundar followed his gaze and smiled. 'No, but they were lucky enough to escape the Kristal Cave and have been blessed with good fortune by their gods. You should never bet against a lucky man,' Hundar whispered.

Azrael grinned. The phrase was scrawled across the walls of every inn in Mercia. 'But the gods are fickle, they will take away their gifts and blessing on a whim,' he whispered.

'The new gods would never act so, they are gods of honour who reward the diligent and faithful,' Hundar replied. 'Er… we are talking about the new religion, aren't we?'

'Of course,' Azrael replied with a slight smile on his lips.

Hundar touched the side of the warlock's dirt-covered face as he looked into his companion's eyes with concern, 'You people always tread such a thin line.'

'Not by our choice, I assure you,' Azrael laughed. 'I think it might be best if we all go.' He traced the outline of a dragon carved into the stone. 'This temple is dedicated to Fafnair. The spirit of the Hiwan river and he will not like it being defiled so.' Azrael nodded towards Feitar as he reclined on a fallen torstone, while his handmaiden poured him a goblet of finest Sunnan wine.

Hundar watched the camp for a minute. The fires had finally been lit. A succession of bubbling black cauldrons had been hung on chains dangling beneath the tripods as the smell of 'all-sorts' stews began to waft through the camp. He shook his head, 'I do not think we will be going anywhere until daybreak; the men are hungry and the wounded need to rest.'

'This is a very bad idea,' Azrael warned. He laid his hand on Hundar's shoulder. I will stay with you. You will have need of my magik before the sunrises.' He turned his head to one side, listening to the still mountain air.

'What do you hear?' Hundar asked, squinting passed the Kristal Mountain.

'The thunderdrums are sounding in rapid beat. They are celebrating...' Azrael whispered.

'Helfire,' swore Hundar, 'that is never a good sign.'

EIGHTEEN

Name - Meloc

Location - The Underground Passage, Kristal Mountain

Allegiance - The Mercian Warbands

The falling sunlight flickered, casting shadows across the top of the vertical shaft, illuminating a series of grooves and deep scratches which criss-crossed the crumbling tunnel walls. The clawing odour of rotting musky flesh lingered. The smell was fresh and reptilian. Meloc climbed quicker.

'I can see the top now,' Meloc shouted as he wiped the sweat from his forehead, his chest heaving with the effort of the climb. He would have used spellkraft but for the puffing Wergend officer below him. Meloc was loathed to have the sun-kissed, athletic captain thinking he was not manly enough to perform such physical tasks without the use of magik. He reached a narrow ledge almost at the top of the shaft, gasping for breath as his hands snatched at the grassy undergrowth which disappeared over the rim of the shaft.

'I may need a bit of assistance to climb over here,' he called to Kasian, who was glowering and muttering to himself, several spirals of stone steps below him.

Meloc squinted into the light and saw the tall, thin shape of Lord Haukar silhouetted black against the noon sky.

'Who goes there, speak and be recognised,' the Eastern warlord demanded.

A relatively friendly face peered over the edge of the shaft. 'Stand down, my Lord, it's the Wergend captain and Meloc. They must have escaped the implosion,' Councillor Hundar reasoned.

'The guards will help you out. Pass up the galdor weaponry first,' Haukar ordered.

The guards stared at the well suspiciously. Its entrance was black, untouched by the last rays of the setting sun. Apart from the panting and rustling of the two climbers, the well was silent, but a dormant sense warned the men that there was something evil lurking down there. The militiamen whispered to themselves and slowly edged away from the entrance.

Haukar shook his head at the soldiers in disgust. 'I need some real men. You!' He pointed to a militiaman with a jagged cut across his forehead. Dried blood covered half of his once youthful face, 'Go to the village perimeter and bring me some warbandmen.'

The youth nodded and disappeared among the lengthening shadows of the torstones. There was a scraping sound and a scream from inside the tunnel.

'Get me out of here now!' Meloc shouted. 'The walls are collapsing.'

'Is there anything down there with you?' Haukar frowned, peering over the well entrance.

'No, my Lord,' Kasian replied. 'It is just the weight of the warlock, causing the walls to crumble.'

'Are you calling me fat?' Meloc raised a fine, black eyebrow. His slender frame containing not one ounce of spare flesh.

'No,' Kasian replied. 'I'm calling you are unfit, un-muscled, and ill-used to climbing. I want you out of this tunnel before your scrapings bring the walls down upon me.'

'Where is the Serpent's Breath?' Haukar demanded.

'We will explain all when we are safe,' Kasian replied, his dirt-stained hand appeared over the edge of the shaft.

Involuntarily, Lord Haukar took a step backwards.

'Here, take my hand,' Azrael said as he stood by the well opening. The searching hand grabbed his wrist. He braced his feet against a fallen stone and pulled Kasian from the opening, then fell backwards into the ring of watching militiamen.

'Thank you, warlock,' Kasian said gruffly as he knelt by the well entrance, his right hand feeling inside the darkness.

'Got you!' he winced as a bolt of electricity coursed through his body as he hauled Meloc from the well.

Meloc sat next to the hole and shook the charge from his hand. His eyes flashed amber as they adjusted to the hazy twilight of the Mercian night.

'Detain them!' Haukar ordered as he pointed to Meloc and Kasian. They were instantly surrounded by a ring of silver leaf-bladed spears.

Kasian and Meloc exchanged troubled glances as they slowly raised their hands.

'We are known to you,' Kasian stated. 'Lower your weapons. I am a Captain of the Order of the Wergend. You have no jurisdiction over me.'

Two warbandmen raised their spears and stepped to the side as Lord Haukar entered the circle. He ignored Meloc. 'I see you have escaped the passages, so I assume your mission is complete but where are the Galdor Weapons?'

'They were stolen, my Lord,' Captain Kasian answered, thumping the left side of his chest with his fist, and bowing to the warlord.

'But that's impossible!' spluttered Chief Feitar as he ambled over, the half-full glass of wine still in his hand. 'Only members of the King's private council knew of their location.'

The ground lurched violently.

Several of the warbandmen fell against the groaning ground, their spears rolling loose from their grip. A bridging stone fell from its supports and crashed onto the ground, as a deep roaring rose from beneath their feet. The ground began to bulge and shake as a stream of soil and stone began to trickle down the protruding sides. There was another roar and the bulging soil exploded, sending super-heated stones high into the night sky above the temple. The soil rained down. Men screamed at the slightest touch of the mud as it burnt the skin from their exposed flesh. The ground trembled again as more soil crumbled down into the widening gap.

'Climb onto the stones!' Haukar yelled to his panicking men as the soil in the middle of the circle disappeared to reveal a huge, carved greystone shaft. Smoke rose from the hole and burnt the air as wisps of grey ash fell across the entrance to the under temple. The men wrapped scarves around their faces as the hot air scorched their lungs.

Lord Haukar wiped beads of sweat from his forehead as he stood on a fallen torstone craning to see down into the under temple. The sound of claw grating on stone echoed through the silence.

'To arms!' Haukar shouted and drew his sword.

One huge, green dragon claw appeared over the top of the pit. Its long talons digging into the soil.

Feitar opened his mouth to scream but Sergeant Dygg slapped his calloused hand over his mouth and dragged the chief to the floor. 'Lie down and don't move.'

Feitar nodded, his mouth still covered, his eyes open wide in terror.

A second enormous claw appeared and Fafnair raised its head. Unblinking green eyes glared angrily at the Welfasten men.

'To arms men, catch it before it takes to flight, and burns us all to death,' Lord Haukar shouted. He jumped from the stone and charged towards the dragon followed by the remaining Eastern warbandmen.

The dragon leapt from the passage. Its back claws grabbed Lord Haukar and flew high above the temple.

'Archers have a care, shoot the beast but not Lord Haukar!' Sergeant Dygg shouted as he leapt across the crumbling earth.

The longbowmen loaded their bows and tracked the dragon as it hovered overhead. The flapping of its great green wings almost blew the men from their feet. The fallen ash rose in choking clouds blocking out the last rays of the sun and cast a shadow across the ruined temple. The lead longbowman lowered his bow and shook his head. The archers returned their arrows to their ornate leather quivers, slipped the bowstrings over their heads so the bows hung diagonally over their backs, and drew single-edged long knives from their belts as they took hold of anything strong enough to survive the wind.

The dragon shrieked, revealing a deep red mouth full of serrated white teeth as it dropped Haukar. His limp body smashed on the ground below, splattering blood across the stones. Fafnair flew around the temple as the Welfasten men ran for cover, a black shape silhouetted against the blazing orange sunset.

'Watch out!' Hundar screamed as the dragon stopped circling and dived, his long body twisting around the torstones.

Fafnair's hind claws snatched two warbandmen as they tried to flee the temple and threw them against the standing stones. The men bounced off the stones and lay motionless as blood began to pool around their broken bodies.

The dragon soared upwards.

'Quick, form on me!' Sergeant Dygg shouted, slipping the great round shield from his back and stepping in front of the chief.

'Helgods!' Hundar swore and grabbed the helmet, shield, and sword from a fallen warbandman as he ran to join the sergeant.

The remaining city guards and warbandmen slipped off their shields and ran towards their sergeant. The first row of soldiers formed a circle and knelt, holding their shields in front of them, as a second row stood above them and covered the heads of the first with their shields. The silver points of spears and arrowheads appeared from gaps within the shield wall.

'Hey… what about us?' Meloc shouted from behind a crouching dogbush. Azrael crawled next to Meloc.

'I think we've been forgotten,' Azrael whispered.

'A dragon will not hurt his own,' Dygg called out. 'You will be safe.'

'Faen! Do we look like bloody dragons?' Meloc muttered as he wriggled further beneath the bush.

The sound of distant thunder rolled above their heads as a gust of wind blew across the temple.

'He's turned! Fight for your lives. Men of Mercia do not run from any enemy,' Dygg shouted. He banged his sword on his shield and roared the ancient battle cry of the Eastlands, 'Ut..ut…ut' up at the dragon.

The rest of the wall roared in unison, banging on their shields, daring the dragon to attack.

Fafnair dropped from the sky and circled above the wall, just out of the reach of the spears.

'The noise must have scared him,' Kasian said in disbelief as he crawled between the two warlocks.

'Hey! Why aren't you over there?' Meloc whispered nodding towards the shield wall.

'Umm...' Kasian replied with a slight smile, 'it appears that the Wergend are as unwelcome as the people they chase.'

NINETEEN

Name - Meloc

Location - The Temple of Fafnair, Kristal Mountain

Allegiance - The Mercian Warbands

Fafnair soared into the sky and hovered. The backdraught from its wings ripping the low-lying mountain bushes their soil.

The men of the shield wall were almost blown from their feet.

'Hold your position! You are men of the Eastlands. You will stand firm, and you will fear nothing!' Sergeant Dygg screamed over the wind.

One long shout of defiance ran through the shield wall as the men braced themselves to meet the dragon.

'Dygg is crazy if he thinks long knives will pierce dragon scales.' Azrael shook his head.

'And what would you have him do?' Kasian frowned, 'tell the men they are doomed and to pray to their god for forgiveness of their mortal vices?'

Azrael blushed and looked away.

'Can't you cast a spell or something?' Kasian whispered to Meloc. 'You seemed to have knowledge of a great many spells in the passages. Once we return to Welfasten, I will be fascinated to learn how you came by such knowledge. According to our reports, you were expelled from Fregna Tower after only one term.'

Meloc shrugged.

'What can I say? I'm a quick learner,' he said, meeting Kasian's gaze, a slight smirk on his face.

'Well, do something,' Kasian ordered as he saw the

shimmering green scales of the dragon's underbelly glow red. A gust of super-heated wind burnt their faces. 'And now would be a good time to do so. Dragonfyre and death is upon us!'

'So, I don't suppose they taught you anything useful in the Tower?' Meloc asked Azrael.

'Funnily enough no; fighting dragons, counts as battlemagik and as you know as well as I, the battlemages were purged in the reign of King Torvald and their spellkraft lost,' Azrael whispered.

Meloc paled as a hidden memory flashed through his thoughts.

He saw flames in the darkness.

He saw a mob of villagers standing in an angry ring around his thatched round house. They appeared in his dreams as faceless grey shadows dressed in dirty brown cloths and armed with clubs and staffs. The mob held torches that flamed through the night as they demanded his father, Morax, to present himself to the village headman for trial.

His father's crime had been discovered by a nameless Seeking Officer based at the Wergend stronghold of Heilagar Fortress. She had been updating the lineage charts of the executed battlemages, to ensure no progeny of the tainted magikal bloodlines survived.

Morax was the only known surviving son of Marchosias, Lord of Goethia, Commander of the Thirty Legions of Magik. Lord Marchosias had perished at the battle of Goethia Plains, at the closing of the Eldor Age. It had been the final battle in the War of the Magiks. The temples of the battlemages had united and rebelled against the tightening of state control against the magikind, triggered by the horror of a gift gone terribly wrong.

Vana, the gift of light in the dark of the Mercian night, had terrified the galdorless, enraged the holy orders, and brought the attention of the Star Council. The warlocks had been accused of heresy and plotting to overthrow the natural order of Mercia. Their tribal temples were destroyed, and the temple priests were arrested. While hundreds of warlocks disappeared in night raids and magikind children were removed from their families and sent to the newly built Fregna Tower for magikal assessment. Few were seen again.

The remaining warlock temples had bound together in a desperate fight to create a magikind homeland in the sparsely inhabited Greylands to the north of the kingdom. It had been their doom. The uprising had ended in the bloody rout of the magikborne at the Battle of Goethia Plains by the combined allied forces of the Kingdoms of Dunmuirlun and Mercia. To achieve the victory, the allied forces had used the Galdor Weapons, a defence created by the battlemages to defend Dunmuirlun, against the magikind. It was rumoured, that in turning the weapons against their masters, the weapons themselves had become cursed and brought hatred and distrust down upon the two once friendly nations.

Morax and his wife, Ealith, had escaped the purge of the battlemages to live quietly as peasant farmers in the village for over twenty years. Until under the full moon in the season of the corn, when Captain Muspell and his troop of Southern Wergend soldiers had arrived in the village and denounced Morax as the offspring of a battlemage.

Morax had accepted his death with honour.

Meloc swallowed as he remembered how his father had

kissed his mother and embraced him. He had smelt the harvest on his father's clothes. 'Be brave my child,' Morax had whispered as he put on his finest blue woollen tunic and the ornate leather belt his mother had given him on the day of his marriage. He squeezed Ealith's shoulder as he left the house.

Morax had died first. Attacked by the terrified mob of villagers, while he knelt and begged Captain Muspell to protect his wife and child. They had left him bleeding to death on the dirt path.

Captain Muspell had taken a sealed proclamation from his shoulder bag and read his orders to the villagers. The clan of the Marchosias were classed as that of battlemages and sentenced to death, without mercy, under the Recantation of Magik laws.

The Wergend soldiers had held the ring of villagers back as Muspell stamped a fastening seal on the front door of the little house. Then he placed bushels of corn around the door, took a torch from the nearest villager, and threw it onto the thatch. The fire ran across the dried reed roof, covering the house in a choking grey screen of smoke.

It was Morax's dying gift to his family.

Ealith had wrapped Meloc in a woven blanket, pressed her amulet into his shaking hands, and whispered, 'Be safe and survive, my love.' Then she picked him up and threw him through the tiny back window of the house into the darkness of the grass fields, just as the roof collapsed into their home.

His mother's screams had lasted only seconds but had been burned into Meloc's consciousness for a lifetime.

A loud scream brought Meloc back to the present. He watched, blinking the tears from his eyes as Fafnair twisted so its head was facing downwards towards the shield wall. The night sky around the dragon shimmered with heat as the dragon roared and plunged downwards. A sea of red fire streamed from its jaws, burning a cindered passage through the stone circle, and towards the company.

The fire exploded against the shield wall.

The soldiers manning the left flank screamed as their wooden shields exploded into flames and their leather uniforms welded onto their arms. Their faces blistered with the heat. The dragon breathed again. Its flames passing across the shield wall.

'Maintain the wall,' Dygg screamed as he collapsed onto the ground, as red flames danced around him. Dygg watched as his wooden shield rolled away and then closed his eyes.

The intense heat melted the skin from the sergeant's body. Satisfied, the hungry fire burnt itself out. All that remained was a whitened skeleton inside a smoking uniform.

The shield hit a small stone and clattered onto the ground.

The soldiers looked at their fallen sergeant in horror, dropped their shields, and tried to flee the temple. Several, caught by a second wave of dragonfyre, were incinerated as they ran forming black shadows upon the towering stones.

Kasian pushed both warlock's faces into the ground and closed his eyes tightly as a wave of superheated air rushed over them. The heat burnt black holes through their clothes, blistering the back of their bodies.

The leaves of the dogwood bush blackened and crumbled; its ash taken by the swirling air.

'By Wergennis' blood!' Kasian cursed. 'Do not move. It will seize the running first.'

Meloc and Azrael nodded.

The dragon roared and circled above them.

Kasian propped himself onto his elbows and scanned the carnage. The shield wall was destroyed, and the temple littered with the charcoaled remains of the Welfasten company.

'We need to find cover in the trees down there,' Kasian pointed to the knoll of oakly trees, covering the eastern slope of the Kristal Mountain, as he crouched behind the skeletal bush.

'When has trying to outrun a dragon ever been a successful plan?' Meloc muttered.

There was a scuffling behind them, and they turned to see Councillor Hundar drop a perspiring Chief Feitar behind them.

'I can't believe you forced me to come to this... this helhole. I'm going to die here and it's all your fault. You must get me out of here.' Feitar grabbed Kasian by the collar and shook him.

'Let go of me,' Kasian said quietly, in a voice filled with disgust. He looked up at the dragon. The disturbance had been noticed. It had dropped lower in the sky its long green neck weaving through the ruined remains of the temple, sniffing loudly as it searched for fresh meat.

'Stay very still,' Kasian whispered.

Fafnair turned towards the survivors, its amber eyes gleaming through the swirls of ash and smoke. Feitar jumped up and ran towards the mountain path. 'Save yourselves!' he screamed as the dragon gave one flap of its wings and flew towards them, its talons stretched, ready to snatch the fleeing chief. Feitar screamed in terror and fell to the floor, sobbing in a foetal position.

'May the goddess protect me!' Kasian swore and thumped the ground with his fist. He leapt up and drew his sword as he ran to defend the chief. He pushed his sweaty dark brown hair from his eyes as he stood in front of Feitar, bracing himself for the attack.

'You must save the chief,' Hundar grabbed Azrael in alarm, pleading with the prostrate warlocks. 'Afterall, he is your cousin,' he added casting a sideways glance at Meloc.

'Just because we are somewhat related, it doesn't mean I like the man,' Meloc whispered.

'If the King finds out that one of his appointed officials died without you coming to his defence, you will be executed without trial, as a traitor to Mercia. He placed the royal seal on the Anti-Mercian Treason Act at last month's meeting of the Star Court,' Hundar said solemnly.

'Faen!' Meloc groaned.

Fafnair dived talons first at the sobbing chief. Kasian slashed across the dragon's feet, with a borrowed sword but the blade merely bounced off the dragon's talons. The dragon twisted in the air, its tail whipped around, and knocked Kasian from him feet, hurling him against the tallest torstone. The sword fell and clattered against the stones.

'Save me!' screamed the chief, as the dragon hovered above him, its giant green wings spanning the diameter of the stone circle.

TWENTY

Name - Meloc

Location - The Temple of Fafnair, Kristal Mountain

Allegiance - The Mercian Warbands

'Azrael be safe!' Councillor Hundar called out as he leapt up from the dogbush. He grabbed a spear lying next to the blackened remains of a fallen warbandmen and ran towards Feitar.

'What the hel are you doing? Come back… now!' Azrael shouted as he watched in horror as the councillor stood in front of Feitar, his borrowed spear pointed towards the dragon. Fafnair roared and swooped downwards, his amber eyes fixed hungrily on Hundar.

'He is an adviser not a soldier. He will get himself killed. This is madness!' Azrael groaned.

'We're all mad for coming here. This is not our fight, let's get out of…' Meloc whispered.

'*Rigning*!' Azrael shouted and hit the floor with his open palm. Instantly, a black shadow fell across the temple as dark clouds appeared in the starlit sky. The shadow of the clouds grew bigger until they covered the waking stars, and the first drops of rain began to fall. Fafnair hesitated, its razor teeth barely two feet from Hundar, as he sensed a spell had been cast.

More clouds raced across the sky and joined together to form a dark grey ring which began to turn slowly, becoming faster with each rotation. White flashes of electricity crackled between the clouds. The sky rumbled and the ruined temple shook. A bolt of lightning leapt through the darkness and hit the stone circle. A vertical torstone split in half and collapsed onto the soldiers hiding beneath it. Their screams and cries for help hidden by the thundering sky. A silver flash streaked through the clouds towards Fafnair. The dragon screeched, flapped its wings, and flew backwards. The lightning bolt ripped through the space where the dragon had been and exploded into the ground below. Bush and grass were incinerated, while around them a firestorm burned orange in the night.

A deep growl sounded through the sky as large drops of rain began to fall.

Meloc sneezed and shivered as he wrapped his cloak tightly around his body. 'What were you trying to do? Wash the bloody dragon?' Meloc asked as he sat on his heels in the mud.

'I thought it might put out his fire,' Azrael answered, the rain making white streaks on his soot-covered face.

The rain grew heavier and poured across the mountainside, picking up the cremated remains of the fallen, creating rivers of blackwater, cursed by the violent death of the ashes they contained, while the waven grass, which had sprung up in the cracks and paths around the stones, shrivelled to brown and withered.

A deep, growling sound came from behind the warlocks.

'Oh faen!' Azrael groaned as he turned to see Fafnair soaring towards them, his breath turning the sheets of rain into amber-tinged clouds of steam.

'I think he actually likes the rain, after all he lives down a bloody well!' said Meloc. 'We need to end this, before we either get burnt to death or die of exposure.'

Azrael looked rather crestfallen. 'It's a spell I use for watering the crops in the Midheim. It's the strongest one I know.'

'I might know of something slightly stronger,' Meloc winked at Azrael as he slammed his palm into the mud and shouted, '*Vídda-holar.*' Instantly, a black circle appeared in the centre of the temple. The circle began to spin and bulge into a sphere. The mud lying beneath the circle began to steam and bubble. A nearby torstone began to wobble, the side nearest the sphere bent inwards, and disappeared.

Fafnair screeched in alarm and flew upwards, trying to avoid being caught in the sphere's energy field.

A loud horn sounded through the rain as a huge metal spear arced over the temple and clattered against the rock littered mountainside. Seconds later a contingent of mounted, navy-cloaked horsemen cantered up the overgrown path towards the temple.

'And I thought things couldn't get any worse,' Azrael groaned and nudged Meloc.

'Oh look! The King's Own Horsehelm have arrived… better hide the honey wine and lock up the women,' Meloc tutted. He nodded to Azrael. The irises of both warlocks enlarged slightly as the amber galdor flames flashed from them. The sphere disappeared and Azrael whispered an incantation and the wheeling thunderstorm eased to that of a more natural light rain shower.

Meloc breathed a sigh of relief – all traces of magik were gone. He grabbed hold of Azrael's sleeve and pointed towards a fallen stone. 'We should be safe under there.'

Azrael nodded.

They both crawled through the mud towards the stone.

'Don't move,' a martial voice growled.

'Hel!' Azrael cursed as he felt the point of a spear press

against his back and raised his hands.

'We are really not lucky today!' whispered Meloc.

'Bring up the Thunderer and kill me that dragon,' the officer demanded as a cart emblazoned with the black raven in flight, pulled by two huge warhorses rolled across the ground.

The Thunderer was a bolt-thrower, an overlarge crossbow, made of sturdy oak pieces fastened together with iron plates. It was mounted on adjustable feet in the back of the cart. Its main body was grooved and slanted downwards. The body contained the bolt weight, a metal cylinder with a hooked end, through which the crossbow rope was passed through. A rope at the end of the bolt weight was attached to a turning wheel. A thickset horseman began to turn the wheel. The bolt weight groaned and moved to the bottom of the bolt thrower, pulling the crossbow rope taut. Another horseman placed a thick-pointed spear in the groove above the rope. He stood back and raised his hand.

'Release the bolt!' shouted the officer.

The thickset soldier let the wheel run free and the spear sprung into the air.

Fafnair screamed as the bolt hit his tail and he flew higher into the night sky. A shimmering green dragonscale thumped onto the ground, just in front of the officer's feet. Major Sverd picked it up and tossed it to his messenger. 'Stow this in my saddle boy, it will be a fine gift for the King.'

Chief Feitar uncurled himself and quickly stood up, smoothing down the front of his mud-ridden robe. 'Thank the gods you have arrived. As I said to Councillor Hundar, the King's Horsehelm always overcome their enemy. Didn't I just say that Hundar?'

Hundar nodded, letting his much smaller spear drop as he

stood next to the chief, 'Yes indeed, chief, you always say that.'

Major Sverd stared at the two officials. 'I was sent by the King, for the galdor weapons. I trust you have them?'

The chief's ruddy face paled. 'Er… Unfortunately, they were stolen, er… years ago apparently.' He looked at Captain Kasian and then across to Meloc.

The captain sat on the ground, his back against a vertical stone, his face covered in a mixture of blood and dirt. 'We both went down to the underground passages and saw for ourselves. The box has been broken. There were no weapons.'

'And yet they were guarded by a dragon and protected by traps only known by senior officers of the horsehelm and the Star Council. They could not have been stolen,' the major growled.

Feitar looked from the lieutenant to the captain, his face frowning in concentration. 'Er… that's what they told me anyway. I don't know if it was true. I never even wanted to come here in the first place. Him and his warlock forced me to come here using magikcraft,' he pointed an accusing finger at Kasian. 'They must be in league with the Dunmuir. They are traitors. I personally, have witnessed that warlock perform illegal acts of magik.'

Sverd nodded at the chief. 'I see. Men arrest the officer and that warlock.'

'But I haven't done anything!' Meloc shouted as two of the horsehelm dismounted and approached him, horse whips in hand.

A Wergend officer with wild blond hair tied back with leather cord, appeared behind the warlock, yanked his hair backwards, and stamped an anti-magik seal on his forehead.

Instantly, Meloc's legs gave way. He was dragged to his feet by the two horsehelm and hung limply between them.

'We have done nothing wrong. You have my word as a Wergend officer,' Kasian said as he stood up, holding onto the stone with one hand for support.

'Well, we will see if you are telling the truth soon enough,' Sverd growled. 'But a Wergend officer working with an unmysnstered, unbound warlock outlaw…' he nodded towards Meloc, 'does not look that innocent. The truth will be extracted from you, and you will both be executed for treason.'

'You cannot arrest me. I am an Officer of the Wergend. I work under the sealed orders of the King and Grand Master Heilagan, the head of my order. You have no jurisdiction over me,' Kasian said, stepping backwards as two riders of the horsehelm approached him, their long blond hair flowing from beneath their domed helmets. Kasian's hand hovering above the hilt of his borrowed sword.

'Captain Asgot, you know me. I am no traitor to the order,' Kasian glanced over to his fellow Wergend officer who was watching silently, his arms crossed.

'You were found working alongside an unlicenced warlock. The wickedness of magik has corrupted you. You are a disgrace to the Order of the Wergend. Take his sword and bind his hands, you will be tried and punished for your betrayal,' Asgot said and nodded his head slightly.

Two of the horsehelm leapt at the captain, knocking him off balance. Kasian crashed heavily, pinned to the floor by the horsemen as Asgot removed his sword.

'This is not even your sword,' Asgot said examining the blade. 'It is unblessed and tainted with its owners' blood.' He dropped the sword and looked down at the kneeling officer in disgust.

'Get off me,' Kasian growled as he struggled to shake the horsemen from him.

'Accept your capture with dignity, Kasian,' Asgot said.

'You are being detained under the provisions of the Anti-Mercian Treason Act,' Sverd stated and kicked Kasian in the stomach. Kasian grunted and gasped for breath.

'Stand him up,' the major ordered.

The two horsemen pulled Kasian to his feet.

'If there is one thing I cannot stand, it is a traitor,' Asgot whispered in his ear. He stepped back and punched Kasian in the jaw. Kasian slumped unconscious between the guards.

'Bring up the prison cart.' Sverd ordered. He signalled for his horse. 'Move out men. We have wasted enough time here. Corporal Sker take three horsemen and bring the prisoners to Fastness dungeon. I'm sure the warlock will feel quite at home there.'

'But aren't you going to escort us back to Welfasten?' Feitar asked in horror. 'What if we meet the Dunmuir?'

'We head north-east to destroy the bridges that cross the Kerlauger river. It will delay the whole Dunmuir advance and give the Southern warband a chance to increase the fortifications around Fastness Fortress. You are most welcome to join us,' Sverd raised his hand, and signalled his men to move out.

'But that is a suicide mission. You will meet the advance head on,' Feitar paled. Quickly, he recovered and shook his head sadly. 'I would gladly fight to protect my beloved Mercia but for my people. They need me. The honour of fighting the Dunmuir will not be mine, just yet. I must return to Welfasten and review the city defences,' Feitar replied as he backed away from the mounted warriors in alarm.

'And it's not like the Dunmuir battlemages can use magik or anything to create *krystal bridges*,' Meloc commented.

'Get that damn warlock out of here!' Sverd shouted at the guards.

Two pairs of gnarled hands grabbed his shoulders and manhandled him into a wooden cage, iron anti-magik seals welded to its bars, perched on top of a cart.

'Well, well, a warlock without a wrist guard. You are lucky the major is so lenient; if it were up to me, you and your people would be killed on sight,' hissed Corporal Sker.

Meloc looked at his left wrist and cursed. He pressed himself against the back of the cage.

Corporal Sker shoved his sword through the gaps, its point ripping through Meloc's fragile robe and cutting his chest. The warlock yelped with pain and the guards roared with laughter.

'Let me go. I'm trying to save the city, you bloody halfwit,' Meloc hissed.

Sker smashed his fist through the bars of the cage. Meloc tumbled backwards, falling against the unconscious Kasian.

They followed the others down the overgrown path and away from Fafnair's kingdom, until it reached the mountain foothills and opened out onto the flatlands of the Midheim where the ragged path joined the great road. Sverd raised his hand, and the horsehelm took the north-east road, while the prison detail and the remains of the Welfasten company turned south.

'Do not fear. I will appeal your case before the king,' Azrael whispered as he rode passed, mounted on a small bay mare. Sverd watched the horsehelm file past him and beckoned the scarred guard to approach and whispered something in his ear.

Then he dug his heels into the flank of his warhorse and cantered after his men.

Meloc felt his heart stop for a second as the guard turned and stared at him. An ominous feeling made the warlock shiver as a cold night wind tugged at their clothing. He did not think he would be alive long enough to hear his case go before the King.

TWENTY-ONE

Name - Meloc
Location - A Galdorhus, Welfasten City
Allegiance - The Mercian Warbands

Meloc startled awake. Sweat was pouring from his forehead and his heart pounded in his chest. His eyes casting dancing amber shadows against the cobweb-draped ceiling. Quickly, he blinked the magik from his eyes and looked around him. The room was empty. He breathed a sigh of relief and sunk back into the pile of empty hessian sacks which had made up his bed. The left side of his face felt sore. Tentatively, he touched his cheek. The hot pain of a fresh burn stung his face and made him wince.

He frowned as he tried to recall what had happened.

He remembered watching the two grey horses who had been pulling the prison cart whinny with fright and bolt into the woods, the wooden prison cage lying smashed against a towering oaken tree. He saw the surprised face of Corporal Sker staring at him, his eyes wide open in terror as a large dark stain oozed across his chest.

'Scitte!' Meloc swore as he sat up in bed. The Welfasten company had been destroyed.

A stream of fire had burnt its way through the convoy. He remembered watching his portly cousin run screaming into the woods, his cloak ablaze. Then lightning crackled across the sky and the scene vanished. The last thing Meloc remembered was two unblinking green reptilian eyes. The waterdrek had led the Dunmuir forward units straight to their position. Fafnair blamed them for the desecration of the temple and the loss of his treasure, and a dragon's vengeance is swift and deadly.

Meloc shook the thoughts of Fafnair from his mind. He was safe, for the moment at least. He stared around the dishevelled room. Its walls sloped inwards, following the diagonals of the roof. A small, round window had been cut into the wood and a circle of sunlight shone onto the dirty wooden floorboards catching a cloud of rising dust in its rays. Beneath the window was a small, wooden door, half the size of a grown man. In the middle of the door, someone had carved a rune depicting the lower half of a vase turned on its side, a *petthro*. Meloc breathed a sigh of relief. Somehow, he had remained tethered to the galdor network and transported himself to a galdorhus: an underground network of illegal, sigil-protected safehouses used by magikind in need of protection from the Crown.

He had not visited this one before and tapped the blue tattoo on his forearm for luck, hoping it was not located in land controlled by the Dunmuir.

A battered table stood by the wall. It was covered in open, leather-bound books with straining spines. Meloc wandered over to the table, hoping to find a clue to the galdorhus' location. He picked up one of the books and blew a layer of dust from its cover. It was the *Saga of Hijálmarr*, a rather tedious tale of a heroic Mercian battlemage from the Eldor Age. Sitting precariously on the right corner of the table was a white candle, its plain wooden holder covered in dried wax drips. Beside the candle was an inkpot, quill, and several scrolls of parchment paper. Meloc unrolled a scroll and read the first sentence, 'A Rebuttal of the Mercian Anti-Magik Laws.' It was heresy and being caught with the document would mean instant execution. Meloc started to roll the scroll up but then he sensed a change in the galdor energy. He scanned down the scroll and a wave of sickness rose from the pit of his stomach as he watched his name being written in black ink. The scroll had been cursed and he was now a signatory to heresy and treason. If the scroll was ever found, he was in no doubt that his execution would be long and painful one.

A loud snort came from the darkened corner of the room. Meloc spun round and peered through the darkness. A figure was lying on the little wooden bed, wearing a rough cotton cream undershirt. A pair of old black boots stuck out past the end of the bed.

'Oh, bloody hell!' Meloc exclaimed.

Quickly, he gathered up the scrolls and books, and tip-toed over to a carved wooden chest half-hidden beneath a grey woollen blanket which flopped over the sides of the little bed.

The chest was small. Its lid engraved with a deer, a daemonic looking bird, and two snakes entwined in a series of 'S' shapes. Meloc stared at the little chest. The heads of the snakes rose out from the box and turned towards him, their forked tongues flickering, as they tasted his presence in the air. Their eyes glowed amber as they began to sway from side to side.

Slowly, Meloc began to move in harmony with the snakes.

He pinched his arm. The pain broke the spell. The snakes hissed angrily at him and shook their tails in warning.

A skittering sound came from within the chest and a river of tiny red spiders began to surge through the keyhole. The spiders swarmed over the front panel of the box and fell onto the floor. Meloc stamped on the nearest spider which made a sizzling sound as it melted into the floorboards. He lifted his foot and cursed as he noticed a one-inch hole had been burnt into the wood. Then he examined the bottom of his boot. There was a somewhat larger hole burnt into its leather sole. He put his finger through the hole and felt his foot. Somehow, he would have to steal some money to either repair them or buy new boots. Either way he doubted that Kasian would approve.

One of the snakes lashed out and caught a scurrying spider which melted in its mouth, dripping green venom across the table.

Kasian groaned and began to thrash about. A bad dream would soon pull him from his sleep. Meloc gathered all the magikal documents under one arm, raised his free hand above the chest and whispered the word, '*Sorma.*'

An amber haze glowed across the chest and the smell of lavender permeated through the dusty air. The snakes wavered unsteadily and then fell backwards, becoming carvings on the chest lid once more and the scurrying noises inside the box stopped.

Meloc breathed a sigh of relief and whispered, '*Opna,*'

The lid creaked open.

Kasian sat upright. 'What was that?' he demanded as his hand reached for the hilt of his sword. His sword belt was empty. A look of horror flashed across his soot-stained face as he searched the bed for his missing sword.

Meloc threw the magikal documents in the chest and slammed the lid shut. Then he smiled innocently at the officer. 'Ah, you're awake at last. I was beginning to wonder whether you were going to sleep all day.'

'Uy! May the Goddess have mercy on me. What time is it?' the officer asked. 'I must get back to Heilagar and make my report to the Grand Master before the orders of treason and theft are announced. You will come too and explain what happened, even though you are a known warlock, and your word means little, but it might help. I need a sword. I cannot go before my order without one, it is forbidden. I must be ready to fight for the goddess at all times.'

Kasian leapt out of bed, stopped, and looked around the attic room. A confused frown on his face. 'Er... where are we exactly? The last thing I remember was meeting the horsehelm. Have we been brought here under guard?'

Meloc shook his head.

'Your sword is lost, and things have become slightly more complicated. As we took the southern road, the convoy was set upon by Dunmuir scouts. It was a massacre. We were lucky though; the prison cart was smashed and the anti-magik seals broken. I managed to spell us to safety.'

Kasian looked at Meloc in surprise and bowed. 'Umm... I see. It seems I owe you my life, warlock. Thank you for saving me. It is surprising, but then these are surprising times.'

'I need to find a sword and then we must ride straight to Heilagar Fortress and explain this series of events to the Grand Master,' Kasian decided.

'And that would be a very interesting conversation,' Meloc commented. 'Not only have we lost the galdor weapons but now we are the sole survivors of a Dunmuir attack. Even I think we are looking a bit suspicious.'

'The truth will exonerate us,' Kasian said as he opened the old wooden door and walked down a rickety staircase. 'Mind you,' he looked back at Meloc, 'You have used illegal magik on several occasions which I will have to write in my report, but at least you will not be hanged for treason.'

'Thanks,' Meloc replied, a slight smile on his lips. He had no intention of accompanying the officer to the Wergend stronghold. Meloc followed Kasian down the staircase and slipped through a narrow doorway which led onto the cobbled courtyard below the galdorhus. A loose roof tile was lifted by the breeze and smashed against the cobbles, missing his head by a fraction of an inch.

'That was close!' exclaimed Meloc.

'I cannot tell whether you are blessed or cursed by your god,' Kasian frowned rubbing his stubble.

'Neither can I,' Meloc grinned as he stepped over the rubble.

'I recognise this place. We are back in Welfasten but what has happened here?' Kasian asked.

The once noisy city was silent.

Meloc shrugged his shoulders, 'The Shady Leaf is full any time of day.' He crossed the cobbled street and tentatively opened the door of the alehouse.

Broken wooden tables and benches spewed across the straw floor. The alekeeper lay slumped across the rough plank he once used to serve drinks on. His customers, lying amongst the debris, showed the raw red wounds of men hacked down by heavy swords. In the far corner, two northern warbandmen lay face down in a pile of broken benches.

'They are all dead,' Kasian announced turning over a blood-stained body, two black arrows protruding from its back. 'We should leave,' he whispered. 'The city has fallen, the Dunmuir may still be here.'

Meloc nodded and crept across the cobbled courtyard of the alehouse, slipped on a pool of congealing blood, and skidded into a stack of wooden crates piled up against the courtyard wall. He fell face down in the dirty straw half-hidden by the broken crates. A man lay a few feet from him, his face staring upwards but seeing nothing, four arrows were embedded into his bare chest. A small sword lay loosely in his right hand.

At least the stable master had died with honour.

A sudden gust of cold wind lifted the straw and dust off the courtyard. A small feather, half-matted into the dried blood, fluttered in the quickening breeze. It had been dyed purple.

'The King's bodyguard, the Purple Guard fought here,' Meloc whispered, pointing to the arrows.

'Umm…' Kasian ran his hand through his dark brown hair. 'But why would the Purple Guard come here? They seldom leave the King's side. And if they had defended the city from a Dunmuir attack, where are the bodies of their fallen? Something is not right, let us leave this place.' He marched through the courtyard, making for the garrison stables.

Somewhere a broken door slammed in the gusting winds and a flock of crows swooped down into the courtyard in one flapping black cloud; their sharp beaks ripped at the twisted corpses of men, women and children lying scattered against the cobbles. Meloc looked away in disgust and ran to catch up with the officer.

The dirt and straw scattered across the cobbles lay in eulogy to the once bustling city. Wooden houses flanked both sides of the streets, their overhanging upper stories peered down at him. He could sense their outrage. Why was he still alive when their beloved families lay slain on their floors?

'I'm sorry,' Meloc whispered guiltily as he headed for the stables.

The rising wind blew the straw covering the courtyard into a miniature whirlwind and the hanging shop signs began to groan in lament for the dead.

A black, bulging cloud appeared in the sky as a dark shadow passed over the city.

Meloc looked at the threatening cloud. He sensed myrkir hidden in its darkness and hurried into the stable.

'Here, I have saddled a horse for you,' Kasian whispered, his voice lowered as if he did not wish to disturb the dead.

'Hel! You almost gave me a heart attack!' Meloc jumped, clutching his chest. 'Why do you Wergend always have to creep up on people? I don't know who will try to kill me next: mysterious masked soldiers, the Purple Guards, angry ancient spirits or the Dunmuir!'

'Sorry,' Kasian replied, 'but we need to leave this place, and quickly.' He tossed the reins at Meloc and began to saddle a large bay warhorse that snorted and stamped its hooves impatiently.

Gingerly, Meloc mounted the small, black mare who had been watching them while chewing on some hay it had pulled from the net which hung lopsidedly from a nail in the wooden stable door. Meloc grabbed the reins and dug his heels into her side. The horse sighed and trotted into the cobbled street.

'Ey! Wait for me!' Kasian shouted.

Meloc half-smiled as he heard hoof beats clatter after him. Perhaps he was not so repulsive after all…

TWENTY-TWO

Name - Meloc
Location - Cripplegate, Welfasten City
Allegiance - The Mercian Warbands

Cripplegate was the smallest and least well-guarded gate on the Welfasten city wall. The arched gateway was protected by a thick oak portcullis and two solid slated-iron gates. Above the gateway were the battlements, which overlooked the flow of traffic in and out of the gate and joined onto the main city wall. Two huge, fierce-looking ballistae crossbows were mounted on the battlements and stood silhouetted against the spreading red dawn. Round fortified towers stood either side of the gate, bulging out from the city wall.

Kasian slowed his horse to a stop and frowned.

The portcullis had been raised and the heavy gates stood ajar. An unnatural silence had descended on the gatehouse which normally bustled with a steady tide of incoming peasants, the sick of various social stations, and assorted chained prisoners.

'Scitte! This horse is more wild pony than trained warhorse,' Meloc swore as he tried unsuccessfully to slow his horse to a walking pace. Kasian tutted and grabbed the reins as Meloc cantered by. Instantly, the horse stood still and began to chew on some of the straw which had blown across the cobblestones.

'Show off,' Meloc muttered.

'And what daemonry is this, I wonder?' Kasian mused as he

stood in his stirrups and peered through a lower arrow slit on the right tower. 'Why was this gate not damaged in the fighting? And where are all the dead?' He rubbed the dark, two-day old stubble on his chin and shook his head, 'I fear something unnatural, probably magikal, has occurred here.'

Kasian dismounted and tied his horse to an iron ring on the tower wall.

Meloc's horse sniffed the early morning air and began to circle, shaking its head unhappily. He quickly dismounted.

Kasian rummaged through his leather satchel and brought out a small opaque magnifier; a piece of glass filled with flickering lights encircled in an iron casing. Four elongated crows with open beaks had been etched into the iron.

'This is the *Sight of Heroc*,' Kasian said as he held it up and watched the dancing lights inside the magnifier glow brighter. 'Only nine of these remain. The rest were mislaid within the vaults of Heilagar Fortress. I was awarded the great honour of being chosen to carry one.'

'Really?' Meloc said raising one fine eyebrow. 'I suppose the rest went missing around the same time as the Serpents' Breath then. The security of your order is terrible. Do you know that? But I guess at least that's one thing I won't get blamed for.'

Kasian threw the warlock a withering glance. Then he stared into the glass and whispered, '*Heroc*... show me what magik has been cast.'

The glass glowed.

The bright morning sky darkened as a silvery crescent moon arced across the sky and shone above the city.

They watched as shadowy wisps of past images began to appear around the gate. Cries and orders swirled around them.

A small orange orb appeared over the top of the left guardhouse and slowly floated towards them.

An arrow whizzed through the darkness, narrowly missing Meloc's head as it thudded into the gate.

'Quick! Turn that bloody thing off!' Meloc yelled as he tried to grab the magnifier, his eyes casting amber shadows across the gates.

'Do not worry warlock. I know you have cast many, many illegal spells,' Kasian said as he held Meloc at bay.

The shadows began to take more corporeal forms. A man, his face hidden beneath a dark cloak, hacked at something lying on the ground with a long dagger. A howling dog ran through the open gate. A flash of metal was caught by the moonlight, as a black cloaked figure ran towards them, his sword raised above his head. His cloak opened slightly as he ran to reveal a bright purple lining.

'This cannot be!' exclaimed Kasian. 'He wears the purple of the King's Royal Guard. He must have stolen it from a dead body.' He shook his head in disgust and kissed the amulet which hung around his neck as he whispered a prayer for the dead.

'Watch out!' screamed Meloc as he pushed the surprised officer into the alley next to the right guardhouse. They fell against the cobblestones as the Purple Guard ran past them, chasing the ghosts of the dead.

'Sometimes the *Heroc* shows us things which we cannot explain,' Kasian said solemnly as he stood up and put the magnifier back in his bag. 'It is best to leave such things to the goddess.'

'A very Wergend idea,' Meloc smiled as he sat on the cold stones.

The smile faded from his face.

'Oh krap!' He swore as the forgotten orb floated down the alley. It began to pulsate and enlarge, its edges straining to contain the swirling gas within.

'It's going to explode, cover your eyes!' Meloc shouted, hiding his face in his arms.

'What magik is this?' Kasian shouted as he fell next to him.

'This is not warlock magik!' Meloc yelled. 'It is a *Megin Trap* set by the Wergend.'

'But that is not possible. No Wergend would set a trap without first placing a sigil on the floor to warn their brothers.'

'I see. Well, I think someone must have forgotten…' said Meloc raising an eyebrow. 'Any idea what is going to come out of it?'

Kasian shrugged. 'Casting *Megin* incantations is above my rank. Only temple masters are entrusted with learning the tenets of the *Megin*. However, I think we had best be on our guard. I do not think whatever comes out of it will be friendly.'

There was a burst of white light and the orb disintegrated revealing a huge grey Wergend brother complete with helmet and lowered faceplate. He held his sword raised before him as he marched towards Meloc and Kasian.

Kasian leapt to his feet, pulling Meloc up by his shirt collar.

'Run!' he yelled, 'that is a member of the Fallen Guard. He has been called from his travels through the Sumorlands to continue his fight against the darkness and will kill anything that has come into contact with magik.'

Meloc opened his mouth to protest but Kasian manhandled him further into the alleyway.

Its footsteps echoed through the silence as it followed them.

'I hope you have a plan?' Meloc panted as he tried to keep

up with the much fitter Wergend officer.

'Wergennis will always provide for her children,' Kasian said as he stopped outside a tiny wooden door embedded in the alley wall. 'Praise the goddess! This must be the escape exit from the guard tower.' He knocked three times on the door and turned the iron ring.

The tiny door stood fast.

'Daemonios!' he cursed. 'It's been sealed.' He took a large ring of strangely shaped black keys from his bag, selected a skeleton key with an overlong bit, and tapped the door. A keyhole appeared in the wood just above the ring.

'By order of the Wergend Command, you must lay down your weapons and submit to your punishment,' ordered the Fallen Guard.

'But I am a Wergend officer!' Kasian shouted at the phantom.

The guard hesitated as a white light flickered in the darkness behind his faceplate. 'That is a falsehood. You were accused of treason and found guilty. You are dishonoured and are no longer part of the Wergend Order.'

'But we have not been tried yet. I have the right to appear before the Council of Heilagar,' Kasian shouted.

'It was the Council who passed your sentence,' stated the Fallen Guard as he leapt forward and slashed down at Kasian with his two-handed broadsword.

Kasian grabbed the dagger hidden inside his boot as he sprang to his feet and parried the blow. His sword arm buckled with the force, and he felt something inside his elbow snap as muscle ripped from bone.

'Wergennis' grace!' Kasian groaned, shaking his head. 'My sword arm is useless.' He swapped the dagger to his left hand

and crouched lower.

The phantom lunged forward.

Kasian leapt backwards, his back pressed up against the door. Then he ducked beneath the Fallen Guard and lunged upwards, his blade went straight into the phantom's neck. The guard made a gargling sound and fell to his knees, clutching at his throat. He collapsed onto the cobbles as his form exploded into wisps of orange smoke.

'Finally, we have a change of luck,' Meloc breathed a sigh of relief.

The orange smoke reformed, split into two, and darkened to grey.

Two Fallen Guards rose from the smoke.

'Faen! It's the *Torfalt* curse. Strike one down and two others will take his place,' Meloc whispered.

'Yes, I think that is obvious warlock,' Kasian replied. His face had turned ash grey and sweat began to trickle down his forehead.

'Are you alright?' Meloc frowned. 'Do you want me to heal your arm?' He touched Kasian's arm.

The officer shook Meloc's hand away. 'Mortal pain is a gift from the goddess. It tells us we are still alive,' Kasian gasped as he rummaged through his shoulder bag. He pulled out a thick woollen wrapping and passed it to the warlock. 'Here, if you want to help, make me a sling.'

Meloc nodded and tied the ends together. Then he looped the wrapping around Kasian's head.

Kasian winced as he carefully placed his damaged arm in the sling.

'Are you sure you don't want me to cast a healing spell?' Meloc asked.

'I would rather cut my arm off with a spoon,' Kasian replied. 'My body must be kept pure from the taint of magik.'

Meloc tutted and rolled his eyes.

'However, if you know of any spells that send the dead back to their resting grounds, now would be a good time to cast them,' Kasian said as he watched the two Fallen Guards approach.

'No… but I can unlock a few doors,' Meloc winked. He knocked on the little door and it swung open.

'You could have done that earlier,' Kasian grimaced.

'Oh, but where is the fun in that?' Meloc grinned as he held the door open for Kasian. As soon as they were safely through, he touched the door and whispered under his breath. Instantly, the door was surrounded by a shimmering orange veil.

'That should hold them for a while at least,' Meloc frowned as heavy blows began to hammer the shaking door.

'Hurry up! We must find the front door before they realise there's another exit,' Meloc said, heading along a narrow corridor towards the main entrance.

'Wait!' said Kasian. 'We cannot go yet. Treachery has been committed here. I can feel it. We have been wrongfully cast in the roles of villains. We must search the guardhouse and find out what is happening. Then perhaps we will lift the stain of dishonour from our names.'

Meloc shrugged. 'To be honest, it doesn't really bother me. I just came to warn my cousin this city was in danger and unfortunately, I was right. Once we leave Welfasten I will travel north-west to the Sea of Iskaldur and sail beyond the reach of the Two Kingdoms. I want no part in this war.'

'I see,' said Kasian thoughtfully, 'so there is to be a parting of our ways. Thank you for your help warlock, you have been

a more useful companion than I could ever have imagined.'
Kasian held out his good arm. Meloc nodded and he grabbed
the officer's arm in a comrade's farewell.

'Go with the luck of the old gods,' Meloc said solemnly.

'Umm…' Kasian shook his head and gripped Meloc's arm
tighter.

Meloc frowned and tried to pull his arm away. Quickly,
Kasian snapped a rowan band over his wrist. The runes etched
onto the band glowed, and the wood tightened.

'Scitte!' Meloc cursed. 'What is this!' His eyes blazed
amber as he tried to cast the band from his wrist.

Kasian half-smiled as he pulled up his sleeve and showed
Meloc a similar looking wooden wristband on his good wrist.

'Do not try to vanquish the *Samian Confine*. We are
joined… even in death, lest you get some ideas, until we are
released by a temple master.

'But why the hel would you do such a thing?' Meloc
demanded, trying to squeeze his hand through the wristband.

'We cannot go against the wishes of Wergennis. Our path
together has been chosen by the mother goddess. We must
regain our honour or die trying,' Kasian said solemnly as he
crept up the spiral stone staircase which ran up the middle of
the guard tower.

'But I'm a warlock!' Meloc shouted as he followed the
officer up the stairs. 'I have no honour to lose in the first place!
I refuse to be party to some Wergend suicide mission. Release
me or face the consequences.' The dark stone staircase began
to shake. Several stones became loose and smashed into the
lower floors.

Kasian smiled. 'Release is impossible. I do not possess the
skill and if you kill me, you will have to carry my cold dead

corpse around until you find a temple master willing to release the *Confine*. Now shall we carry on or stand here and wait for the Fallen Guards to kill us both?'

Meloc closed his eyes and the amber energy dissipated from his body. 'You have no idea what you have done,' he whispered to Kasian's back. The captain ignored the warlock and marched up the staircase.

The staircase opened into the guard's living quarters at the top of the tower.

A dying candle flickered, sending dancing shadows roaring across the empty room.

The parchment case had been broken; its scrolls scattered. While half-eaten plates of food lay abandoned on the heavy wooden table in the centre of the room. Its wooden benches upturned to form hasty barriers; their undersides covered in sword slashes. A solitary leather boot stood in the centre of the room; its owner lost.

'What trickery is this?' Kasian whispered as he walked through the remains of a dinner half-eaten, which now lay smashed across the guardhouse floor. He clutched his amulet. 'But there are no bodies… I sense myrkir at work here.'

He crept towards the weapons rack. It stood half-empty, one of the swords abandoned on the floor. Kasian picked it up. It was heavier and less finely balanced than his lost sword, but it was a killing blade. He slipped it into his sword belt.

'Praise the goddess. I am whole again,' Kasian breathed a sigh of relief. He picked up a lighter blade and handed it to Meloc. 'Here… arm yourself warlock.'

'I don't need one,' Meloc replied, crossing his arms.

Kasian laughed. 'I thought only old nags and children sulked. Take the sword, it may save both our lives.'

Begrudgingly, Meloc took the sword and glared at Kasian.

A breath of wind blew through the arrow slit.

The candlelight flickered and died as the wind picked up the scattered scrolls and tossed them across the empty room. It was not a good omen. A purple feather caught by the wind hovered for a moment, then landed, caught in a spot of congealed blood.

'Let us be gone,' Kasian ordered. 'There is nothing for us here.'

He felt his way down the spiral staircase and walked through the larger main guardhouse door which led onto the courtyard. The ornate oak gate, carved with a relief of beggars receiving alms from the generous city merchants and nobility, began to creak slowly in the breeze.

'Wait here,' Kasian whispered, 'and make no noise.'

Cautiously, Kasian made his way towards the sound. Then he stopped and stared at the entrance in confusion. Someone or something had lowered the portcullis. Even though the gate was open, their way out of Welfasten was now barred by a tonne of forged iron latticework. He ran his fingers through his hair as he pondered how to open such an impregnable barrier. Gingerly, he put his foot in one of the lattice holes and tested its strength. A low, deep whirring sounded throughout Cripplegate as the untethered portcullis raised rapidly upwards disappearing up into the gatehouse.

Kasian jumped from the portcullis and rolled onto the cobbles below, shielding his left arm. The portcullis juddered to a noisy halt and plummeted downwards.

'*Stayay!*' Meloc shouted. The portcullis shuddered to a halt and hovered six feet from the ground.

'What did you do?' Meloc demanded. 'We were meant to

be quiet. That noise is enough to wake more of the dead! We need to get out of here before whoever did this comes back.'

'I think that would be best,' Kasian nodded as the echo of the Fallen Guards footsteps became louder.

TWENTY-THREE

Name - Meloc
Location - Cripplegate, Welfasten City
Allegiance - The Mercian Warbands

Meloc eased himself into the saddle, the leather groaning under his weight. He sensed a change in the energy of the city. Black trails of myrkir began to ooze from the Cripplegate walls. He stood in his stirrups, desperately searching for the source of the dark magik.

A shadow moved past the arrow slit at the top of the gatehouse and silver flashed in the orange sky. Meloc's horse panicked and bucked. The reins flew from his grasp, and he desperately grabbed at the mare's mane. Kasian ran over and calmed the frightened horse.

'Have a care. You may need these,' Kasian said as he handed the reins back to Meloc.

'Thanks!' Meloc muttered, blushing scarlet.

An arrow slapped against the cobbles, missing the warlock's head by inches.

'A black flighted arrow! The Dunmuir are here. We must leave now!' Kasian shouted as he slapped Meloc's horse on the rump. The black mare leapt forward, galloping wildly through the half-open gate, and onto the mud track as the unfortunate warlock bounced precariously across his saddle.

The little road led onto the majestic grey stone highway which swept across Mercia, linking the four great cities of the kingdom. The roads ran from Heilagar Fortress in the north-west to Ableakan in the east, spreading northwards to Stonefall Fortress and southwards to the seat of Kings, Fastness

Fortress. The highway was seldom empty. It was the main thoroughfare for the King's armies, munitions, merchants, and the few dazed survivors fleeing the Dunmuir invasion in the north. It was also a road they could not take. Meloc pulled on the mare's reins and the horse whinnied in panic as she veered to the left. The small mare stumbled, almost losing her footing on the tumbling stones, as she galloped up a small, stony track heading to Hauger Hill, a picturesque gathering of tall oaken trees which looked disapprovingly down upon Welfasten City.

Meloc reached the top of the hill and spurred his horse onward. An invisible force tugged at his arm, and he flew from the saddle, landing heavily on his back. His right hand stretched out behind his head, seemingly stuck to the ground. Meloc lay there for a moment, winded and gasping for breath. He tried to pull his right hand towards him, but it was stuck fast. He turned towards his errant hand and swore. The runic writing on the wristband was glowing amber.

'Faen!' he swore again and grabbed a handful of grass, ripping it up from its roots in frustration. He had strayed too far from the captain and the *Samian Confine* had been activated.

'Damn the Wergend!' Meloc groaned as he lay there and watched as his horse proceeded to walk straight into a bush and rake the branches with its strong, yellowed teeth. After a few contortions, which would have even impressed the harlots and patrons of the Crusty Mound, the dirtiest alehouse in Welfasten city, he managed to sit up. Meloc paled as he saw the captain spurring his big bay horse uphill as an arc of arrows soared through the sky.

Kasian was followed by a troop of Fallen Guards who strode up the hill seemingly oblivious to the arrows raining down around them. Every so often an arrow hit its mark and a Fallen Guard collapsed to the ground, only to split in half and rise again.

Meloc's horse, growing tired of its meal, turned its head inquisitively and watched the noisy approach of the bay, its hooves sending up small showers of pebbles.

Kasian smiled with relief as he saw Meloc and rode over to join him. He blinked the sweat from his eyes and wiped his face with a dirt-stained sleeve.

'That was definitely close!' Kasian gasped, panting for breath as his horse turned in circles, 'but we can outride the Fallen, however, their numbers will grow until the incantation ends.'

'And when will that be?' asked Meloc.

'When the compline and evening penance has been performed,' Kasian said, cradling his bad arm.

'So, in about twelve hours' time then? This is going to be a very long day,' Meloc said shaking his head.

A loud horn sounded in the west.

'Well, we seem to be very popular all of a sudden,' said the warlock drily.

Kasian stood in his stirrups, craning his body over the horse's neck. A unit of Purple Guards bearing a hanging black raven pennant flag appeared from the beech woods, which sprawled below the hill. They turned up a narrow path in single file and headed straight for the hilltop.

'What now!' Kasian said as he watched the horsemen approach. 'The prison convoy must have been discovered, and we have been blamed,' he said shaking his head.

'That's typical. The warlock is always blamed for everything,' Meloc said rolling his eyes.

'Well, that is not without precedent,' Kasian commented. 'But if you are going to cast some illegal magik, now would be a good time.' He unsheathed his sword and turned his horse to meet the guards.

Meloc rolled his eyes. 'I am not some court magician that performs tricks on request you know.'

Kasian half-smiled. 'No, indeed you are far too coarse and ill-dressed to ever appear at the Kings' Court.'

Meloc grinned and began to rub his hands together muttering magik under his breath.

The Purple Guard reached the hilltop and began to circle around the little copse.

'Guards close ranks,' ordered Lieutenant Drithenhold, their commanding officer. His face covered by a face shield inlaid with gold, his eyes lost in shadows, and his mouth set in the arrogant slant of someone born to power and money.

The large grey warhorses wove in and out of the trees, closing the circle around the fugitives.

Meloc yawned and then sighed, deliberately and loudly.

'How dare you! You piss-peasant! Guards inward wheel!' Drithenhold screamed.

The Purple Guards turned their horses, so they faced the fugitives and lowered their spears. Kasian and Meloc were trapped. The big bay neighed in fright and reared onto its hind legs. Kasian was caught off guard, gripping the reins with the fingers of his broken right arm, while holding his sword with his left. He tumbled beneath the circle of horses.

'Kill the traitors!' the Lieutenant ordered.

Kasian rolled into a tight ball as broad-leafed iron spearheads tried to skewer him to the ground as he grasped for his fallen sword.

Meloc bent over his saddle as a spear hurtled over his head. He sat up, his eyes glowing amber and blew across his palm. The air around his hand froze into tiny particles of ice, suspended twinkling in the morning air. '*Frosinn-Kom,*' Meloc shouted. The ice crystals enlarged and formed a white wave which rolled across the knoll.

The two Purple Guards nearest Meloc were touched by the wave of ice. They sparkled as ice crystals spread across their bodies and their horses. They opened their mouths to scream for aid but were frozen into statues before they could utter a sound.

'Keep away from the whiteness and bring me the heads of the traitors!' the Lieutenant ordered.

Kasian shouted a warning. Meloc half-turned just in time to see a huge, two-handed axe raised above his head. The rider roared and smashed his axe downwards. The warlock lunged to the side and tumbled from his horse, which whinnied in fright and galloped through the circle, heading back to the safety of its city stables.

Kasian's fingers grasped the hilt of his borrowed sword as he dragged himself to his feet.

'Draw your sword, we will cover each other's back. Get behind me,' Kasian shouted across to Meloc.

'Kill the traitors!' Drithenhold yelled as he levelled his spear directly at Meloc's face. Kasian drew his dagger and threw it at Drithenhold. The Lieutenant screamed and swore as the blade cut into the exposed black trousers which peered out from his mail coat. Drithenhold gritted his teeth as he pulled the blade out. A young serving woman in a grey robe, carrying a heavy cloth satchel, rushed forward to attend to the wound.

'How dare you!' he hissed. 'Guards take them prisoner. They do not deserve a quick death in battle.'

The Purple Guardsmen grinned as they stuck their spear shafts in the saddle sheaths and dismounted, their swords raised.

'Get down,' Meloc shouted as he pulled Kasian down onto the ground next to him. Then, covering his face with his arm, he whispered '*Skoldur.*' Instantly, a wall of galdor glowed around them. A volley of heavy sword blows bounced off the wall. The guardsmen looked uneasy, and the blows lessened, fearful the warlock would unleash another deadly attack.

'Hold your ground!' Drithenhold ordered. 'The wall will fail as all magik does. Hand me my spear.'

He took the spear and hurled it into the wall.

The wall buckled and repaired itself.

'How long can this magik last?' Kasian whispered to Meloc as more spears thudded into the galdor wall.

'Well about two more minutes at this rate,' Meloc panted wiping the sweet from his face.

'May the goddess protect us,' said Kasian shaking his head.

'You are not very good at this magik casting, are you?' Meloc tutted and raised his hand against the inside of the wall, pouring the remains of his galdor energy into it.

TWENTY-FOUR

Name - Kasian
Location - Hauger Hill overlooking Welfasten City
Allegiance - The Mercian Warbands

A strong gust of wind rushed screaming through the shaking trees sending a cloud of green leaves into the air as it smashed through the spear wall. The horses whinnied with fright and backed away from the rippling trees.

Slowly, a black mist began to envelop the hillside.

'Guards have a care! Magik has been cast. Mount and form a line on me!' Lieutenant Drithenhold shouted as he turned his horse to face the mist.

His men mounted and circled their unwilling warhorses into a line across the hilltop.

The riders leant over their saddles and whispered warnings to one another. The air became electrically charged as if a thunderstorm was stirring.

The warhorses stamped their feet and shook their manes.

The probing breeze vanished, and the hill held its breath. The world became quiet; caught in the elongated pause before a battle.

Then time accelerated, noises became louder, and colours shone brighter as a drumbeat sounded from within the mist.

The *Skoldur Wall* collapsed.

Kasian leapt to his feet, his attention split between the trees, which had grown unnaturally still, and the line of Purple Guards.

'They are coming through. Get down quick! We don't want any part in this,' hissed Meloc, grabbing Kasian by the trouser leg.

Kasian frowned in confusion as he followed Meloc's gaze into the swirling mist. He nodded and lay back down against the cold grass. Meloc rolled over to him. His naturally white face was grey, his vivid blue eyes circled with black rings.

'*Maldición*! Are you still battleworthy? Your use of magik has depleted your strength, I see,' Kasian shook his head. 'It is a great shame you are not a stronger warlock.'

'And that's all the thanks I get for saving your miserable life?' Meloc tutted. 'Next time I will cast my shield wall and leave you on the other side!'

Kasian tapped his wrist. 'That would not be one of your best ideas warlock. Remember we are bound in life… and death until our release. When the battle begins, we should take cover by the standing stones over there,' he whispered, pointing to a broken circle of stones, a relic of the old religion, half hidden by the oaken trees.

The sky groaned and rumbled, then split in two, leaving a jagged black rip in the clouds which began to bulge and darken. The wind sighed and breathed again, whistling around the soldiers, pulling at their uniforms. The horses staggered wild-eyed as they tried to keep their feet.

A flash of lightning tore across the sky and an unseen army charged.

'Have a care men! The Dunmuir are coming through. Show them the might of the Purple Guard and watch them fall beneath our feet!' Drithenhold shouted.

The hornsman sounded the alert. The Purple Guard shouted as one as adrenaline surged through their bodies and they lowered their spears.

A brigade of Dunmuir horsemen leapt through the rip and

landed heavily at the base of the hill. Their black battlehorses melted into the darkness of the rising mist, so that only their red eyes which glared through black nose plates, were visible. They snorted smoke as their black hooves stamped impatiently on the trampled grass, hungry for flesh. More and more black-cloaked horsemen poured through the rip.

A bolt of lightning flashed across the damaged sky, illuminating a unit of Draigar warriors for an instant. Some carried heavy iron flails each containing three balls pierced by sharp black spikes, while the others were armed with double-headed axes, too heavy for normal men to wield.

Then the last of the Dunmuir horsemen landed with heavy black longbows slung across their backs.

There was a high-pitched scream and the Dunmuir formed four lines which spread across the base of the hill. The centre of each line parted as General Vargal rode to the front.

A row of lightning strikes shot down from the sky which glowered and growled. There was a loud crack and the smell of oaken. The hilltop blazed red for an instant as the tallest oaken tree on the hilltop stood smoking, its trunk split in two. General Vargal leant over his saddle and watched as two Fallen Guards were hit by raking lightning strikes as they climbed up the hillside. The Fallen Guards blackened and crumbled to piles of ash. Moments later four guards climbed out of the ash piles.

'Well, this just gets more entertaining by the second.' The General raised his hand and shouted, 'Battlemage, to me!'

The Dunmuir battlemage spurred his horse forward, his face hidden by a heavy black hood. The battlemage's body armour was lighter than that of the horsemen. It was made from teardrops of dark leather sewn together to form a breastplate and a matching kilt made from thick leather flaps. A short sword hung from his wide leather belt.

Drithenhold cursed under his breath and then shouted, 'They have a battlemage. Men raise your shields and have no fear. You are protected.'

The Purple Guard slipped the round wooden shields from their backs and raised them in front of their bodies. The shields were painted in white and purple quarters. A black arrow sigil had been painted in the corner of each white quarter.

'That's a minor health sigil,' Meloc muttered, running his hand through his wild hair. 'It will offer no protection against the spells of a battlemage. They will be slaughtered. We should warn them.' He opened his mouth to shout a warning but was stopped by Kasian slapping his hand over his mouth.

'I am sure their young lieutenant is well aware of that,' Kasian whispered in his ear. 'It is better his men die unafraid with honour rather than to run away in terror. Do not forget to die in battle is the greatest honour,' Kasian let go of Meloc and kissed his amulet.

'Hmm...' Meloc tutted as he wiped his mouth with his sleeve.

'Oh, I think you just frightened the Mercians,' Vargal half-smiled. 'The Fallen Guards are on the wrong side. Don't you agree, Hevisla?'

The battlemage bowed to the General. His eyes glowed amber as he raised his hand to the sky and then pointed towards the Fallen Guards. '*Erasso,*' he said as his fingers glowed amber.

The Fallen Guards stumbled as if hit by an unseen force. Amber flames erupted around them. They fell to the floor, crumbled to ash, and rose again their numbers doubled, their eye slits glowing amber as they strode through the flames and knelt in front of the General.

'Destroy them,' the General ordered. The Fallen Guards drew their swords and continued to climb towards the hilltop. Vargal ran a black gauntleted hand through the greying wind and licked the air. 'Other magik has been cast here. There is a warlock close by.' A thin smile crossed his face, just visible under his black visor, as he turned his horse to address ranks of Dunmuir, 'It appears we will have more sport today. Kill them all except their warlock. I want its magik.'

The Dunmuir force thumped their black leather breastplates.

'And give no quarter to the Mercian scum,' Vargal said in a quiet voice filled with disgust.

'Yes General!' They shouted; their gaze fixed upon the thin line of Purple Guards.

Vargal signalled to the drummasters, their huge thunderdrums mounted each side of the magically enhanced, monstrous looking horses. Their overlong faces swaying from side to side as they eyed the Purple Guard hungrily, the largest drumhorse roared, saliva dripping from its jagged, razor-sharp teeth.

The drums sounded, their ominous low beat echoing through the hillside. Vargal raised a fist to his head. The Dunmuir behind him howled and shook their weapons in response.

'Archers away,' the General screamed. An arc of black arrows launched into the sky and fell on the guardsmen. Several horses whinnied and collapsed as their unprotected flesh was struck by arrows, their riders tumbling heavily to the ground.

'Catch the horses,' Drithenhold yelled but his voice was lost as thunder rolled across the dark grey sky. The terrified riderless horses galloped down the hillside.

'Scitte!' he muttered, wiping the sweat from his eyes. 'On your feet,' the Lieutenant ordered the fallen riders. 'Sergeant Grym,' he looked down at a muddied figure cradling his arm. 'Take the fallen riders and archers. Create a left flank by the trees.'

Sergeant Grym bowed. He pulled several of the fallen guards to their feet and stumbled towards the trees. Drithenhold signalled to his second sergeant. 'Tressur, form an eastern flank over there.' He motioned towards a muddied field sloping away from the knoll.

'But Syr,' the Sergeant frowned. 'It's on the lower ground, we will be fighting upslope.'

'I know,' Drithenhold shouted as he ducked as another rain of arrows poured down from the sky, 'but at least in three parts we will divide the arrow fall.'

Tressur bowed and raised his sword. 'Blue watch to me.' he yelled and turned his horse, galloping towards the field.

An arrow arced from the sky and pierced Drithenhold's mail coat. He flew backwards in his saddle and then steadied himself, twisting the arrowhead from his chest and throwing it on the ground beneath his horse's hooves. He stared across the field to the black-cloaked Dunmuir General barely a hundred feet away from him.

General Vargal raised his sword, and the drumbeat quickened. 'Ten gold coins for the soldier who brings me the purple pennant,' he said staring at the young golden-haired flagbearer standing next to Drithenhold.

'Lower your spears and prepare for battle and glory!'

Drithenhold commanded. 'Fight for your mothers, wives, and children, or die the death of cowards! Ride hard and break their line. Guardsmen walk on!' He patted his horse's neck and clicked the horse onwards. The hornsman sounded the walk to engage and the rest of the line walked forward. The sounds of leather creaking and jiggling metal filled the silence as they began forward march.

'Charge!' Drithenhold shouted as he dug his heels into his mount's sides and the horse jumped forward, galloping towards the Dunmuir lines. The rest of the battalion roared as adrenaline coursed through their veins as they charged.

'Fools! They rush to their doom,' Vargal hissed. 'Hevisla stay by my side.'

He stood in his stirrups and raised his sword above his head. 'Dunmuir charge and do your worst!' the general shouted as he pointed his sword towards the purple line.

The roars of the Dunmuir horsemen filled the air as their battlehorses' leapt forwards.

'Quick!' Kasian whispered. 'Go now!'

Meloc and Kasian leapt to their feet and ran southwards towards the stone circle. The ground shook and the sky thundered as the horsemen galloped into each other.

A scarred Draigar armed with a spiked mace drove through the lines smashing his mace down upon two guardsmen. The crests of their helmets were beaten inwards. Both riders fell unconscious to the ground and were trampled by the churning horses. The scarred horseman sat watching the riders die for too long. A Purple guardsman rode behind him and sliced his head from his body. The head plopped onto the ground and rolled downhill, as the guardsman was set upon by two Draigar swordsmen.

There was a shout and the sound of galloping as Tressur and the Blue Watch rode in from the east at full gallop and wheeled behind the Dunmuir line. The nearest Dunmuir horsemen turned their horses to face the new enemies but found themselves caught behind the two Mercian flanks.

'Archers away,' Sergeant Grym ordered. Eight arrows shot through the woods aimed directly for General Vardal. The glint of their arrowheads caught as a white vein of lightning flashed across the sky. Quickly, Vargal raised his round black shield as the eight arrows pinged into its wood.

Several riderless horses galloped passed him. A fallen Dunmuir horseman screamed as his horse bolted, his leg caught in his stirrup dragging him across the battlefield.

Another flight of arrows fell around the General, hitting his personal guard. The guard collapsed onto the floor an arrow sticking out from his eye.

'These Mercians are taking too long to die!' Vargal hissed. 'Battlemage, summon me an eldstormurdrek.'

'But General, such dragons cannot be controlled.' Hevisla frowned.

'When I want the opinion of a mage, I will ask for one,' Vargal hissed. With preternatural speed his gloved hand grabbed the warlock's neck and pressed hard. 'Do not question my orders again.'

Hevisla grabbed at his neck and gurgled.

The General smiled and released his grip.

Hevisla bowed and took several steps away from the General, rubbing his throat as he whispered, '*Dreki-kominn.*'

Meloc looked out from his position beyond the standing

stones. His alabaster white face flushed red as the electrified air burnt his cheeks.

'We should be safe here until the battle is done,' Kasian said as he crouched beside the warlock.

The mangled body of a bloodied guardsman landed on the ground directly in front of the stone circle. Instantly, the corpse was set upon by the hungry Draigar battle horses. A bloodied guardsman ran over sword in hand to defend the body of his fallen comrade. He screamed for help. Meloc stood up but was pulled back down by Kasian.

'This is not a fight we can win,' he whispered. 'We cannot die until our mission is complete.'

Sergeant Tressur galloped over to the fallen guardsmen, circling his whip through the air, and cracking it in front of the feral horses.

'Begone, you foul hel creatures,' he shouted. Tressur lunged forward in his saddle and gasped as something hit his back. He tumbled from his horse onto the fallen guardsman. A grinning Dunmuir horseman leant down from his battlehorse and ripped the heavy battle axe from the sergeant's back as he rode passed.

'Purple Guard, form a line on me!' Drithenhold shouted across the battlefield. The one remaining hornsman blew the recall. Its sound almost lost among the shouts and crashes of iron blades. In the distance, a high-pitched screech echoed through the hillside.

The Fallen Guard clamoured through the bodies towards the Lieutenant.

Drithenhold clutched his chest with one hand as the sword fell from the other. He swayed unsteadily in his saddle. The blood from his chest ran down his legs, dripping from his stirrups.

The hornsman leapt at one of the Fallen Guard, slashing at him with a short sword. He looked down in horror as his blade passed through its body. The Fallen Guard picked the hornsman up by the front of his mail coat and threw him high into the air.

Meloc watched in horror as the broken body fell onto the sloping field.

Drithenhold slipped from his saddle and fell onto the blood-drenched grass. The remaining guardsmen looked around in alarm, their line half-formed as they searched for orders.

A deafening screech pierced the sky as a grey shape appeared in the fire-tinged sky and circled above the battle. White lightning flashed across the sky turning the clouds navy blue. An enormous shimmering grey dragon was caught in the flash. Its wings were made from stretched grey skin and ended in huge black talons. Two glowing amber eyes shone from its head, as the dragon watched the battle. It shook its head. The spiked bone plates which ran from its head along the ridge of its back to its tail shivered. The dragon took a deep breath, gulping up the air. Its grey belly expanded and turned an iridescent blue.

'Krap! An eldstormurdrek. It will destroy everything that moves,' Meloc whispered.

'Quick get underneath my shield,' Kasian said raising his round wooden shield.

'Seriously?' said Meloc raising one fine black eyebrow.

TWENTY-FIVE

Name - Meloc
Location - Hauger Hill overlooking Welfasten City
Allegiance - The Mercian Warbands

The eldstormurdrek watched the battle below as it hovered in the air. Its wings beat faster, creating a vortex which twisted through the battlefield. The updraft bent the trees, ripping branches from their trunks, and tossing them into the air.

'Look to the sky!' Sergeant Grym screamed as he ran out from the oaken trees, waving his arms. The left side of his face was bleeding from a deep cut on his cheek. His voice was lost among the screams of the injured, the shouts of the living, and the heavy clunk of weapon on weapon.

'Helgods!' he swore as he ran towards the fallen hornsman lying in the churned mud, a large red stain spreading from his mail coat. Grym manhandled the horn strap from the dead man's shoulder and blew three times.

The surviving guardsmen glanced in the direction of the horn.

'Look to the sky!' Grym shouted, pointing towards the dragon.

The eldstormurdrek screeched and breathed a river of white-tinged fire through the battlefield. The dragonfyre cut a path of death through the battlefield as men and horses were consumed by flame.

Meloc watched in horror as the sergeant caught the full force of the blast. His skin bubbled and peeled from his bones as his remains collapsed into the mud.

The dragon screeched again and flapped its wings as it

soared above the clouds.

A blackened path six feet wide ran through the centre of the hill. Smoking survivors both Mercian and Dunmuir screamed in pain as the dragonfyre continued to burn the flesh from their bones. The air smelt of charcoaled bodies as drifts of ash fell silently across the hilltop.

Meloc stood up, his clothes and hair covered in ash.

'What are you doing?' Kasian ordered. 'Get down, now! You will be seen and killed or worse and I do not fancy being chained to a corpse.'

'*Rigning*!' Meloc shouted as he raised his hands towards the sky.

The thunder rumbled away, and the clouds fell lower. Their white seams darkened to grey as they began to rain. The hungry fires scattered across the battlefield died and plumes of choking smoke rose into the air, covering the hillside in a veil of white.

'Retreat to the city!' Orvar, the remaining guard sergeant, ordered as he pointed to Welfasten. The sergeant rode through two unseated Dunmuir horsemen, knocking them to the ground, as he galloped towards the city road.

The surviving guardsmen watched the sergeant leave, his words lost in the noise of battle.

'We are all doomed,' Orvar muttered as he glanced over his shoulder to see his remaining men still fighting on the battlefield. He leant back in the saddle, pulled his horse to stop, and turned. His figure fading in and out of the drifts of smoke. The sergeant raised his sword above his head, its blade pointing towards the city, 'Purple Guard, make for the city!' he yelled. A shaft of sunlight caught the blade of his sword and flashed silver.

The surviving guardsmen saw his signal and fought their way from the battlefield, spurring their horses through the swirling smoke. The sounds of their horses' hooves clattering along the stony road seemed to echo through the battleground.

'What are they doing?' Meloc said in alarm as he fell to his knees panting on the ground. His galdor energy spent.

'They do not know they are riding to their deaths,' Kasian said shaking his head. 'Stay down, lest we join them.'

'There can be no survivors,' Vargal said as he watched the Purple Guards flee from his position on the hilltop a little way back from the fighting. He raised a black gauntleted hand and signalled the reserve forces to follow them.

The eldstormurdrek swooped below the clouds, its serpentine grey head piercing through the white smoke, it grabbed a Dunmuir horseman in each foot, its black talons piercing through their breastplates, and tightened its grip until the men stopped screaming. The dragon opened its mouth to reveal its orange-tinged lining and screeched. The sound blew the smoke from the centre of the battlefield. The Dunmuir horsemen struggled to control their terrified battlehorses as the enormous dragon flew overhead and released its grip on the lifeless bodies which thudded into the mud below. The dragon drew a breath, sucking the air from the hillside. Its abdomen extended and flickered blue as its reptilian amber eyes stared menacingly at the general.

'Battlemage, get rid of that bloody eldstormurdrek!' Vargal shouted in alarm. He waited impatiently and then scanned the battlefield for Hevisla.

The battlemage stood in the mud, a carbonized statue of himself.

The eldstormurdrek flapped its wings. A gale blew through

the battlefield. The statue disintegrated into grey ash and was taken by the wind. Another stream of dragonfyre burnt everything in its path. The remaining men and horses screamed in terror, choking on the drifts of ash and smoke. The flames missed the general by inches. He threw his burning cloak to the ground and glared up at the dragon.

A Dunmuir officer rode up, the side of his face burnt and blistered by dragonfyre. 'My General, the dragon will destroy us all. Such a beast should never have been summoned,' he said as he watched the dragon rip two escaping horsemen from their saddles and toss them into the fire.

Vargal grabbed him by the throat and twisted. The corpse slid from the horse.

'A Dunmuir general never makes mistakes,' Vargal stated and stared at his bodyguards.

Silently, they raised their fists to their chests and bowed. Vargal stared impassively as the dragon flew upwards to restoke its fire. 'I think it's time to end this. Your majesty, grant me your privilege and bestow unto me Dragonsdoom, the mighty spear of Kings,' he said, bowing to the wind.

A silver rip opened in the sky and an iron-barbed spear flew through the clouds, landing between the general's feet. Its blade was twenty inches long and as thin as a knife. It was decorated in silver leaves and hollow red yelling berries filled with dark green seeds. The pretty berries produced the deadliest toxin in the five kingdoms. A sudden frosted wind breathed across the blade and the berries burst open. Black sap spread across the blade and dripped onto the group below, which steamed as the poison ate through the soil.

The dragon screeched again and dived beneath the clouds, circling the battlefield, fire pouring from its mouth. The

Dunmuir horsemen were trapped within a ring of flames. The dragon dived to grab a survivor, running screaming from the inferno. Vargal screamed, his eyes bulging beneath his helmet as he launched the spear into the air with enhanced strength. The poisoned spear pierced through the dragon's hindquarters.

The eldstormurdrek screeched. The dragon's wings stuttered for an instant as it plunged lower to the ground as its serpentine neck twisted round and ripped the spear from its body. The remaining horsemen covered their heads with their hands as the injured eldstormurdrek flew overhead, its wings beating unevenly as it turned north towards the Witian Mountains and disappeared.

Vargal strode through the fire. He picked up Dragonsdoom and hurled it back into rip in the sky. The sky rumbled and flashed white as the spear disappeared. The General walked through the battlefield and sat on a collapsed stone which formed part of a forgotten stone circle. The fire ring died; its caster vanquished but everywhere smaller fires burned and danced between the twisted corpses and the crying injured.

Kasian put a dirt-stained finger to his lips and crouched lower behind the standing stone. Meloc put his hand over his mouth trying not to breathe. The acrid smell of myrkir permeated the General's clothes. It pricked his eyes and burnt his throat.

Vargal signalled to his sergeant to approach. 'Kill the injured and then collect the bodies. Take them directly to the Welfasten Gate portal and dispatch them back to Dunmuir. Our doitimages may have use for their corpses.'

The sergeant clenched his jaw and bowed, then signalled to his men and they began to drag the Mercian bodies both living and dead from the battlefield.

Kasian relaxed slightly and slumped against the standing stone.

Vargal sprang from behind the stone and lunged at Kasian, the blade of his sword bouncing from his mail coat. Kasian twisted away and sprung to his feet, drawing his sword with his uninjured arm. Vargal lunged again. Kasian parried but was too late, the sword blade went through his thigh. Kasian gritted his teeth and pulled his leg from the blade, sweat pouring from beneath his helmet. Vargal smiled. Kasian frowned and turned to look behind him.

A black cudgel swung towards his face, and he collapsed into the ground.

The horsemen holding Meloc's shoulders, pulled him to his feet. Meloc kicked and struggled but was no match for the musclebound soldiers. 'Die in flames!' he screamed. The Draigar horsemen looked at each other in horror and dropped him as they warily raised their shields.

'*Eldur!*' Meloc shouted. His eyes flickered amber for an instant and faded back to cobalt.

'Pathetic,' smiled Vargal grabbing Meloc by the face, 'but still, your galdor energy might be of some use. Tie him up and gag him. Then send him back through the gate.'

'What about him?' the sergeant pointed to Kasian, lying face down in the ground.

'Leave him to die. We have wasted far too much time here,' Vargal ordered. 'We ride to Welfasten.'

TWENTY- SIX

Name - Sergeant Orvar
Location - Welfasten City
Allegiance - The Mercian Warbands

The leading party of Purple Guards pulled their horses to a stop at the bottom of Hauger Hill and stared at Welfasten City in confusion. Sergeant Orvar circled his frothing mount and followed the gaze of his men.

'The gate is open,' a dusty-faced rider gasped. 'The city has fallen.'

There were murmurs of agreement.

'But I heard nothing at this morning's briefing,' Orvar said stroking his long red beard as he stared at the city.

'Look the flags are still flying,' a young rider pointed to the triple mountains on a background of green. The symbol of Mercia.

There was a slicing sound as the air around the riders was cut in two. The boy frowned slightly as he fell forward in his saddle and slipped to the ground. A black spear embedded in his back. His horse whinnied in terror and galloped along the road heading towards the safety of Welfasten City. Another spear flew through the air. The rider next to Orvar fell from his horse a spear sticking though his neck.

The riders circled their horses in panic.

A wave of arrows hissed through the air and slammed into the road several feet behind them as the sound of creaking leather, jangling chains, and the hoof falls of the warhorses echoed behind them.

Several Purple Guards wheeled their horses to the left and

galloped back beneath the hill, making for the safety of the beech woods. A horn sounded and the left flank of the Dunmuir horsemen broke their line and chased after the guards. The Purple Guards were caught a quarter of a mile from the woods and fell to Dunmuir arrow and sword.

Only their horses escaped alive.

'Scitte!' cursed Orvar as he kissed the amulet hanging around his neck. 'May their spirits be found worthy.' He circled his horse as he addressed the survivors. 'If we are fated to die at least we will die with honour defending Mercia. We make for Welfasten!'

The remaining men nodded and followed Orvar as he spurred his horse onwards and galloped into the city.

'Shut the gate!' Orvar shouted over the sound the snorting horses and stamping hooves. He grabbed a passing rider and pulled him closer, whispering in his ear, 'Geirod... the city is too silent. This feels like a trap.'

Geirod nodded, as he struggled to control his horse. Its eyes rolling in terror as it refused to venture further into the city. 'We have ridden to our doom. Death surrounds us. The horses sense it.' He reached down to pat the horse's neck.

Orvar nodded and gripped his young nephew's shoulder tightly. 'You are a messenger. You must survive and warn the King. Welfasten has fallen. Now go and find a quiet gate to leave by.'

'But what of you uncle?' Geirod frowned as he reached out and grabbed his uncle's thick leather coat.

'I will die here in battle and join our glorious forefathers. Now go!' Orvar whispered. The two men embraced. Orvar nodded at his nephew, slapped his horse's rump, and watched his nephew canter down the empty street. Then he wheeled his horse and stared through the gate as a line of black mail coated horsemen approached the city.

'We must shut the gate now!' Orvar yelled at his men. He could see the men in the gatehouse struggling to turn the wheel mechanism which released the chains and closed the doors. Corporal Fellir, the man mountain, tried to prise the wheel into movement using the blade of his two-handed great sword, but it was stuck fast.

Orvar ground his teeth together as he watched his corporal remove his sword and begin to beat the wheel with a wooden bench.

'Save your energy Fellir,' he ordered. 'The gate has been cursed. No man can close it.'

'The gods have deserted us!' Fellir shouted and threw the bench against the guardhouse wall. 'What do we do now sergeant?' he asked.

Orvar could see the desperation on his face.

'We fall back and die with honour, and we will take as many of these Dunmuir monsters with us as possible. The longer we hold them here the more time we give for the southern defences to be strengthened. Men form a circle on me!' Orvar shouted. Adrenaline soared through his veins like a wave of burning heat. He ripped off his leather mail coat and roared up at the clouds. The rest of the platoon roared back at him, drew their swords, and shook them at the approaching enemy.

The Dunmuir horsemen burst through the open gate. The Purple Guards who were still trying to close the gate were hit by their battlehorses. Their bodies were thrown against the city walls and then fell to the floor leaving trails of blood. Behind the Dunmuir horsemen rode the Draigar, their battlehorses snorting and stamping, enraged by the scent of Mercian blood.

The Dunmuir horsemen formed in lines inside the gate. Three Draigar warriors dismounted and walked slowly through the lines, holding their great swords with both hands, their points glinting in the sunlight which streamed between the white seams on the grey clouds.

'Dismount and release the horses,' Orvar ordered. The horses were good and trusted soldiers of Mercia. They had served the unit well. There was no need for them to die in battle.

The riders nodded to the sergeant and dismounted, quickly threw off their saddles and whispered a final goodbye to their mounts. Orvar fondly rubbed his horse's long brown ears.

'Make haste, go back to the stables at Fastness Fortress. May your arrival send a warning to the King.'

The horse's ears twitched and then lay back against its head. The freed horses galloped through the approaching warriors and past the lines of Dunmuir horsemen.

Vargal's lip twitched in amusement as he watched the horses stampede from the city.

Sergeant Orvar took a spear slung across his back and hurled it high into the air. Its point turned downwards and fell inches short of the black boots of the oncoming Draigar warriors.

'The goddess Herja will take you all!' he screamed. The men behind him roared and ran screaming towards the Draigar. The magically enhanced warriors carved the air in two as the oncoming guardsmen fell to the floor.

'Bring that one alive.' Captain Vargal ordered pointing to the sergeant. 'Kill the rest.' He dismounted and tied his horse to the gatehouse door. Then watched as the three Draigar warriors approached the remaining Purple Guards.

'Attack!' screamed Orvar as he charged the three warriors. The middle warrior twisted his hand to the right. Orvar was flung through the air and hit the wall, falling with a thud onto the cobbles below.

The warriors to the right and left slashed through the guard ranks, their black boots were wet with Mercian blood. They unsheathed pointed jagged daggers and proceeded to turn over and check each of the fallen guardsmen for signs of life. There would be no prisoners.

Orvar was hauled to his feet and dragged over to the General. He could not move his legs but could still feel the waves of pain radiating through them. His face glowed red as sweat ran down his forehead but he said nothing as he stared defiantly at the General.

'I can see pain in your eyes,' Vargal smiled. 'Tell me where the galdor weapons are, and I will make your death come quickly.'

'And you can go to hel, I will tell you nothing. You can cut off my arms and legs and I will still tell you nothing. I am a soldier of the King, and you are less than a heap of dung,' Orvar spat into the general's face.

Vargal punched him hard in the stomach.

Orvar doubled over, grunting in pain, then stared up at the General through defiant, red-rimmed eyes.

'To be honest, I believe you,' Vargal said. 'But I have no intention of limb dismemberment. A memory spell is quicker and far less messy, bring me another battlemage.'

His bodyguard nodded and disappeared. A minute later he reappeared with a diminutive battlemage wearing a dark green hooded robe which covered her face.

The mage pressed two fingers against Orvar's forehead. '*Opich minni*,' she commanded.

Orvar screamed as a tight band of pain encircled his brain. Then he felt nothing.

'Very good. What is your name?' Vargal whispered.

'I am Orvar, Sergeant of the Purple Guard company at Fastness Fortress. Son of Orvas. Son of Orvat.'

'How fascinating...' smiled Vargal, 'and where are the Galdor weapons?'

'They are hidden somewhere in the underground passages beneath the Kristal Cavern,' Orvar replied.

Vargal stabbed him in the heart. The two warriors holding Orvar stumbled backwards in surprise.

'Useless,' Vargal muttered. He signalled to his bodyguards to drop the body.

'Do we ride to the cavern, my Lord?' asked one.

'No...' growled Vargal. 'I have a witness to the fact that the caverns are empty. The Galdor Weapons have been removed. Wolf Company stay here, burn the bodies, and help guard the city. Dragon Company... we ride on. Somewhere in this peasant-littered, filthy country is a cache of weapons more powerful than anyone can imagine, and King Alfarinn wants them found.'

TWENTY-SEVEN

Name - Meloc
Location - The Road East
Allegiance - The Mercian Warbands

The prisoner possession marched onwards. Their hands bound behind their backs; their necks yoked with loops of rope which were tied to a longer rope that joined all the prisoners together. The rope line held thirteen prisoners of war. All in some way important to Dunmuirlun. Meloc glanced behind him and watched as the bannerol bearing the mountains of Mercia was taken down and the blue banner bearing the white drek of Dunmuir was run up. Welfasten City was lost.

Meloc thought he could hear the screams of men, but was unsure, for the wind from the distant mountains roared loudly, ripping at his clothes, and howling in his ears.

'Move on, Mercian-scum,' a guttural voice ordered as Meloc was pushed in the back. He stumbled forward, the yoke cut into his neck, and he gasped for breath. The guard laughed and moved on down the line.

'Have a care,' whispered a voice from behind. 'If you fall you will pull everyone down with you.'

'Oh sorry,' tutted Meloc. 'I'd hate to inconvenience anyone.'

The voice behind him laughed quietly. 'Not a warbandman then I take it?'

'Er… no, I'm a warlock,' Meloc paused waiting for the negative response.

'So… you were not seconded to Fregna Tower and yet you are still powerful enough to be wanted by the Dunmuir. You have my interest warlock. What is your name?' said the voice.

'I am Meloc of Goethia. Son of Morax.'

'I am honoured to meet you, Meloc son of Morax. I am Anders, son of Lord Thorvald of Stonefall.'

'What news of Stonefall?' Meloc whispered as he watched a huge Dunmuir guard stride down the line, a black leather flail in his hands.

'The fortress fell two nights ago,' Anders growled.

'I'm sorry,' Meloc said as he shook his head, thick black curls flopping across his face.

'We were betrayed but I will take revenge for the fallen,' Anders vowed. They fell silent as another Dunmuir guard walked past them, his whip hand raised and ready to strike. A hooded figure at the front of the line stumbled and fell. The guard marched up the line and dragged the figure to its feet.

'So, master warlock can you cast spells?' Anders whispered.

'Er… yes, that would be the definition of a warlock,' Meloc answered.

'Well then…' said Anders, 'undo my bonds and let me escape. I will not live the life of a dog while my country falls to darkness.'

'If I could, I would have,' Meloc whispered. 'I've tried but I cannot access any galdor energy. It has been blocked. I think it's this stone thing around my neck.' He nodded to the triangular shaped stone amulet hanging around his neck which glowed slightly in the gloom of the broken sky.

'You may be right,' replied Anders. 'Kick the man in front of you.'

'What?' said Meloc. He looked at the mountainous warbandman in front of him. 'But he might kick me back.'

'That is a risk I'm willing to take,' Anders replied.

Meloc shook his head and kicked the man as hard as he could in the back of the knees. The man stumbled and fell forward. The sudden weight pulled the joined line of men down on top of each other. The tautness of the rope relaxed, and Anders fell next to Meloc.

'Get up and keep moving you useless Mercian pigs,' an enormous Dunmuir one-eyed guard roared and began to whip the fallen men.

'Quick turnaround,' ordered Anders.

Meloc swivelled round on his knees. Anders leant forward.

'Er… what are you doing?' Meloc asked, leaning away from Anders.

'Stay still!' Anders ordered. 'Do not worry, you are not my type,' he winked as he bit the amulet around Meloc's neck, lifted it over his head, and spat it onto the road.

'Now warlock spell something quickly!' he ordered.

'Er…' said Meloc, staring into the dirt-streaked, bloodied face of the new Lord of Stonefall. His mind blank.

The dark shape of a guard loomed over Anders' shoulder; his whip raised.

There was a crack and Anders fell forward onto Meloc. The line was showered in an explosion of amber light and the rope yoking all the prisoners together disappeared. The once tethered prisoners fell to the ground. Their hands still bound as they struggled to their feet.

'What just happened?' The one-eyed Dunmuir guard demanded, glaring at the prisoners.

'I don't know,' another guard answered. He picked up two fallen Mercian warband officers holding them at arm's length as they tried to escape his grasp.

'I would have thought that was obvious,' Meloc replied.

'Be silent warlock,' Anders warned.

'Lie face down on the ground or die,' the one-eyed guard ordered. 'And gag that bloody warlock!' He screamed, glaring at Meloc.

Two Dunmuir guards flew at Meloc, and he fell forward onto the muddy track. One sat astride Meloc's back and pressed his face into the puddle. Meloc struggled and thrashed with his legs for a minute and fell silent.

'You're killing him!' Anders shouted.

The guard released the grip on Meloc's head and yanked his hair, pulling his head from the puddle. Meloc coughed and choked, spitting the mud from his throat. 'He ain't dead he's just even more dirty,' the guard laughed.

Meloc turned his head towards Anders and winked. '*Gefa út*!' Meloc screamed. Another flash of amber lightning snaked across the fallen convey. The rope binding the prisoner's hands fell to the ground.

'Men of Mercia arise! Now is your chance. Kill or be killed!' a familiar voice shouted.

The prisoners stood up, picked up any weapon the surrounding woods could provide and ran at their guards, with the savage desperation of the doomed and the mad.

A blood-soaked figure ran from the trees surrounding the muddy road.

'Quick get up!' hissed the man, dragging Meloc to his feet.

'Scitte! Captain Kasian is that you? You look halfdead,' cursed Meloc in surprise.

Kasian nodded. 'I have been tracking you since the battle, a Wergend officer does not leave its charge or its mission unfinished. Quick we must go… Now!'

'But shouldn't we stay and help?' Meloc asked, looking at two warbandmen as they tipped a guard over and began to beat him with rocks they had found by the wayside.

'The warbandmen seem to be looking after themselves,' Kasian stated. 'We have a greater mission. The future of Mercia depends on us.'

Anders stared suspiciously at Kasian. 'What mission can a Wergend officer, and a warlock have that has joined them together so?'

Kasian looked the strong warband lord up and down. 'Our mission is secret, but we need an extra sword. We are searching for the Serpent's Breath. They are the only things that will stop the invasion.'

'But I thought they were hidden and only to be used for emergencies,' Anders said as he grabbed a passing Dunmuir guard and threw him to the floor. The fallen guard was immediately set upon by several bloodthirsty prisoners.

'Half the country is under the Dunmuir yoke, and the great fortresses fall one by one. There is no greater emergency,' Kasian replied.

'I see…' nodded Anders. 'So, where exactly are these weapons?'

'We are not sure, but I am certain the mother goddess will guide our way,' Kasian replied wincing as he tightened the blood-soaked rag around his thigh.

'But definitely not in the Kristal Caverns where they are supposed to be,' Meloc replied, stepping quickly to one side as a jagged rock flew through the air and landed in his muddy footprints.

'You really have no idea?' Anders raised a dirty red eyebrow.

Kasian blushed and averted his gaze.

'That is so typical of a warlock and a Wergend, and this is why you will need the help of a Northern warbandman,' Anders laughed.

Kasian moved to one side. The head of a Dunmuir guard still strapped into its helmet sailed past him and landed in the long grass.

A deep drum sounded from the trees.

'Scatter men. The Dunmuir reinforcements are coming. Make for Fastness Fortress,' a commanding voice called out. The last of the Dunmuir guards were despatched. The men grabbed any weapons they could and ran into the woods.

The drumbeat sounded nearer.

'We need to leave before we are overrun, magik us away!' Anders commanded.

Meloc shook his head. 'One of the Dunmuir drums is playing in a *spillt* melody. It dampens the galdor energy field.'

'Then I suggest we had better leave now,' replied Anders rubbing his stubble.

Kasian and Meloc nodded, and they disappeared into the surrounding trees.

TWENTY-EIGHT

Name - Meloc
Location - The Midheim River
Allegiance - The Mercian Warbands

The light green shrub grass changed to the rich emerald tones of the rolling meadowlands as the companions travelled into the floodplains of the Midheim River. The Midheim, in contrast to its north-western cousin, was a huge, lumbering river which meandered its way south-eastwards, creating the rich fertile farmlands of Southern Mercia.

Meloc felt his chest tighten as the repressed memories of his destroyed childhood threatened to surface. Quickly, he reburied them.

'Are you alright warlock?' Kasian asked. 'You have gone pale? If you faint, I cannot carry you.'

'Don't look at me,' Anders replied, 'I'm not carrying him either.'

'No one needs to carry me,' Meloc growled as he jogged through the fields. Several screams rang out in the distance as the Dunmuir guards caught a group of fleeing prisoners. Startled, a flock of rookends took to flight, circling above their heads. The rookends stared down hungrily at the three companions. Even from half a mile away they could smell the dried blood sticking to the fugitive's skin and clothes.

Anders drew his sword and raised it skywards. 'Come and feed on me at your peril, monster birds.'

The birds cawed once again and wheeled away.

'Maldición! They have our scent. They will be back when they sense we have weakened,' Kasian said, watching the birds fly off. 'They will pluck the flesh off the bones of the dying. I have seen it before.'

'So, are all Wergend guards this cheerful? Or is it just the southlanders?' Anders enquired. 'Have no fear, I will have to be very dead before the rookends feed on my corpse.'

'They won't feed off mine,' Meloc grinned. 'Rookends hate the taste of the magikborne.'

'I do not think that is anything to boast about,' Anders winked at Kasian.

Kasian tutted and brushed past a particularly vicious looking stinging weed. 'Are you sure we are going the right way? By my sight we will reach the great roads by nightfall, roads which would be best if they were avoided.'

'If we want to travel south, we need to cross the great roads,' Anders replied, his hand resting on his stolen sword. 'I am not scared of anything we may meet along the road.'

'And anyway,' grinned Meloc, 'I know a shortcut. We will reach the great roads before nightfall, have no fear.'

'I am a Wergend officer. I fear nothing,' Kasian snapped as he marched stiffly through the grasses.

Anders and Meloc exchanged amused glances and ran after the officer.

The meadow fell away to reveal flat lands lined with wilder grass and dark green shrubs. A line of ashling trees rose from the shrubs, their branches moving softly in an unknown breeze. Ivy leaves ran across the ground, twisting around the oaken trunks as spongy green moss dripped from their branches.

'This wood is old. The old religion was practised here. I can sense it. We must move quickly, before the old gods stir,' Kasian said kissing his amulet.

Meloc bent down and pushed a clump of ground ivy to one side, to reveal a squat sandstone statue of a woman with a huge belly and pendulous bosoms. 'This way,' he said as he disappeared behind an enormous oaken tree.

'But if we go in there we will be cursed!' Kasian said.

'I think we are bloody well cursed anyway,' said Anders pushing Kasian into the woods.

A slight path ran between the moving trees.

Anders reached out to touch a branch but Meloc touched his arm and shook his head. 'It's best not to wake the trees,' he whispered.

Anders green eyes widened, and he quickly walked on. Meloc smiled to himself and patted the rough trunk of a tree as he passed by.

'The galdorless are just too easy sometimes,' he smiled to himself.

The companions walked silently through the woodland path. In the distance, towering above the treeline stood Konungur Cross, one of the great crossing points of the King's Way whose sweeping grey stone roads bisected the kingdom.

Anders signalled them all to crouch down in the woodland undergrowth as he watched to see whether the roadway was deserted.

The road began to tremble as the sound of galloping hoof beats was carried on the wind.

'Who's that?' Meloc began to whisper but was cut off as a calloused hand clamped tightly over his mouth. Anders put his finger to his lips and shook his head.

'What news from Welfasten City, Birger?' a disembodied voice inquired.

Meloc twisted free of the hand and peered around a creeping

dogwood bush. Anders groaned inwardly and pushed Meloc firmly back into the shadows of the woodland. 'Keep out of sight. Remember we are outlaws!' He hissed at the scowling warlock.

'Welfasten was betrayed and has fallen to the Dunmuirherr, Syr Haukel,' replied the captain. His crowned raven crest glinting in the morning sun.

'Sard!' Syr Haukel swore.

'We have reports that the Dunmuir partisans, a warlock named Meloc and his accomplice, Wergend Captain Kasian, have joined forces with Anders of Stonefall and are taking the Galdor Weapons back to their master, Alfarin of Dunmuirlun,' the captain replied grimly.

'Have no fear. My brother will hunt them down before they reach the border,' Syr Haukel replied. 'I must report back to Dreagur Tower and then rejoin my battalion.'

'A safe journey to you, Syr Haukel, and please send my greetings to your brother.'

'Thank you, captain. I will. I am sure Lord Haukar will be waiting as impatiently as ever for my report,' he smiled ruefully. Syr Haukel shouted to his unit of warband warriors.

They wheeled and galloped down the southern road.

Captain Birger sat and watched the Easterners depart. Their white bannerol snaking through the grey morning sky. He whispered an aside to his sergeant, who nodded in agreement.

'Prepare to advance at the canter... Canter!' The sergeant yelled, and the Horsehelm spurred their horses back towards their base at Fastness Keep.

Anders let go of Meloc and cursed bitterly, 'Scitte, we are wanted traitors.' He ran his hand through his hair. 'We must seek an audience with the King and clear our names.'

Meloc grimaced. 'The Horsehelm are the King's private army of spies and thugs. If they said we did it, it comes straight from the Royal Council, and if we go to the King without completing our mission, we are as good as dead anyway.'

'So, we just need to find the weapons, while hiding from both armies who want us dead; then, if we are still alive, we can go to Fastness and hopefully persuade the King to clear our names,' Anders sighed.

'Yes, and in doing so get him to admit that it was he who lost the Serpent's Breath in front of his whole council,' Meloc muttered sarcastically. 'Still, I'm sure we will be dead long before things ever get that far.'

'You know of where these weapons are?' Kasian asked as he took a jar of ointment from his satchel and winced as he rubbed a grey looking paste on his wounds.

Anders stared at Meloc. 'How do you know where they are?'

'I feel their whispers calling on the breeze,' Meloc replied. 'The further southeast we travel the stronger their voice becomes. The weapons have been found and hidden beyond the mountains of Austurlun, but I don't know why.'

'So, the Dunmuir are hunting for the weapons in Mercia while they are in fact a lot nearer their home,' Kasian replied. 'The gods move in the most mysterious of ways.'

'So how do we find these weapons then?' Anders frowned. The warlock smiled and shook his head, 'I think we will have to follow the whispers and hope whoever is keeping them will release them to us.'

'Well, we can certainly hope but I doubt the request will be favourably received. It would be best if we took the weapons in a more informal manner,' Anders replied.

'There is a secret way into Austurlun through the mountain passes,' Meloc stated, blushing slightly.

'Can you get us there… unseen?' asked Anders frowning. Meloc sighed. 'Last time I went to Austurlun, I was very young and ate more herbs than I gathered; consequently, my memories of the whole trip are a little blurred.'

Kasian stared at the strange little warlock for a full minute. His eyes widened with surprise.

'But the private consumption of herbs containing magical properties is strictly forbidden. Exactly how many other crimes against the new religion have you committed?' Kasian asked shaking his head.

'Do you really want to know?' Meloc grinned.

'Perhaps it would be best if I know nothing,' Kasian smiled slightly and cautiously crept onto the huge stone highway which transected the kingdom.

He turned and looked down the highway, squinting into the early morning sun. There were no heavy hoof beats vibrating through the cobbles. In the distance, grey shadowy people wandered aimlessly along the road, refugees from the fighting in the north-east, looking for a haven and finding none.

'Let's go quickly, we are too exposed here, we must leave the highway as soon as we are able,' Anders whispered, signalling to the distracted warlock. Meloc got up slowly and Anders pulled him to the side of the road, so they walked in the shadows of the trees. The trees began to moan, and their leaves rustled as news of the intruders spread along the lane and into the semidarkness of the ancient woodland.

Flying unnoticed, high above their heads an iridescent turquoise drakefly circled twice and then headed southwards towards Fastness Fortress.

TWENTY-NINE

Name - Meloc
Location - The Southern Road
Allegiance - The Mercian Warbands

The King's Highway stretched like grey branches across the four corners of Mercia. It had been laid in the time of King Ferdamor the Hammer during the Eldor Age. Ferdamor had fought the minor kingdoms of Mercia, sweeping through the country in a wave of bloodshed. Those kingdoms who capitulated without raising arms were allowed to live under his rule, while those who fought for their freedom were butchered and their villages put to flame. And so, Mercia had become one country under the rule of Ferdamor, born from a legacy of blood and fear.

The highway had been built as a rapid response to local uprisings. Legend said each of the large white stone slabs laid along the road's surface represented the death of a Mercian, killed under Ferdamor's tyrannical rule, the slabs serving as their nameless tombstones. Needless to say, most Mercians preferred to use the ancient winding mud tracks, for fear of the road. Over the decades the great highways had become the sole preserve of warbandmen, robbers, and the desperate.

The stones softened as Meloc walked over them. He could feel his boots sink into the slabs as he moved. He looked back to see a line of his footsteps indented across the stones in red.

They were being followed by a blood curse.

He thought about telling his companions but decided against it. Kasian would probably insist on some sort of Wergend cleansing routine, which no doubt would involve being stripped naked and having a bucket of ice water poured over him, and then being forced to drink some sort of foul-tasting sludge.

Anders would just laugh in his face.

The air became heavier as the highway passed the Murmuring Woods. A narrow mud track ran from the road into the trees.

'Let us take the path through the woods,' Anders said. 'The Highway is too dangerous to travel on. It will be watched.'

'I agree,' said Kasian. 'We have few friends and many enemies; we need to take leave this road.'

'Yes, we'll travel through the ancient woodlands, not around them like everyone else in the kingdom. I'm sure it will be much safer…' Meloc muttered to himself as he followed his companions into the Murmuring Woods.

The Murmuring Woods consisted mainly of primordial oak trees which huddled together for protection. The centuries of galing winds and freezing winters had twisted their branches and stunted their growth. They had grown so dense that even on the brightest day the wood remained cloaked in shadow.

Everything in the wood lay carpeted in a bright green moss which climbed the trees and crept along their branches, covering the boulders which slept upon the ground, and soured the air. The spongy woodland floor writhed and crawled. Leaves lay abandoned, gradually decaying until they became part of the black crumbling soil. Hidden underneath the decaying twigs and muddied stones, the insect population buzzed and thrived. Ants, cockroaches, and spiders scurried everywhere, busily covering the moss laden trees in a moving, teeming membrane.

The woods were alive, too alive.

The air smelt vaguely burnt as the wind carried the smell of death down from the great mountains of the North.

'Helgods! This road goes on forever,' Anders exclaimed, slashing his sword into the rustling vegetation which seemed to be growing denser the further they walked.

The sound of high-pitched bells rang through the silence.

'Temple bells,' smiled Kasian in relief. 'We must be nearing a religious house. Perhaps we can rest there, we seem to have been walking for hours.'

'I don't think that's a good idea,' Meloc said scanning the wall of brooding plants. 'We should stick to the path.'

'You have taken on an even more unhealthy appearance. You need to rest, we all do, besides they might have honey wine,' Anders smiled as he stepped from the road and began to cut his way through the endless undergrowth, as he headed towards the sound of the bells.

The sun fell slowly, its light filtering through the overhanging canopy and casting shadows across the browning woodland floor. Anders wiped the sweat from his forehead as he pushed his way through a thorny redberry bush and abruptly tumbled into an overgrown garden, which backed onto a derelict, wooden shack.

An enormous thud echoed through the deserted garden.

Anders turned to see Meloc lying face down in the long grass. Kasian hauled the fallen warlock to his feet. The soft ringing of miniature bellflowers gently jingled around them. The grasses swayed in time with the sound. In the far distance, the racing white waters of the Midheim River gurgled as they rushed past, hurrying to leave the Murmuring Woods.

'What is this place?' Kasian asked. 'It is no religious community… I sense it has been touched by evil. Is it a warlock lair?' He grabbed hold of the amulet which hung around his neck.

Meloc gave a half-smile. 'I can assure you there's only one warlock here, but I can feel the myrkir energy. It's calling from within the sound of the bellflowers. This, however,' he pointed to a tumbledown shack hidden amongst the pointed leaves of giant myrtle bushes, 'was a storehouse for a smuggler out of Iskaldur.'

Anders raised his sword. 'Is he here?'

'Yes,' Meloc replied. 'He never left. I think we should go now and try not to disturb that which lies sleeping here.'

'I agree,' said Kasian. 'We will not stay long but I just need to fill my water bag.' He walked over to the little well standing quietly by the crumbling shack.

Meloc shouted a warning, but it was too late. Kasian touched the handle of the well.

The gentle chimes of the bellflowers turned into a cacophony of discordant noise as a black mist began to ooze from the well and seep across the little garden. There was a scrabbling sound and two pale, withered hands appeared over the top of the well.

An angry wind exploded from the well and roared across the garden towards them. The force of the wind threw the companions backwards into the overgrown garden. Anders grunted as his head hit a boulder hidden among the swaying grasses. He lay there unconscious as the grasses began to wrap their blades around him.

Quickly, Kasian rummaged through his shoulder bag and took out what appeared to be two sticks tied together to form an 'X' shape.

'What the hel are you doing?' Meloc screamed above the

wind.

'This is a *Illit Cross*. It is a portal, it will catch the evil spirits and send them back to the cold, dark mists of Hel, where they belong,' Kasian called back as he held the *Cross* towards the well and began to mutter a Wergend incantation.

There was a thud as the creature leapt on top of the little stone wall surrounding the well. Its wild black hair dripping with dead black water. The creature threw its head backwards, so its neck was folded back on itself and opened its mouth to reveal a row of serrated teeth. Then it roared. The noise was deafening. It bent the garden trees backwards and ripped the planks from the walls of the shack and flinging them high into the air. The *Illit Cross* was ripped from Kasian's hand and fell against the ground.

'But I do not understand. The *Illit* does not fail. Perhaps it is broken?' Kasian shouted, his hands grabbing hold of tuffs of grass as the wind threatened to drag him from the garden.

Meloc propped himself up on his elbows and turned his head slowly towards the well. Two large amber eyes glared back at him.

'I think it might have worked. If that was an evil spirit,' shouted Meloc. 'That thing is a bloody fossegrim, and it's not quite dead enough for the *Illit*.'

Kasian cursed and punched the ground with his fist.

'I smell a little warlock… so full of magik. I am coming to get you, galdorsack,' the fossegrim sang softly, its long, forked tongue started to lick at the air as if tasting Meloc's flesh.

Meloc looked at Kasian. The Wergend officer rolled his eyes and nodded his approval. 'Use your kraft and use it quickly, this wind is pulling the flesh from my bones.' Kasian lost his grip and was pulled back ten feet across the grass, yelping as hidden stones ripped across his body. He grabbed hold of a narrow tree trunk and screamed into the wind. 'Do it now!'

Meloc's eyes flashed amber and he raised his casting hand. A bolt of white flew at the well. The oozing steam exploded into a haze of water droplets which hung suspended in the air for a moment before crashing down onto the overgrown garden.

Enraged, the fossegrim flew at him, its hair trailing through the air as its unblinking orange eyes fixed on him. Meloc felt his blood run cold as fear shivered through his body. His mind went blank. His knowledge of spellkraft disintegrated. He felt his spirit rise from his body and fly upwards, so that he looked down upon the little garden. Everything seemed to be happening in slow motion. Anders was almost covered by the weaving grasses, only his face remained visible. A drop of blood trickled from his reopened cut and splashed loudly onto the rock. Kasian looked at him, his mouth and eyes wide open, as his fingers were ripped from the tree trunk.

'Lord Gaderel, help us!' Meloc screamed.

The fossegrim paused.

The name of a forgotten spell fluttered into Meloc's vacant mind.

'*Fréosan,*' he whispered, as he held his breath. The air glowed amber. He crawled backwards, feeling the tall grasses wrap tightly around his trousers as his heartbeat pounded in his ears. Meloc had committed the ultimate magikraft offence. He had cast a spell he could not remember.

The waving leaves on the myrtle bush began to glisten with ice. The wind blew and the leaf disintegrated into a thousand ice crystals. The amber glow expanded across the garden and touched a strand of wild, black hair. The fossegrim screamed in confusion as it became trapped in the amber glow. The amber shadow sparkled, freezing everything it touched creating a garden of shimmering ice sculptures. The dwarven apple tree splintered and shattered against the frozen grass.

Meloc frowned as he tried to locate the fossegrim among the sparkling white ice sculptures of the garden. His eyes widened in horror. The creature was too powerful to be trapped by his magik for long and had disappeared.

'You're close, though, I can feel you,' Meloc said as he walked across the frozen garden, his crunching footsteps leaving a trail of green as he went.

A light glinted from the cottage roof.

Meloc froze.

The fossegrim leapt from the cottage roof onto Meloc's back, biting down into his neck.

Meloc screamed and grabbed at his neck as he fell onto his knees, blood pouring through his fingers.

The creature gripped Meloc's forearms tightly, pinning him to the ground. The fossegrim leant over and hissed into his ear. 'Your death will arrive shortly, but I think I will play awhile with your friends, their deaths will be slower and a lot more painful.'

Meloc glanced over at Anders, lying helpless, almost hidden by the frozen grass. Kasian trapped mid-scream as he was dragged into the woods. Anger surged through Meloc's body. He grabbed a beechling leaf and pressed it over his wound. Instantly, the wound tingled and froze. He would not bleed out just yet. A jagged stone sparkled in the frosted garden in front of him. He grabbed the stone and with the last remains of his strength, threw the creature from his back. The fossegrim landed on its back in the ice, the extreme cold momentarily pinning him to the ground.

Meloc leapt onto the creature and hit it in the face with the stone.

The creature laughed. Its face folded in and rebounded back. Then it threw Meloc from its chest and jumped high in the air crashing down onto the warlock's abdomen.

Meloc groaned and felt the air fly from his body as he grasped for breath. The creature sat on his stomach with both hands around his throat. Meloc tried to pull the damp fingers from his neck. His legs thrashed in the crushed grasses trying to topple the creature, but the fossegrim just laughed. Meloc's hands fell from the creature's arms. He clutched at the dying grasses as he felt his chest tighten and constrict. He mouthed a final spell under his breath, but the galdor ebbed to nothingness and his eyes turned blue. Pain seared his crushed throat and he struggled for one final breath.

The garden faded to black.

THIRTY

Name - Meloc
Location - The Smuggler's Cottage
Allegiance - The Mercian Warbands

The fossegrim went rigid, its eyes lost their amber glow as they widened, and the creature fell forward. Its face frozen in a death mask of surprise. The wind vanished and the twisting tall grasses shrunk back into the soil.

A flock of rooks took flight and wheeled through the air in a black cawing cloud.

Cautiously, Meloc opened one eye and breathed a sigh of relief. A shining dagger was lodged firmly in the creature's back. Its wooden grip etched with a single mountain design surrounded by a series of runes granting the thrower good aim, an honourable death, and a sharp blade.

'When you have finished playing with that creature, perhaps you can help?' Anders called.

His left arm was free, but his body remained within the woven grass tomb of the bellflower enchantment and was slowly sinking into the black earth beneath the waving grasses. Kasian put one hand around the narrow trunk of a bending elmit tree and reached out to Anders with the other, their fingertips brushed against each other. The ground wobbled and Anders was sucked further down into the mud away from his reach.

'Malediction!' Kasian cursed. 'Why is this land so cursed with magik?'

Meloc blinked, startled at the interruption. The fossegrim was pinning his legs against the treacherous grasses. He tried to heave it onto the grass, but the creature fell through his arms in one gelatinous mass.

'Warlock! A bit of help any time before I drown would be good!' Anders shouted as he tried to grab at the overhanging grasses and pull his way out of his sticky tomb.

Meloc muttered strange words under his breath, and the corpse flew through the air. Then he thumped his hand on the earth and yelled '*Fresla*!' There was a puff of amber as the myrkir rose from the bellflowers and disappeared. The grass tomb withered to brown, and the soil began to harden around Anders' body.

'Quick pull him out or he'll be stuck fast!' shouted Meloc as he sprung to his feet and raced over to Anders.

Kasian let go of the tree and pulled hard on Ander's free hand. There was a slurping noise and Anders sat up, his entire body covered in black mud. Meloc grabbed Anders other hand and they both pulled.

The captain was catapulted from the mud and collapsed onto the ground next to the woven tomb, panting.

'Faen! I thought the flowers had me. To be killed by a flower would be worse than death itself! I think my father would descend from the Valholl and kill me again with his bare hands!' Anders gasped as he wiped the sweat from his forehead with a muddy hand.

'Come, we have stayed too long. I hear the whispers in the woods; our presence is known to all, and forces have been dispatched to meet us on the Southern Road. We need to cross the Midheim River by nightfall,' Kasian said grimly.

'The Wergend never have any good news, do they?' laughed Anders. He stood up and stretched, sending a shower of dried mud over his companions. 'Right... let's go then. I refuse to be captured by either side until I have cleared my name and regained my honour.'

He picked up his sword from where it had fallen on the brown grass, sheathed it, and marched into the woods. A second later he turned around smiling sheepishly, 'Er… which way is it?'

Kasian shrugged.

'What would you two do without me,' Meloc tutted. 'It's this way,' he pointed. 'I can feel the river calling.'

'Why doesn't that fill me with confidence?' Anders frowned as he watched Meloc disappear into the trees.

'Because it's daemonkraft,' Kasian said shaking his head as he followed Meloc.

They walked in single file through the creeping thorny undergrowth, which tore against their trousers.

Unblinking pale eyes watched their progress from within the tree canopy as the sounds of the river rippled through the dense woodland.

After an hours' walk through the woodland shadows, the path opened onto the banks of a huge, deep blue meandering river. The riverbanks were covered in lush green grass which leant over to touch the water. Sprinkled among the grasses were tiny white moon flowers, their petals closed, ready to unfurl with the rising of the moon. Anders stepped around each flower, careful not to disturb any hidden magiks.

'I think you're safe from moonflowers,' Meloc laughed.

'Hmm...' Anders replied grimly. 'I am not risking being murdered by another flower.'

'Ejem, is there a spirit in this river too?' Kasian asked staring suspiciously at the river.

Meloc closed his eyes and raised his hand, feeling the waves emitted from the river. His hand felt wet and icy cold. He opened his eyes and stared at his palm. Cold, green water dripped from his fingertips. It smelt of decaying flesh rank mixed with a tinge of sickening sweetness. Meloc wiped his hands on his trousers. 'There is nothing left alive in that river,' he said grimly.

'And that's good news... for once,' replied Anders.

Kasian nodded.

'Even so,' warned Meloc, 'it would be best not to let the water touch you.'

'We will use the steppingstones,' said Kasian making his way towards a series of reclining granite slabs. There were large gaps between each slab to allow the tumbling waters of the Midheim to pass by unhindered. However, the river waters did not like the granite intruders and tried to rip pieces from the sleeping stones as they rushed past. Consequently, each year the gap between the steppingstones increased as the thundering waters reclaimed its riverbed.

The surface of the slabs glistened in the fading sunlight, damp and treacherous underfoot. Meloc jumped tentatively from stone to stone. Mercian legends spoke of the disappeared, people who had fallen into its racing waters never to be seen again. The fight with the fossegrim had drained him physically and magikally. He needed time to recover and prayed the crossing would be uneventful. Meloc carefully stepped from stone to stone. After a day of running for his life, he didn't smell too pleasant but neither did he have any desire to wash in the khaki waters of the Midheim.

Anders brushed past him as he bounded from stone to stone.

Meloc squealed and fell forward onto his hands and knees inches from the edge of his slab. He panted and peered into the swirling water beneath him. He felt something in the water glare back at him. Meloc paled and sat back onto his heels.

'There's something in the water, watch out!' he warned. Anders tutted and jumped nimbly onto the last granite slab. Meloc watched in mounting horror as the captain slipped on the slimy green algae which lay across the stone, hidden in shadows cast by a group of twisted willow trees crouched near the riverbank. Anders eyes opened wide with shock as he skidded into the waiting waters. He splashed to the surface, waved at Meloc, and started toward the riverbank.

Meloc breathed a sigh of relief and jumped to his feet.

The last stone cannot be trusted.

He lowered his gaze to the riverbank and whispered under his breath hoping Kasian was too busy extricating Anders from the river to notice his unnatural eyes. Meloc leapt high into the air and landed delicately on the riverbank. Kasian frowned at Meloc but said nothing as he hauled Anders from the fast-moving waters.

'Something's got my foot!' Anders screamed, kicking out at the water.

'Don't let go of him!' Meloc screamed as he bounded over. Kasian fell forward, his arm outstretched over the grassy bank as Anders was pulled backwards into the river.

Meloc swore and rushed to grab Kasian's legs before he disappeared into the churning waters.

'Don't let go!' Meloc screamed. His eyes burning amber as he gazed below the surface of the viscid waters.

He knew the Midheim travelled from the mountains of Mivir in the Northeast carrying its galdor lode, bringing magikal energy to the adjoining lands. Meloc stared into the river. He could see no galdor presence. The magikal crystals had been ripped from her waters. In their place an emptiness filled with hate. The Dunmuir must have filtered the crystals from the river before she entered Mercia, and in doing so accidentally freed the river's spiritual energy. The released energy had then condensed into a more corporeal form and this form was enraged.

Meloc's eyes glowed stronger and he gasped. At the bottom of the riverbed, he could see grey-eyed, blanched faces of the dead staring up at him. Their feet were tied to the towering riverweeds on her bed. Tiny flakes of shimmering galdor leeched slowly from their bodies as they became one with the river. Almost hidden in the murky darkness of the riverbed, the spirit of the Midheim glared hungrily at Meloc. Her huge blue eyes staring through him as if he were mere prey. She turned and darted to the far end of the seaweed forest, pulling Anders further into her lair.

Meloc watched in horror as Anders disappeared among the forest of grey, lifeless bodies. He ran his hand through his hair as he squinted through the frothing waters searching for the warbandman. He leaned further over the riverbank, wobbling precariously while holding onto a hanging willow branch. A wave of water crested on the far bank and crashed against the river, forming a tidal wave of angry water which rolled directly towards him. If a drop of this water landed on bare skin what little supply of galdor he had left would instantly vanish. He cursed and jumped out of the reach of another surging wave. As soon as the waves broke over the bank they retreated to the river, leaving empty grey scars devoid of all life. Meloc rushed back to the side of the bank, carefully avoiding the dark puddles forgotten by the river. The gigantic seaweed trees parted, and he spotted Anders, his legs tied to a shaking seaweed stem, desperately slashing at his ties.

'If you can bring the spirit to the surface,' said Kasian rummaging through his shoulder bag for the *Illit Cross*, 'I will send it back to where it will do no harm.'

'If it ever works,' Meloc murmured looking at the *Illit* suspiciously.

'Que?' Kasian replied. 'You will have to speak louder.'

'Nothing,' replied Meloc innocently.

He closed his eyes and summoned the remains of his galdor energy and raised his upturned hand towards the river. A small hand tightened around his boot. He spun around and saw a blue tinged arm extending towards him from the biggest puddle. Wavy fingers began reaching out from all the puddles left behind by the retreating waters. He was surrounded. From deep within the waters, he heard the spirit laughing as she sensed victory. The watery fingers began pulling at his boot and Meloc jolted his foot away, the boot leached to grey.

Another hand appeared and grabbed at his hole-ridden sock. Meloc leapt back from the prodding fingers and screamed. 'They are surrounding me!'

'Cast a spell then,' Kasian shouted. 'Hold the water while I find my *Illit Cross*.' He looked worried as he rummaged through his ancient shoulder bag.

'I am almost out of galdor energy. I don't think it will hold!' Meloc shouted back.

'Just do it warlock before the captain drowns!' Kasian commanded. 'We need his sword, or our mission is over.'

Meloc tutted. The Wergend as usual cared more for their mission than anyone not ensnared by the teachings of their goddess.

He raised a hand towards the river and shouted '*Kyrr.*' A

wave of sparkling amber rolled across the Midheim. The waters stopped, caught as they crested, by the still spell.

The river spirit glowed amber. The spell collapsed. Black cracks ran through the stilled seaweed sculptures, which broke into jagged pieces and floated away on the quickening undercurrents. The river's surface melted into water once again. Meloc whooped with joy as Anders burst through the surface of the water.

Quickly, Kasian hauled the warrior onto the riverbank.

The temperature of the river began to heat. It bubbled with rage. Angry waves crashed against the bank, trying to regain their prize. Anders lay choking and gasping for breath for a minute and then dragged himself to his feet. 'Let us get out of here, I think we made her mad!' he gasped.

'I think it was the Dunmuir who did that. 'You smell awful, a cross between mould and wet dog!' Meloc choked, holding his nose. An overpowering odour of dank, stagnant water clung to Anders' clothes. It was not a good omen.

Anders looked down at his mud-stained clothes and laughed, 'You make a good point warlock. Even I think I need a bath. I just need to find an attractive serving wench to scrub my back.'

Kasian shook his head. 'If you are acquainted with the teachings of the goddess, you will know a pure body without a pure soul is meaningless. Scour your own body and then repent your sins.'

'What! You mean self-flagellation? I've seen one of your whipping parties. To be honest, I'm not into that sort of thing, but if a big-chested woman comes at me with a whip I would give it a go,' Anders smiled.

'You have completely failed to grasp the concept of

repentance and humility,' Kasian growled.

'So how many big-chested women have you turned down then?' Anders grinned.

'All of them,' Kasian answered. 'My body is pure. It is saved to be used as a vessel for the goddess.'

'Yes, I've been used by a few inn goddesses too,' Anders nodded. 'Some of the best leave weekends I've had.'

'He means he's a virgin,' Meloc said, a slight smile twitching on the corner of his lips.

'Really?' Anders replied. 'They are bloody rare in the Midheim! I had heard the rumours about the Wergend order but thought they were more suggestions than actual rules,' he laughed.

'I will pray for your spirit,' Kasian said solemnly.

'That will require a lot of work on your knees,' Anders grinned as he marched up the narrow path into the woods of the northern bank of the woods.

Kasian stared after Anders and shook his head.

'Warlock, can you walk unaided?' Kasian questioned turning to Meloc.

Meloc tried to stand but exhaustion hit him, and he stumbled and fell.

'Not that much,' Meloc wheezed. 'I need to replenish my galdor supply.'

'Very well, I will carry you then,' Kasian stated as he squatted down. 'But do not touch my bare skin. It feels unpleasant.'

'The feeling is mutual,' Meloc replied as he climbed on the Wergend's back.

THIRTY-ONE

Name - Meloc
Location - The southern banks of the Midheim River
Allegiance - The Mercian Warbands

The southern bank of the river was more open than its northern counterpart. counterpart. The banks of the Midheim were lined with straggling green bushes and white blossomed creepers which crept over the low-lying plants and twisted around the trunks of the fluttering elmit trees.

Several mud paths led from the riverbank into the dappled forest. The forest contained a mixture of birchlings whose branches filled with quivering light green leaves and spreading squat elmits. Here and there the thick gnarled trunk of an oaken towered above its neighbours, splitting the canopy and allowing the remains of the sunlight into the woods. While large greening boulders, the remains of ancient floods lay scattered over the forest floor.

'This is a good place,' Anders coughed. 'The ground is flat and the water fresh. I think we should rest here for the night.'

'I agree, to travel deeper into the forest at night is too dangerous. The evil things which lurk in daytime shadows are freed to walk among the living. Besides the warlock is much heavier than he looks,' Kasian said as he unceremoniously deposited Meloc on the ground.

'You collect the wood, and I will start the fire,' he ordered Anders.

'Yes Syr!' Anders gave the Wergend officer a mock bow. He winked at Meloc as he wandered off to search for unwanted branches fallen beneath the rippling trees.

Kasian went to the riverbank and collected an armful of smoothed river boulders which he placed in a circle on the floor. Next, he rummaged in his bag and took out a little metal box embossed with dancing flames.

Meloc rolled onto his front and watched the Wergend officer with interest as he twisted the lid to one side to reveal a long match. The stem on the match was brown and twisted in a corkscrew shape. Tiny words almost invisible to the naked eye had been inked on the stem. The match head was black and had a clawing, chemical smell.

'This is a *Tinderkassa*,' Kasian said with pride holding the match up for Meloc to see. 'It was carved from Eldtré, the tree of fire, which Lady Wergennis, gave to our order. With her blessing, it will light anything.'

Meloc stared at the match. The words written on the match began to move and spiral up the stick. Unless the Goddess Wergennis was a practising warlock, no blessing could achieve that. However, he could sense no galdor energy store in the match.

'Here's the tinder,' Anders grinned as he dumped a collection of sticks and dried leaves next to the stone ring. Carefully, he created a base for the fire using the sticks and kindling. Then he placed the dry grass and leaves on top of the kindling.

'Move aside,' Kasian ordered, 'the flames sometimes burn fiercely with the might of Wergennis.'

Anders and Meloc shuffled backwards and watched in fascination as Kasian took the match and struck it against one of the twigs. The twig exploded into flames. Quickly, Anders added more kindling to the fire.

'That is a useful match, have you got a spare?' Anders

asked.

'No,' replied Kasian carefully replacing the match in its box. 'It is a blessing from the goddess to her followers.

'Pity,' replied Anders, 'still holy fire is good enough for me.' He began to strip off his clothes.

'What are you doing?' Kasian cried out in horror.

'I'm getting naked,' grinned Anders, 'you don't expect me to spend all night in these wet clothes, do you? I hope my body doesn't make you uncomfortable?' Anders laughed as he lay his clothes over a large boulder resting near the fire.

'Er no, it's just that nudity is frowned upon in the order,' Kasian said blushing as he adverted his gaze.

Meloc looked at the warriors' taunt stomach muscles and bulging biceps. His legs were rippled like tree trunks. Anders looked more like a messenger from the gods than a mortal man and he knew it. Meloc smiled.

Something in the fire called to him and reluctantly he pulled his gaze away from the warrior's chiselled body. He felt drawn to the fire. He raised his hand and felt a slight shock as he connected with the remains of galdor energy.
He frowned and stared a Kasian's back as he busily prepared a pot of stewed vegetables.

'Well, well, frijemden… strangers,' a guttural voice sneered from behind the group of ancient willow trees clinging to the riverbank. A flicker of yellow crossed the sky as a startled wood warbler took flight.

Caught unawares, they were trapped.

Meloc cursed. He had recognised the voice instantly… A svinnar.

The svinnar had been created by a forgotten warlock envoy to give King Awain a more exciting hunt.

Part-wild boar, part-peasant, they had tiny peering eyes, razor sharp tusks, and large foraging snouts covered in coarse pink hairs. They walked on two large, hairy feet and were a squat mass of muscle and bone. Awain had never managed to kill one of these creatures. Meloc doubted he had even tried. Instead, they ran wild in the woodlands of southern Mercia: torturing, eating, or ransoming anybody who they found wandering unprotected through their territory.

Meloc was puzzled: this pack was far from their forest home, and too close to the dangers of the southern road to be a normal hunting party.

'You have no business with us!' Meloc shouted, propping himself up onto his elbows in a vain attempt to look important.

'We are in the service of the King and carry vital information!'

'Scitte!' he groaned as he collapsed back onto the ground, stars spinning around his vision. 'My link to the galdor force is fading, someone has cursed me, my magik is failing.'

Anders stared at Kasian.

'It was not me!' he said indignantly. 'The Wergend do not use such dark magiks.'

'Hmm,' replied Meloc, 'to curse me without my knowledge requires stronger magik than your order possessed.'

Kasian opened his mouth to protest.

'Enough!' Anders ordered. 'Just hand me my shirt! If we are about to be murdered, I refuse to die naked!'

Meloc grinned as he glanced at the frowning warrior. He reached over and pulled the steaming shirt from the boulder and threw it towards Anders, then he collapsed back onto the grass, panting heavily. Anders snatched the shirt and edged closer to the warlock.

Three huge svinnar's grabbed Meloc, Kasian, and Anders by their shoulders and pulled them to their knees in front of their leader.

'I will do the talking,' Kasian whispered. 'I will appeal to their higher calling. No one can deny the will of Wergennis.'

'Velkominn, children of the forest! I am Captain Kasian of the Southern Order of the Wergend. I am sanctioned by the mother goddess, and I am here on an important mission. I must speak to your leader at once,' Kasian ordered.

'Stilte! Silence your mouth,' Antik the Red, the one-eyed, pink-toned Chief of the Forest svinnar roared. He stared at Kasian for an instant, then snorted in disgust and smashed him on the back of his head with a gnarled wooden club. Kasian fell onto the ground.

'I don't think they follow the path of the faithful,' Anders whispered.

'Stilte!' Antik growled as he stared up at the darkening sky. A shadow of fear crossed his face. Soon the last rays of the exploding red sunset would fall from the sky, and the light of Vana would turn the night sky burnt amber. Everyone in Mercia knew it was unlucky to be out under the amber sky for it had been cursed by warlock blood.

'It too dark to walk,' Antik announced. 'We camp here. Tie them tight. Gerdeg stand guard if they move… chop their legs off.'

THIRTY-TWO

Name - Anders
Location - The Clearing, the Murmuring Woods
Allegiance - The Mercian Warbands

'Tie them over the horses. We go now. I smell intruders in forest,' Antik ordered.

'What about my breakfast?' Anders enquired as two pungent smelling svinnar picked him up and lifted him over the back of a stout forest pony.

'What about morning devotions?' Kasian asked. 'If I do not pray to the goddess before the day starts, she will be angry, and misfortune will follow.'

'I think it's a bit late for that,' Anders muttered.

'Never underestimate the wrath of the goddess,' Kasian replied sombrely. 'What of our warlock companion? He seems strangely quiet.'

'Hmm…' replied Anders watching as the unconscious warlock was dragged across the riverbank. 'I think the journey might have been too much for him.'

'Silence human-scum,' the one-eyed guard growled as he slipped a rope under the pony's girth and tied Anders tightly to the pony.

'Move out!' Antik ordered and turned his pony down a well-trodden dirt trail between two crumbling greystone waymarkers. Green lichen had spread across the markers covering most of the ill-crafted words which had been chiselled acros the two stones. A man's head surrounded by serpents had been carved at the top of each stone.

'What or who is that?' Anders whispered.

'This forest has stood for over a thousand years,' Kasian answered. 'That is the image of its protector. Try not to damage his children.'

The svinnar holding the pony's rein, grabbed hold of Kasian's hair and pushed his face against the pony's stomach. 'Be quiet or I eat your tongue,' he snorted.

Kasian sneezed the horsehair from his face but said nothing; the svinnar laughed and pulled the pony onwards.

After an hour jolting through the narrow woodland path the claustrophobic greenness of the dense woodland fell away as the svinnar, and their Mercian cargo entered a clearing. Dark stumps of once proud ancient oaks littered the muddy floor. While the oakens jostled for space around the little camp. They seemed to lean over into the little camp, their thick moss wrapped branches scraping against the woodland floor as if trying to reclaim their stolen land.

The ponies jolted to a halt. Two grinning svinnar guards dragged the companions to an oak tree, which stood just outside the warmth of the small, stone-circled fire of forest twigs and roped them tightly against its scarred trunk. Anders struggled against his bindings, but the ropes were too tight and cut into his bare skin. Kasian sat back straight against the tree, his eyes closed, lips moving in a silent Wergend chant.

Meloc should be able to spell these ropes lose.

The warlock could change the very essence of nature, freezing water, and stop time. His father's warnings floated through his thoughts, *'Never trust the daemonborne. Their magik would destroy the world.'*

But he saved me from the Dunmuir. Perhaps there is such a thing as a good warlock? Anders looked dubiously at the warlock who appeared to be fast asleep.

Another memory flooded into his brain.

He was sitting by the fire high up on the slopes of Stonefall Mountain watching his father instruct a young warbandman, on how to survive in the cold without arms or food.

'Survival is a matter of will. Your will to survive has to be greater than that which wishes to harm you. You are a strong, young warrior. You will survive this test; I have no doubt. Make it back to the fortress within four days and set the north a new warband record, Thorne,' Lord Hamarr had commanded. Then he had embraced the young man, whom Anders had later come to realise was his half-brother, and had marched down the mountain path, calling Anders to follow.

'It is all a matter of will, Father,' Anders whispered. He scanned the svinnar camp, its layout, lookout posts, and its leader.

For a race of humanised wild boars, Antik, looked too human. He stood about six feet tall with long, densely muscled arms and legs. A few waves of ginger hair flopped across his head. Small, heavily lidded black eyes lined with long reddish eyelashes squinted out from tiny cracks in his face. With each new generation the genetic intertwining of the spell had weakened, some had become more human while others more porcine. In a few more litters time, the human branch of the svinnar might even pass for Mercians.

Anders shuddered.

Antik was sitting on a tree stump arguing with two sour-looking subordinates. Every so often they would gesture and grunt noisily in the direction of the prisoners.

A line of forest ants marched over Anders' bare legs, and he shivered as their sting left a red trail across his skin. A nearby svinnar laughed and grabbed his face.

'What is matter? We not good enough for real Mercian? Do we disgust you, pretty blond girl?' he squeezed Anders' face tightly.

Anders felt the creature's hot, putrid breath on his face, and his stomach heaved. Revulsion soared through his body, and he kicked the svinnar hard between the legs.

The svinnar roared, grabbed hold of Anders' hair, and took a long hunting knife from his rough skin belt. 'I think I have supper now,' he grunted.

Anders' squirmed and tried to kick the knife from the creature's hand. 'Meloc wake up and help me!' he shouted.

Meloc groaned and turned his head towards the struggling warrior. Anders glanced towards the warlock and his heart sunk. The warlock's eyes were cobalt blue. The curse must have unmagicked him. Black vinelike marks were spreading across his face and hands as the curse began to spread through his body.

There was a heavy thud.

The svinnar's tiny eyes bulged with surprise as he fell face first into the dirt. Antik wiped the blood from his dagger on his torn trousers. 'No one is touching the prizes!' he ordered.

The rest of the herd roared in agreement. Antik strutted into a rough canvas tent, dragging the fallen svinnar behind him.

Anders breathed a sigh of relief as sweat poured down his back. His damp shirt clung uncomfortably to his body. He took a deep breath and forced himself to concentrate on the encampment.

From his position, Anders could view the rough camp in its entirety. Some svinnar were idling by the cooking fire drinking réamwíne. He could see the thick creamy liquid frothing over the sides of the boar tusk vessels and dripping down their faces as they drank. At the edges of the camp, several grunts kept watch, eyes scanning the black depths of the forest for intruders and perhaps dinner, Anders shuddered. There were nasty rumours circulating Mercia about the svinnar and their eating habits. Many travellers had gone missing in the Murmuring Woods, and when the Purple Guards were sent to investigate, they had found nothing.

The missing had just vanished into the dense forest air.

Anders watched as a rotund svinnar ripped the flesh off a roasted deer leg and began chomping though the sinew and bone. He turned his gaze from the hungry grunt to the far side of the camp, where a big black cooking pot was being prepared. Leaves, berries, and mushrooms all gathered from the forest were thrown into a bubbling liquid. The cook, a huge svinnar with a scar running down the length of his face, started sharpening a serrated knife while staring at the groggy Meloc.

He needed to create a distraction.

Anders cleared his throat and shouted over to the fat cook,

'Hey fatso…what good do you think killing us will achieve?'

'A fine meal!' The chef sniggered and the rest of the herd, who were lying by the fire, roared with laughter.

Anders gulped and decided that this was not going to be a very productive line of argument.

A deep horn sounded through the forest and the resting svinnar jumped up grabbing heavy wooden clubs and fierce looking, hook shaped knives. A red-faced lookout rushed over to the canvas command tent and ran inside. Seconds later, he reappeared with Antik, blood dripping down his stubbled chin.

The horn drew closer.

A legion of the King's Own Horsehelm burst through the trees and rode into the camp, their raven standard waving through the air as they trampled the camp back into the forest floor.

'Thank the gods!' Anders breathed a sigh of relief as he recognised the men. It was Birger's company.

The herd huddled around their leader; weapons held at the ready as the Horsehelm circled the camp. The horn sounded again, and they wheeled their horses around to form two lines as their commander, Captain Birger rode into the camp. Behind him rode Councillor Hundar, a cloak of lincoln green, covering his spotless chainmail shirt.

'Front line dismount,' Birger ordered. Leather creaked and sword clanked against chainmail as the first line dismounted as one and handed their reigns to their counterpart. A sergeant helped the councillor from his horse.

'Councillor Hundar, my lord, praise the god Tyr you are here!' Anders called out, smiling in relief.

Hundar's eyes narrowed as he walked over to the warband captain. 'How dare you address a loyal member of the Star Council!' he slapped Anders across the face with his gloved hand, 'You are a traitor and a coward.'

Anders reddened and stared at the councillor in dismay, 'I am not a...' he stopped, his voice breaking as the point of a Birger's sword pressed against his throat.

'I am not interested in your excuses,' Birger hissed. 'Lord Hamarr was a great man and died a hero of Mercia. You will suffer the death of a common criminal.'

'And remember, Antik, if we find them, they will have to be brought to trial,' Hundar said looking towards the svinnar leader. 'The King wants this matter attended to discreetly for fear of distressing his loyal subjects.'

Partially hidden by the deep shadow thrown from Hundar's warhorse, Azrael slid noiselessly from the saddle of his chestnut pony. He slipped the thin iron wristguard from his casting hand. Anders frowned. This was not the sort of behaviour he expected from the warlock envoy to the Star Council. Azrael put a finger to his lips and crept through the twisted oaks towards Anders.

'This is so typical of Meloc. Completely selfish! I'm sure he got cursed deliberately so he would not have to do any work,' Azrael whispered to Anders, who flattened himself against the tree trunk, trying to avoid touching the unbound royal warlock. Azrael half-smiled at the captain and then turned towards Meloc as he blew gently into his casting hand.

His hand began to glow faintly amber.

Anders closed his eyes and prayed for a good, quick death. The black vine which had spread across Meloc's forehead fluttered. Its leaves fell from the vine and disappeared. The vine retracted back down Meloc's neck and disappeared beneath his clothes.

'The curse is breaking, I will…' Azrael whispered.

'Watch out!' Ander's eyes flashed open in alarm.

Birger grabbed Azrael by the collar of his tunic and threw him against a tree, his forearm pressed tightly against the court warlocks' throat. 'Saying goodbye to a dear friend, are we? Just remember who owns you, warlock,' he hissed. Azrael made a gurgling sound, his face getting redder, his hands clawing at the arm.

'Captain Birger! That's the wrong warlock!' Hundar called out. 'You are meant to be my escort. Come here now and bloody well escort me!'

Birger glared at Azrael then released the royal envoy. Azrael fell to the ground, gasping and rubbing his neck as Birger stalked back over to the councillor.

Flanked by a ring of well-armed horsehelm, Hundar approached the huddle of cowering svinnar, only Antik stood his ground, staring defiantly at the humans. 'Why aren't these traitor's dead yet?'

Antik stood his ground and looked at him, his deep-set black eyes full of hate.

'We keep them fresh for many dinners. We take arms today and legs tomorrow, good eating for week.'

'Very well, I will not deprive you of a meal. Just make sure there is nothing left to identify their bodies with,' Hundar answered. He turned his back on them, his fine green cloak flapping into their leader's face as he called for his horse and trotted off into the forest, followed by the horsehelm.

Azrael scurried out from the safety of a crouching dogbush. The collar of his black tunic had been ripped so that his tunic flapped open, revealing an old grey undershirt. A ragged scratch ran across his left cheek, partly hidden by strands of long black hair that had escaped from his ponytail. In the time it took for a sand grain to drop in an hourglass, Azrael rushed forward to Meloc, placed his hand on the warlock's head and whispered some ancient words.

Meloc sighed.

Azrael, ran to pick up his wristguard, his face fell as he snapped it into place, and he quickly mounted his pony. Azrael cast one final look at Meloc and cantered off unsteadily into the forest.

THIRTY-THREE

Name - Anders
Location - The Murmuring Woods
Allegiance - The Mercian Warbands

Anders was relieved to see Meloc's face had lost its curse mark and had turned a slightly healthier alabaster tone. Survival is a choice, he thought grimly. He watched the svinnar cook stir the giant cauldron and a shiver of fear passed through his body.

'Is it really wise to cook us here? The horsehelm may return at any moment,' Ander asked.

Antik stalked angrily over to Anders and grabbed him by the throat with one gigantic, clawed hand, squeezing until he was unable to speak. 'Perhaps you speak true words boy but speak again and I take your tongue.' He looked over to the groups of idling, muttering svinnar. 'We go home to our women,' the chief ordered.

Antik was catapulted sideways as one of his strongest subordinates, Donncha the Snout-nosed barrelled into him.

The two landed in a heap next to Meloc, who jolted awake.

Quickly, Meloc drew his legs into his chest as the two svinnar wrestled beneath the tree. Antik roared, long-pointed canine fangs flashing as he threw the challenger from him. Then he leapt onto the stunned Donncha, headbutting him in the face. Cheers and roars echoed through the little camp. The rest of the herd formed a circle watching the sudden fight with delirious excitement, banging their clubs on the ground, and chanting in monosyllabic grunts.

'What is happening?' Kasian whispered, ducking as Donncha's free leg braced against the tree and heaved his body upwards catapulting Antik over his head. Antik landed on all fours. His tiny black eyes bulging as he snorted angrily at the pretender.

'Leadership battle,' whispered Anders. 'Antik was humiliated by Birger. When he didn't fight the Horsehelm, he showed himself as weak to the herd. Duck!'

Donncha raised himself up onto his elbows, blood dripping from an open cut running across his forehead. Antik leapt onto the stunned Donncha. He groaned, winded. Antik sensed his opponent's weakness and put two muscular hands around Donncha's throat, roaring his domination throughout camp. The herd snorted with delight and banged their clubs harder against the shaking ground. Antik stood up and roared, the roar was taken up by his followers, and echoed through the forest.

'Eat and then we pack the camp!' Antik roared, his face flushed red with victory.

The watching herd surged forward and set upon their fallen comrade.

Anders looked on in horror at the squealing mass of bodies in front of him. The smell of fresh blood turned his stomach. Beside him, Meloc looked ashen and sweaty. He smiled weakly at Anders, then turned and was sick against the trunk of the oak.

Two porcine svinnar with flopping strands of ginger hair approached Anders, knives in hand, smiles twisted across bloated pink faces smeared with fresh blood. Anders closed his eyes and whispered a pray to his god as he prepared to die. The thick ropes binding him to the rough tree trunk were sliced in two.

The warbandman fell forward and was unceremoniously dragged across the dying forest floor and left next to the ponies. Kasian and Meloc were thrown down beside him. The ponies wheeled around, spooked at the sudden noise and heavy hooves cluttered around their faces.

'I'm getting tired of this,' Meloc moaned as one by one they were thrown over the forest ponies. He looked over towards the bare oak tree.

Kasian raised his head to answer but Twigg, the larger svinnar, rushed over to him, grabbed his hair, and pressed his face roughly into the horse's girth. Kasian coughed and spat horsehair from his mouth.

Meloc smirked.

'Prisoners do not talk!' Twigg hissed in Kasian's ear. His breath stank of old blood. Kasian shivered and said nothing.

'Move out! Tonight, we dri-nk!' Antik roared. The herd cheered and roared in agreement. Twigg watched Anders, almost daring him to speak, and grabbed the reins of the straying cooking pack pony.

'So, you know the royal warlock?' Anders whispered. 'Have you attended court?' he frowned trying to recall Meloc at past royal gatherings.

Piercing cobalt eyes glanced at him and quickly looked away. Anders grimaced as he saw Meloc redden,

'I saw him at The Signings,' Meloc muttered, an angry glint flashing through his eyes.

Every magik creature hated The Signings. The first of every month every known magikal creature in Mercia was required to attend their nearest Wergend Chapel House to be checked, processed, and registered. The same process occurred for all the livestock brought into the walled cities. Those magikborne found unbound or without travel orders were immediately classed as Skelmir warlocks. The Skelmir had two fates: they were either sent to Eldingar Tower in the north for their unmynstering and then set free, or the ones considered too dangerous were sealed and sent south to the dungeons of Fastness Fortress.

Once in Fastness, they were never heard of again.

Anders looked across at Meloc, his pale unbound right wrist was clearly visible against the brown of the forest pony and wondered how he had escaped.

Meloc raised an eyebrow and flickered the fingers on his unbound arm. The meaning was clear. Hundar and the Horsehelm had missed their chance, but he would not.

Antik let out a ferocious roar and slowly lowered his head, ready to charge anyone who disagreed with his plan. The ponies circled and pulled against the naked dogwood. Dozens of pairs of anxious eyes fixed on their chief. Abruptly, the herd burst into activity, stamping out the fire, turning over the cauldron and tying strangely shaped cooking pots and bedding to the ponies' backs.

The herd then left the clearing and disappeared into the overgrowth, following a tiny track hidden amongst the twisted oak trees. The ponies walked hesitantly over the climbing ground, stumbling over the moss-covered stones that lay abandoned on the tiny trail. Eventually, the dwarven oaks gave way to taller birch trees that loomed over the living forest with a disdainful indifference.

Insidious, spongy moss had silently conquered the low forest, its floor enveloped in a thick blanket tainting everything it touched with light green spores. Rotting black branches lay scattered across the forest floor as the forest grew over them, reclaiming the fallen and carrying its spoils back into the earth. The failing light of the afternoon gave the dark green, mossy growths clinging to the birches an almost luminescent glow. Anders watched the unending blanket of moss and cursed. His stomach and ribcage were sore from being thrown against the pony with each uneven step. The smell of the pony and its mildewed leather saddle made him sneeze, and his eyes started to itch. He struggled to remove his hands from their bindings. The ropes binding his wrists were too thick and bit into his skin every time he tried to move.

He cursed again.

This day could not get any worse.

The cluttered forest fell away to reveal a ramshackled, sprawling settlement hidden in a clearing cut deep within the depths of the forest. It was difficult to see where the hamlet ended and the forest began, for the wooden buildings were covered in a cloak of ivy.

Leeshy Alehouse seemed to welcome its adornment crouching down onto the forest floor, merging into the green. The door of the inn opened to reveal its large, green-tinged owner, its wild brown hair matted with twigs poking from it.

'We come with food!' Antik shouted to the alekeeper.

'Good, good, very nice... young things... tasty,' the alekeeper muttered half to himself. 'Throw those two in the holding room, my svinnarings. They will keep till evening. Bring the Wergend inside an' we shall see if his goddess really protects him.'

Antik threw his head back and roared with laughter. He took his knife from his belt and grabbed Kasian by the throat. 'Let's see if your goddess protects you from the nathbak.'

'Hold him steady,' he ordered his men as he cut two parallel lines down Kasian's right cheek. Blood oozed from the cuts and dripped onto his uniform. Antik leant forward, the smell of fresh blood was intoxicating as he licked the blood from the cuts.

Kasian flinched.

'Take him to the cage an' string him up outside the pub, we will see who is stronger, his invisible goddess or the nathbak.' The assembled svinnar roared with laughter as Kasian was dragged away.

'Let him go!' shouted Anders, struggling against his guards.

One guard twisted Anders' arm behind his back and pushed him on to his knees. Twigg and a heavily muscled svinnar then dragged Anders over to the open trap door set in the yard just in front of the alehouse.

Anders peered into the musty smelling darkness and struggled violently.

'What's the matter, 'bandman?' The alekeeper shuffled over. His back was bent almost double so that it seemed as if he were perpetually examining the floor. Grey, lank hair hung by the side of his sharp, pointed face while ferret eyes moved swiftly from side to side even when speaking, always alert and checking for danger.

Anders glared at the alekeeper.

A yellow stained, bony finger prodded Anders in the stomach.

Repulsed by the svinnar's touch, Anders pulled away sharply and fell into the gaping mouth of the cellar. A minute later, Meloc crashed through the trapdoor, his fall broken by Anders. The trapdoor slammed shut and there were sounds of heavy barrels being rolled across the courtyard alongside muffled shouts and heavy footsteps. A heavy foot stamped on the roof of the cellar.

'Don't go running off now. We want our dinner!' The

familiar voice of Antik bellowed down at them, roaring with laughter, before marching off to join his men in Leeshy Alehouse.

THIRTY-FOUR

Name - Meloc
Location - Leeshy Alehouse, The Murmuring Woods
Allegiance - The Mercian Warbands

A trickle of amber twilight fell through a crack in the trapdoor catching the rising dust in its muted rays. A dark green mould crawled over the cracked stone walls of the hidden holding room as if trying to escape. The air was dense and musty as if it too were trapped.

Meloc and Anders lay on the cold stone floor of the little room and listened as the sounds of the svinnar grew quieter. Tight ropes rubbed into their wrists and ankles, every movement making them tighter.

Anders cautiously raised his head, testing the firmness of the rope. 'Well, things can't get much worse. Faen! I hope Kasian is still alive. For a Wergend he's not that bad.'

'I feel his presence. He is still with us,' Meloc replied panting heavily. He needed to rest and restore his depleted galdor reserves and do so as quickly as possible. They had two hours at most before darkness fell and the alekeeper returned. An image of Azrael riding through the forest flashed through his mind, but he dismissed it instantly. He would never live it down if the royal warlock had to rescue him twice in one day.

'Helgods!' swore Anders as he thrashed about the floor. He let out a deep sigh and his body relaxed. 'It's no good. I can't break free of these ropes… but I refuse to die being eaten by the svinnar!'

'You are very choosey about how you want to die; do you know that?' Meloc grinned weakly.

'If you had ever met any of my forebears, you would understand why. Can you try to wriggle over here and untie these knots?' Anders asked turning onto his side.

He looked across at Meloc for help, squinting through the darkness. The warlock was silhouetted in the reaching shadows, sitting with his back propped against the wall staring into nothingness. 'Are you alright er… Meloc…?'

'I will be,' Meloc whispered. 'Just let me rest a while.'

An hour past. Anders lay and watched the light slowly cross the stone floor while Meloc mumbled in the shadows.

'Yes!' Meloc announced, his eyes glowing amber through the dappled light.

'Pardon?' Anders frowned.

'I can create magik again,' Meloc breathed a sigh of relief and ropes fell from his wrists and ankles. He rubbed his raw red wrists.

'You can undo ropes? Why didn't you do so before!' Anders gave Meloc an exasperated look.

'Er… There are rather a lot of spells in *The Grimmurlis*, and I haven't used the *Leysa* spell since I enjoyed the delights of Ableakan city rather too much, I ended up tied to the bed with a thumping headache totally naked, and completely broke. I was woken up the next day by a rather loud alekeeper banging on my door and demanding the night's rent,' Meloc grinned.

'Ah yes,' Anders nodded. 'We've all been there.'

In the distance, the alehouse door creaked open and then slammed shut.

'We need to get out of here now,' Anders said. 'Quick untie me!'

Meloc closed his eyes tightly and muttered the incantation under his breath. An orange aura radiated through his body.

The ropes slipped from Anders' body, magik fingers brushing electrical pulses against his wrists and ankles. He stretched his aching limbs and rubbed his wrists.

'Now, any ideas on how we get out of here?' Anders whispered looking up at the trapdoor.

Meloc grinned, 'Don't worry. I can always remember the *ferglast* spell; it's very useful but rather temperamental. Now, hold tight. You don't want to be left behind, do you?'

He held out his pure white, delicate hands and Anders gripped them tightly. Meloc whispered several strange words under his breath and the travellers were engulfed in a flash of amber.

What seemed only a second but could have been hours or even days later, the travellers found themselves lying on the straw covered floor of a very disorderly public house. High pitched squeals of laughter were intermingled with the sounds of fighting and breaking furniture. A drunken svinnar staggered and collapsed onto the floor just in front of Anders and made no effort to get up again.

'Let us go slowly and quietly and avoid any confrontation,' Anders whispered.

'Good idea!' Meloc winked as he vanished through the alehouse door, which now hung by a single hinge.

Anders shook his head as he followed the disappearing warlock.

'You are a lot more powerful than you seem warlock. Perhaps the Star Council are correct, you warlocks are a bigger threat to Mercia than any mortal force,' Anders paused as he rubbed his stubbled chin thoughtfully.

'But the Dunmuir are no mortal force and only magik can defeat magik in the end,' Meloc said as he flattened himself against the alehouse wall.

'And that does not bode at all well...' Anders replied and clasped his herb necklace for luck as he followed the retreating warlock.

Yellow candlelight flickered through the open windows, jumping with every movement from inside the alehouse. A grey moon had risen and sat next to Vana, the ever-shining Star of Mercia, which illuminated both the alehouse and the surrounding woodland in a shadowy amber glow. A tall thick trunked oaken tree stood just apart from the forest trees. Its thick branches fanning out so that the night sky twinkled through its darkened leaves. Something glinted in the moonlight.

'There he is!' Meloc pointed to a man-shaped cage made from iron strips which hung from the end of the thickest branch.

'The Wergend's been gibbeted. Is he still alive up here?' Anders asked doubtfully.

'Hmm,' replied Meloc his eyes flickered amber. 'Yes, I sense his body is alive, but in a low state. I think he's either sleeping or praying.'

Sounds of shuffling and voices floated out from the open door.

'Quick turn it off,' Anders warned looking over his shoulder.

The svinnar cook staggered out of the alehouse and collapsed face down in the muddy track.

'They are my eyes, I cannot turn them on or off,' Meloc said rolling them dramatically. 'Anyway, I think we are quite safe. The svinnar don't seem to hold their liquor that well, must be part of the pig origins.'

'Never say you are safe in times of war,' whispered Anders. 'It brings a curse.'

Meloc half-smiled and shook his head. 'Curses are just magik spells. Nothing more.' He crouched down low in the shadows of the alehouse and then ran over to the oakling.

The gibbet was attached to the oakling branch by a thick chain which had been twisted around the branch and ran down the tree trunk. It had then been welded onto a thick spiked ring which had been hammered into the ground between the bulbous roots of the oaklings. The oakling was as trapped as the prisoner in the gibbet. Twigs fell from its branches and cracked beneath his feet, Meloc touched the tree: its bark was thick and rough, it's galdor energy ran too slowly.

The tree was suffering.

'This tree is in pain,' Meloc whispered to Anders.

'Don't do anything. We'll just get the Wergend and leave quietly,' Anders said shaking his head.

'Is that you?' Kasian called down, he moved, and the gibbet rocked. Its chains groaned and the pieces of iron hanging beneath the gibbet like a macabre windchime clanked together.

'Shh!' Anders said in a hushed voice, quickly glancing over his shoulder. He grabbed hold of the ring and heaved. It did not move. He tried again, his face turned bright red and sweat poured from his forehead. Something in his arm popped loudly.

'It's no good,' he said collapsing not the ground, 'it won't budge.'

'It's magiked,' Meloc said. 'You'll never be able to pull it out.'

'Well, why didn't you tell me before?' Anders demanded

massaging his arm.

'I didn't want to spoil your heroic moment,' Meloc winked.

He put his hands against the tree trunk and whispered, '*Gefa út.*' The gibbet glowed blue through the semidarkness. There was a loud crack as the chain pinged from the ring and unwound itself from the tree. The gibbet crashed to the ground.

A loud grunt following by a series of groans emanated from within the cage.

The surrounding silence evaporated.

Loud shouts and high-pitched squeals came from the direction of the alehouse followed by the sound of breaking furniture as the svinnar staggered to their feet.

'At least you didn't kill him,' Anders said shaking his head as he ripped open the cage and pulled the bloodied Wergend from it.

'Thank you for the rescue,' Kasian wheezed, blinking away the blood dripping from a cut above his eye. 'I did not think I would see either of you again.'

'A warbandman leaves no man behind, it is our code of honour,' Anders said solemnly. 'But let's get out of here. That crash was enough to waken the dead.'

'It could have gone a little better, I suppose,' Meloc nodded.

Anders frowned as he noticed an object caught in the bushes behind the gibbet was glowing slightly in the amber twilight. It was Kasian's leather water bag inscribed with the Antriad, a triangle within a square, the holy symbol of the Wergend order. He passed the water bag to Kasian.

'Thank you,' Kasian smiled weakly. 'This was a gift from my father upon joining the order, I would hate to lose it.'

'I see,' said Anders as a shadow of sadness crossed his face. 'But can you walk?'

'I will walk,' Kasian answered. 'The goddess will support me. We need to find Antik, he took my pendant and bag. Without either we will be helpless.'

Kasian collapsed.

Anders grabbed the Wergend as he fell and heaved him over his shoulders.

'You will have to do without gifts from your goddess,' Anders said as he grabbed Meloc by the shoulder and marched towards the stables adjacent to the alehouse.

The horses had been left in their stalls by the stable hands, who lay passed out over a pile of hay stacked in the corner of the stables. A bottle of cheap honey wine lay on the stable floor, slowly oozing its contents into the hay. A rat who had been licking at the liquid scurried into the darkness.

Meloc eyed the rat hungrily.

Startled, the horses whinnied in fear and started banging their hooves against the stall doors. Anders grabbed the reins of a small bay pony and threw them to Meloc. He heaved Kasian on a big bay mare.

'Ride or die,' Anders said, handing him the reins.

'Thank you,' Kasian replied weakly.

Anders walked up to a heavier more spirited, door kicking warhorse. 'Serve me this night and I will set you free,' he whispered in the horse's grey ear. He walked the stolen warhorse from the stable. Its hooves echoed through the courtyard each time they hit the cobbles.

Meloc and Kasian followed, the courtyard rang with the sound of clattering hoofbeats.

'Stop them!' Antik screamed standing at the doorway of the alehouse, a barbed spear in one hand. He threw the spear. The spear veered in an arc, hit the stable door, and rebounded landing on the cobbles in front of Meloc's pony.

'That was closer than I expected,' Meloc gasped, as he struggled to control his pony who was turning circles, wide-eyed terror.

'You are not lucky, are you?' Anders laughed. 'Let's get out of here!'

The companions dug their heels firmly into the horse's flanks. Anders' and Kasian's mounts sprang into a gallop and disappeared down the muddy track, swallowed by the darkness of the forest canopy. Meloc's pony watched Anders disappear into the forest with great interest and reluctantly cantered after him.

THIRTY-FIVE

Name - Antik
Location - Leeshy Alehouse
Allegiance - The Royal Dunmuirlun Forces

Antik staggered into the night, tankard in hand, 'Scitte! The prizes have escaped. I'll rip their heads off with my bare hands!'

A sudden breeze rippled through the Murmuring Woods, rustling the oaken leaves, and knocking their branches together. Frightened, the roosting rooklings cawed and took flight disappearing into the dark sky.

Hidden beneath the woodland sounds was a deep, slow drumbeat.

'Scitte!' Antik swore again and perspiration dripped down his face. Slowly, he backed away from the wavering trees.

The chain of the fallen gibbet unwound from the oaken tree and slid silently across the grass.

Antik felt the cold stone wall of the alehouse and breathed a sigh of relief.

The chain whipped into the air, seized him by the throat and tossed him into the air. Antik landed with a thud. The chain pulled tight, and dragged him back to the oaken tree, wrapping him tightly to its rippled trunk.

'Your majesty,' Antik gasped as the chain tightened around his throat. 'I serve you good.'

'How dare you speak to me,' a chill voice answered. 'You failed me.'

'No… wait!' he begged. 'I caught the Mercians, and I will get them again. They will not get far.'

'Keep the warlock alive. He will find the Galdor Weapons for me, he feels the Serpent's Breath. Kill the others,' the voice hissed.

'Yes, your majesty. The svinnar will get you the warlock,' Antik nodded.

'Just remember no one lets me down twice and lives,' the disembodied voice hissed.

The chain dropped and Antik fell to the ground rubbing the thick red bruise across his neck. He crawled to his knees and bowed his head. 'The svinnar will not fail you, your majesty.'

'Do not!' The voice was lost, taken by a gust of wind which swept through the courtyard and smashed into the oaken tree. There was a loud crack and the sound of splitting wood as the trunk ripped in two. Its branches smashing into the roof of the alehouse.

One second of surprised silence was followed by squeals of anger and terror as the herd poured from the crushed building.

'Come together now!' Antik roared loudly.

The herd assembled, jostling, and pushing against each other, trying to gain sight of their leader.

'Bring me the alekeeper!' he roared.

The alekeeper was dragged forward by two heavy svinnar guards and thrown at Antik's feet. He knelt; his bony, dirt-stained hands clasped together begging for forgiveness. 'But the two Mercians were tied up, my dear svinnarings! And the Wergend was put in the cage. I thought they were safe 'til dinner. It wasn't my fault they escaped.'

The svinnar leader looked at the cowering human in disgust. Slowly, he took a cleaver from his belt and slashed across the man's throat. He collapsed onto his side. 'I forgive you, alekeeper. But we still have to eat.'

The assembled crowd roared with laughter. Ingolfa the grunter, the former second cook, rushed over to the corpse and started dragging it towards the alehouse kitchen.

'Herd, find the Mercians, kill the soldiers but keep the magikind alive and unchewed!' Antik roared, saliva oozing from the corners of his snout at the thought of raw, juicy, Mercian flesh.

The herd charged from the yard, wheeling round onto the muddy track as they caught the smell of the fleeing Mercians hanging in the empty air.

THIRTY-SIX

Name - Anders
Location - The Daucherlun
Allegiance - The Mercian Warbands

'Warlock ride faster. They're gaining on us!' Anders shouted as he galloped along the muddy path, his horse easily jumping the rotting branches that barred his way. The stunted oakling trees watched in brooding silence and tugged at his overshirt as he rode past them. Frowning faces were etched into their wrinkled bark as they stood watch over the narrowing path.

'We should not follow this path!' called Meloc. 'The trees are not happy.'

'Well, I'm not that happy either,' replied Anders, 'but the svinnar will not dare to stray too far from their woodland home.'

They cantered further down the path as the dense woodscape fell away to reveal the Sleeping Fields of the Daucherlun, a series of ancient burial mounds which spread were across the flat grasslands which lay into the east of the Murmuring Woods.

'We should not enter the Daucherlun,' Kasian whispered. 'It is cursed and without my amulet or spiritual bag we have no spiritual protection.'

The howling sound grew louder.

'Let us hope the pigmen think that too!' Anders yelled as he spurred his warhorse along the track heading into the Daucherlun.

The mounds housed small stone dwellings with narrow tunnel like entrances. The stone chamber was then completely covered in soil, their sides slowly flattened until they reached the field. Over time, a creeping moss had covered the burial mounds, so that from a distance they blended into their grassy surrounds. In the centre of the field was a circle of weathered monoliths, the former Temple of Tivor.

They were built for warriors, the nobility, and the high warlocks in the Eldor Age to keep their bodies protected from the touch of myrkir after death. Now they lay peacefully covered in long moorland grasses which stretched upwards to the horses' knees. However, hidden below the smaller mounds, the ground lay restless, cursed by the treachery of those long dead. These were the tombs of the Order of Tivor, a cult of religious warriors from the Eldor Age sworn to serve the old god in return for immortality. None of the Tivorhelm had died naturally, and their deaths could not be contained by their earthly tombs. For these warriors the promise of immortality had been a curse, transforming them into monsters.

At night, they could be seen wandering throughout the Daucherlun.

A slight breeze blew across the mounds and the tall grasses whispered. Anders frowned and squinted into the amber darkness. Noises coming from the darkness were never good. The grasses rippled as the ground beneath them woke. The earth groaned and bulged, brown soil crumbling down the sides. A spearhead shot through the ground. Anders' warhorse reared in fright, almost unseating him. He looked warily across the fields as the ground throughout the sleeping fields rumbled as the almost-dead awoke as he tried to calm the terrified animal. It neighed in fright as the grass wrapped itself around its legs. Anders dismounted and pulled the horse up to the relative safety of the top of a still quiet burial mound. The horse tossed its head and backed away from Anders, straining against its reins.

'We should not be here,' Kasian said as he dismounted, rivulets of dried blood across his sweat stained face. 'These lands are unholy. There is myrkir here. I can sense it.'

Anders scanned the shadows of the forest. Under Vana's gaze, he could just make out the distant figure of Meloc bouncing up the track below.

'The hunted have few choices,' Anders replied. 'But at least the warlock has managed to keep his seat. Perhaps your goddess is looking after us.'

'All praise the goddess Wergennis,' Kasian said bowing. He did not notice the twinkle in the warbandman's eye or the smile on his lips.

Looking past the uncomfortable warlock, Anders could see an ominous cloud of dust appear as a grey shadow on the starlit horizon, and he felt the ground tremble. The svinnar were coming.

After several long minutes, Meloc reached the burial field and dragged his unwilling pony up the grassy mound. His face covered in sweat and dirt. He stood next to Anders and Kasian as they watched the dust cloud approach. Trackers ran ahead of the main party, their snouts wrinkled in concentration as they followed the intoxicating scents of warm horseflesh and Mercians. Their high-pitched squeals rang through the dusk as chase fever took hold.

The mound groaned and trembled.

A great, two-headed axe thrust through the grass.

'Faen!' Anders gasped.

The axe was held tightly by a huge black leather gauntlet as an ancient leather clad warrior rose from his grave.

'They have awoken,' Meloc murmured, his eyes staring into the night.

Anders gripped Meloc's arm until the warlock squealed,

'We've got to go. Can you get us out of here?'

Meloc pulled his arm away and rubbed it, looking at Anders in confusion. 'The dead are calling, crying out for their revenge,' he said softly. He tilted his head to one side, listening to sounds Anders could not hear.

'He cannot hear you,' Kasian said. 'The old gods are calling out to him.'

The mound lurched violently as a ragged figure stood up, holding a heavy double-headed spear. The spear tip caught Meloch on the arm, ripping his sleeve, and leaving a deep red scratch. Anders quickly pulled the warlock away from the spears reach.

'They are not fully awake. Let us depart silently,' Kasian whispered. Anders nodded and began leading his pony passed the burial mounds.

'Hail the followers of Tivor!' Meloc half-bowed and thudded his chest with his fist.

The near dead warrior turned towards the companions, its large grey eyes staring at them from behind the half-visor. Black soil crumbled and fell from his dulled chainmail as he roared and smashed his axe into the shaking ground. The roar was instantly taken up across the field as more warriors woke.

'This will bring the svinnar down upon us,' Anders groaned.

Terrified, his horse broke free of its ties and galloped through the burial mounds, weaving between the tall martial figures. Slowly, the ancient warriors turned towards the unexpected noise.

There was movement by the borders of the wood behind them. Branches waved and cracked and the ground shock as the svinnar streamed out of the woodlands. Antik led the pack, a carved scythe in his hand. Some of the svinnar ran with weapons in their hands, whilst others charged from the treeline on all the fours, galloping towards the companions, their large, pointed canines visible from their panting mouths.

'Bring me the warlock alive,' Antik ordered. 'Rip the others from arm to leg and eat their flesh.'

A cheer and squeals of delight echoed from the wood as the herd surged into the grasslands.

'Let us leave our enemies to fight each other,' Kasian said. He took hold of Meloc's reins and pulled his pony over the shaking grass and down the northern bank of the mound. At its base were a pile of broken monoliths where the circle had collapsed against the grass. Snaking between two of the smaller stones was an overgrown, dirt path.

'Praise the goddess,' he breathed a sigh of relief and disappeared, lost in the shadows of the narrow path.

The excited squeals of the svinnar pierced the silence of the burial field. The noise of heavy footfalls reverberated through the night.

'The fallen ones have found new sport,' Meloc whispered, the enchantment of Tivor broken.

'At least this will slow them down, why can't the dead just remain dead?' Anders sighed. Meloc's pony flicked its brown tail in his face, and he cursed the pony, the svinnar, the undead cult, and the warlock.

Sounds of squeals and shouts sliced through the air.

'We need to move quickly,' Anders said. 'Follow the pathway, I will guard our rear.' He drew his sword. Meloc and

Kasian nodded and pulled their mounts through the narrow pathway, but with every step the svinnar were gaining ground.

Anders could almost feel their grunting breath on his neck. He glanced over his shoulder and swore as he saw the flickering orange flames of svinnar torches burning through the semi-darkness. He heard Antik scream to his men to divide and fight. Half were sent to fight the undead cultists, while the rest were to hunt their Mercian dinner.

They ran, twisting in and out of the silent monoliths.

'We must free the remaining horses, they do not deserve our fate,' Kasian panted.

'I agree,' said Anders.

'Go home friend, you are released from your duty,' Kasian whispered into his horse's face. The horse nodded, its dark mane flowing in the air and it stamped feet, then turned and galloped off heading towards the safety of the adjacent treeline.

Meloc's pony watched his stable mate disappear into the darkness and snorted. It threw back its head, rearing up on its back legs. Caught by surprise, the warlock stumbled backwards, only to be caught by Kasian. An electric shock jolted them apart. Behind them the squeals grew louder as the svinnar caught their scent on the nighttime breeze and followed them down the path.

'Hmm...' Anders said, rubbing his stubble. 'Let's move.'

Meloc got unsteadily to his feet. He glanced over at Kasian who was staring at him. 'Are you cursed?' he whispered.

'Piérdase... Get lost, warlock,' Kasian growled and ran stiffly after Anders.

THIRTY-SEVEN

Name - Meloc
Location - The Caves of Tivor
Allegiance - The Mercian Warbands

The path stopped.

The companions were trapped against the cold stone of the silent, greystone monolith. Escape was impossible and they could almost feel the hot breath of the surging svinnar on their faces.

Anders felt something grab his shirt collar and pull him into a tiny opening between two towering stones. Kasian clapped his hand firmly over Anders' mouth and Meloc put a finger to his lips. Anders nodded and was released.

'Follow me!' Meloc whispered as he disappeared between the monoliths.

The ground trembled as the herd approached. Dislodged dust tumbled from the tops of the monoliths and showered the companions with thick grey powder, which caught in their throats and pricked their eyes. The great stones muted the outside noise, so it became a dulled echo which rang through the small passageway.

A horn ran out and the herd began to gather on the outwardside of the monolith circle as they tried to locate their prey.

Beads of sweat ran down Anders' forehead as he held his breath, trying to blend into the greystone.

'Don't just stand there! Get in here quickly!' Meloc whispered as he crouched next to a tiny hole in the base of the smaller monolith.

'How am I supposed to get through that?' Anders exclaimed, kneeling next to Meloc as he stared suspiciously at the hole.

The horn echoed through the monoliths and was quickly followed by the sound of hooves and snorts of sweat as the herd tracked the Mercians into the circle.

'I suggest you try very hard,' Kasian stated as he crawled into the hole.

Meloc shot him a sideways glance. 'Too much fine castle dining? Don't worry, I'm sure I will be able to squeeze you through somehow… Do you want me to spell you smaller?' Meloc asked the corner of his mouth twitching.

'Er… no,' replied Anders hastily his green eyes widening in alarm. 'Don't worry, I'm sure I can make it.' He crawled on his belly through the hole, wincing each time the gravelly rocks rolled under his weight.

Meloc watched Anders' feet disappear through the hole. He could feel the earth tremble as the herd approached, he could sense the air grow warm with their frenzied breath. Quickly, he slid through the hole. Once safely on the other side, he pressed his hands against the stone wall and whispered, '*Leigfaira.*'

The wall began to bulge, the greystone moving in and out like a slowed heartbeat.

'More daemonkraft,' Kasian shook his head.

'Yes, and it's saving your life so be grateful,' Anders replied flicking his long hair from his face.

The hole led into a narrow stone shaft which descended downwards beneath the stone circle. It smelt musty and forgotten but beneath the cobwebs and dust the stones glowed faintly, casting amber shadows against the shaft walls.

'What is this place?' Anders frowned as he wiped the remains of generations of dusty spider's webs from his face.

'It's a galdormeetinghus,' whispered Meloc, 'and it's best to keep quiet.'

They walked down the shaft in silence as it opened out into a huge subterranean cavern. Its walls were jagged and wet to touch. Rivulets of water ran across the cavern roof, dripping down the melted waxing stalactites and falling into pools on the rocky floor.

Anders stood open mouthed, entranced by the beauty of the cavern, but Meloc pulled him down a narrow passageway cut into the rock. As they moved, Anders ran his fingers along the wall. It ripped through his skin, and he jumped back in surprise.

Meloc frowned. 'Do not touch the walls. It's glasgot rock and will take the skin from your bones if you let it.'

Dropping his hand fast, Anders stared at the seemingly harmless rock and noticed that it glowed a slight amber as Meloc passed by.

Kasian shook his head. 'Por Dios... and yet more spellkraft.' He raised one black eyebrow. 'You magikind have been allowed to run too free. Your leashes needed to be tightened.'

'Well, I do enjoy a good tight leash...' Meloc winked and disappeared around a turning in the tunnel.

'Umm...' Kasian replied frowning.

Anders bit his lip and hurried after the retreating warlock, carefully avoiding the sharp rocky outlets that tried to grab hold of his undershirt and rip his bare skin as he walked by.

The passage led into a smaller, dust-filled cave. The walls of the cave started to close in on them and Meloc took a step backwards. He could feel the dismay and rage of the spirits who wandered lost and forgotten trapped forever in their subterranean tomb.

Meloc hoped his companions would not notice the grey hands tugging at their shirts, trying to make them topple headfirst into the jagged wall. Fortunately, Anders seemed oblivious to the grotesque, twisted spirits that loomed around him. While Kasian seemed to sense their presence and kept looking around but without his spirit bag he was helpless.

Meloc swallowed hard and walked through a pile of sobbing ghosts in the middle of the cave, then stopped and raised his hand.

'*Synar,*' Meloc whispered. 'Show me the way!'

There was a grating sound as a narrow tunnel appeared in the glasnot rock on the left side of the cave, almost invisible among the cracks and folds of the wall.

The sounds of heavy martial feet reverberated through the underground passages. Dust and small rocks shook free of the walls and fell to the floor, sending clouds of choking powder through the musty air.

'The Tivorhelm are coming,' Meloc whispered.

'Scitte,' Anders looked anxiously over his shoulder. 'They must have broken through the svinnar rearguard.'

'Or they just ran away. Can't they do anything useful?' Meloc groaned as he lifted his hands above his head and quickly slipped between the cutting rock entrance of the tunnel.

'Are you sure that's safe? If it's a dead end, we'll be stuck in there like a wolf down a rabbit hole,' Anders frowned.

'I'm quite sure,' Meloc winked and disappeared into the little tunnel. He knew these caves well. They offered an underground safe haven for warlocks. Some hiding in the caves during the Wergend sweeps, when the unregistered magikborne were hunted down and sent to Eldingar Tower to be unmynistered. While the more militant warlocks used the caves to rest on their way to Austurlun.

The heavy feet stopped as the undead warriors paused.

The companions stood in the darkness of their tiny tunnel. Meloc put his fingers to his lips.

The Tivorhelm stopped outside the tunnel entrance, slashing at the thin air as the ghosts of failed travellers pulled at their armour. The largest warrior raised his two-handed axe and sliced through the ghosts, sending them scurrying to the darkest recesses of the cave. He stood for a moment. His helmet tipped to one side as if listening.

Meloc smiled.

'Don't worry. They will not find us in here. We are protected by spells cast by the great Grand Warlock Gaderel himself and to venture further into this cave is a trap. The cave is a mouth of the earth, the further they go into the cave the narrower it becomes, the rocks become hungrier. The floor and ceiling both teethed with razor sharp rocks, trapping the traveller between their jaws. The only option would be to slide backwards over the sharpened rocks as they ripped through your skin unless, of course, you were stuck fast in the cave, and then death would come slowly in the darkness. It should hold up even undead knights for a good while.'

A hot galdor wind blew through the chamber, unsettling the fallen debris and knocking against the piles of yellowing bones. Meloc felt the wind stinging his eyes and he rubbed them with dirt covered sleeves. He breathed in the rising dust and sneezed.

Six heavily armed Tivorhelm warriors appeared at the mouth of the cave. They marched over to their comrades who were gathering outside the tunnel waiting for their orders amid the rising wind and wailing ghosts. The spearman stood silently, his spear tip pointing to the top of the cave.

Meloc heaved a sigh of relief. 'Let's go,' he nodded.

The spearman turned and stared into the narrow opening of the tunnel. He thrust his spear inside, beating it against the jagged walls. Anders stood on tiptoes as the spear searched inches from his feet. Meloc touched Anders' shoulder and nodded to Kasian. They scrambled through the passage. Behind them came the ominous sounds of metal on rock as the Tivorhelm squeezed through the narrow opening and into tunnel.

'Only those who are attached to the galdor path can enter here unharmed,' Meloc recited.

'Or those reanimated by it,' Kasian said.

The tunnel compressed growing smaller and smaller the further they entered.

'I am beginning to hate these caves,' Anders said as a steady trickle of small rocks fell in front of his face. Sweat poured from his forehead and his undershirt clung to his back.

'Shh…' warned Kasian, 'do not let them hear you say that. You do not want to upset the caves.'

'I wish you wouldn't say things like that!' Anders groaned as he quickly crawled onwards.

Meloc said nothing but kept the light from his activated eyes fixed in front of him as he fought against a rising tide of panic as claustrophobia surged through his body. He would never have used the monolith entrance to the caves, but he had been given little choice. The path was barely big enough for him to squeeze through on his stomach. Amber-tinged rock shadows danced around him, and fear gnawed at his churning stomach as tears streaked white lines down his dirt-stained face. The banging of metal on rock echoed louder as the bodies of the Tivorhelm elongated and began to slide through the passage, oblivious to the tearing rocks and choking dust.

Anders yelped as a gauntleted hand grabbed at his foot.

'They have caught us up! We've got to get out of here!' Anders screamed, kicking at the warrior's visor.

'It's not long now!' Meloc called back. 'Cover your faces!' Meloc put his face against the hard stone ground and thumped his hand against the ground in front of him. '*Forloré*,' he commanded. A blast of wind thundered down the tiny shaft. The Tivorhelm were picked up by the blast and flung against the wall, disappearing in an explosion of black flakes.

'Having a warlock along is rather useful,' Anders grinned.

'But illegal,' Kasian replied as he breathed a sigh of relief. The tunnel jolted and an angry rumbling rose from the depths of the cave.

'Cave in!' Meloc yelled above the noise. 'Move it!'

Meloc felt the cave shudder. An avalanche of rocks crashed onto the shaking floor and an explosion of choking dust rushed through the tunnel. The dust cloud was unnaturally hot and carried fragments of jagged glasgot rock, which smashed into the sides of the passageway and tore away its protruding rocks. Meloc hid his face in his hands as the cloud ripped past his body as it rushed through the tunnel. The discarded dust and dirt gently floated to the ground, covering the inert figures of the three companions in a thick layer of grey.

THIRTY-EIGHT

Name - Meloc
Location - The Caves of Tivor
Allegiance - The Mercian Warbands

Meloc woke to the sound of metal scraping against rock. Laying against the tunnel floor, he was entombed in darkness. He breathed a lungful of dust and choked, sending the dirt and small stones tumbling from his back.

'Warlock you are not dead, get up!' Anders grabbed Meloc's boot and pulled hard.

Anders brushed the stone and powder from the dazed warlock and pulled Meloc up into a sitting position. Two beams of amber shot through the passageway. The glasgot in the walls sparkled and everything was tinged with an orange haze.

An ominous scraping sound echoed through the tunnel.

'They will be upon us soon' Kasian said frowning. 'The rockfall has covered the tunnel ahead, we need to dig our way out and soon. Everyone, start moving the rocks.' He picked up a rock and swore as the rock ripped through his leather gloves.

One drop of red blood fell to the floor.

'Oh faen!' Meloc swore as he rummaged in the rubble.

'What is the matter?' Kasian asked.

'I've lost my right boot. I can't tramp through the caves wearing a sock - the floor is too cold, and rock covered to walk on,' Meloc groaned.

'We cannot wait here until you find your boot!' Anders said looking over his shoulder. 'The Tivorhelm will be upon us. Besides walking barefoot will turn the soles of your feet too leather.' He looked down at his bare feet and wriggled his toes in the dust.

Meloc held out his hand and Anders pulled him up.

'But I don't want leather feet!' Meloc moaned as he brushed the grey powder from his clothes while hopping on one foot.

'Well, hurry up and just magik one if you must warlock,' Kasian said nodding at Anders.

'Shall I make a pile of gold while I'm about it?' Meloc said as he raised one sarcastic black eyebrow. 'Galdor energy can be transformed from one form to another but cannot create or be destroyed.

'Couldn't you just do a copy spell and create a boot from your other one?' Anders suggested.

'I could,' said Meloc rolling his eyes, 'but then I would have two right boots.'

'I see your point,' blushed Anders.

'Well…' said Kasian, 'then you appear to be one booted. Do not worry about the sharp stones, suffering is good for your soul. Your pain will cleanse your darkness away.'

Three black arrows whistled through the air and thudded into the wall just above Meloc's head. Then dissolved to smoking black dust.

'Myrkir arrows,' Anders hissed as he dropped to the floor, pulling Meloc down with him. 'One cut and the myrkir will enter your body and kill you from within.'

Another flight of arrows pinged through the darkness and thudded into the wall where they had been standing.

'We need to get out of here. We are sitting ducks,' Anders whispered as he lay on the floor.

There was a loud whoosh as the glint of an iron spearhead appeared out of the darkness as if in slow motion and brushed past Kasian's uniform as he flattened himself against the wall. Kasian breathed a sigh of relief as he whispered a prayer of thanks to the mother goddess.

'We are trapped. Prepare to die with honour,' he said drawing his sword.

'Oh nonsense!' said Meloc. 'We might not be able to make goods from nothing but the real advantage of being magikborne is that we can blow a lot of things up!' he grinned.

Anders and Kasian glanced at each other uneasily and stepped away from the warlock. Meloc muttered '*Myrkirstorr*' under his breath and a rush of warm galdor wind flowed through the tunnel. 'Watch out!' he warned as he waited for the galdor energy to expand. The passageway groaned under the weight of the spell, and broken shards of rock and stone skimmed over his head.

'Now for the explosion,' Meloc grinned. I would make myself rather small if I were you.'

Kasian and Anders curled themselves into tiny balls, facing the outer tunnel walls and shielded their heads with their arms. Meloc thudded his hand against the stone floor just stopping short of the rockfall as he screamed, '*Sprenga.*'

The centre of the rockfall exploded outward, the rocks smashing to pieces against the wall as a wave of thick choking grey smoke rushed down the tunnel.

Meloc disappeared around a bend in the tunnel. Kasian and Anders hurried after him.

A loud 'Yes!' echoed through the darkness and the constricting rocky tunnel widened into a cavern. Meloc eyes flashed, and a row of wooden torches burst into flames. Anders blinked, the flames burning into his eyes. Kasian grabbed his hand and pulled him around the corner, following the trail of torches.

'Do not get left behind,' he warned. 'There is nothing natural about this place. It reeks of myrkir and where there is myrkir there are monsters. They are attracted to it. It feeds the wickedness in their soul.'

'How do you know of these tunnels, er…Meloc?' Anders asked over the echoes of angry shouts of the Tivorhelm as they dug their way free of the rockfall.

Meloc wiped his face with a grimy hand, smudging trickles of sweat into his dirt-stained face and half-smiled. 'These are the Caves of Tivor… A safe place for magikind.'

'The old tales are true then. My father spoke of these caves, but I thought they were just old wives' tales, told to frighten children at night,' Anders said stroking his red stubble as he looked around the cave in awe.

'So, this is the reason you know active magik spells,' Kasian said grimly. He shook his head. 'My order failed the goddess in its collection of magical creatures. I will atone for this later.'

Meloc shrugged his shoulders and walked into the cavern. The cave stood as big as a fortress hall and the sound of their footsteps echoed into the shadows as the cavern began to vibrate and hum in welcome. Water droplets dripped from inverted pinnacles in the cavern roof, falling into black puddles scattered across its floor. The walls of the cavern were covered with paintings - thousands of pairs of pale hands with fingers outstretched surrounded by clouds of orange or pale cream paint. The hands themselves seemed to glow against the rocky tones of the cave. The ghostly hands were everywhere, and they seemed to move as the walls reverberated with the echoes of their footsteps. Suddenly, all the hands pointed upwards as if trying to push through the rock and reach the surface.

'There is strong magik hidden in the paintings,' warned Kasian. 'Do not gaze upon them.'

'I feel strange,' Anders' said rubbing his eyes. He began to sway in time with the vibrations as they entered his body.

'Do not gaze at the hands they are a magik trap…' Kasian said, his voice trailing off.

'Too late,' Meloc tutted as both companions stood staring vacantly at the cave wall. 'I really don't have enough galdor left for this.'

Meloc sighed and walked over to the side of the cavern, where just below a jutting rocky outcrop, was a small white handprint. He reached out and placed his palm on the spot. It fitted perfectly and a wave of galdor energy shot through his body like a lightning bolt. The wall of hands was a galdor reserve donated by centuries of Mercian warlocks. If the time ever came, this was to be the last stand of the magikind against the Mercian army. It's use for any other purpose was strictly forbidden, particularly when if it involved saving the galdorless from a lingering death.

Meloc peered into Anders' face, amused to see its frozen expression, his lopsided grin showing bright white teeth in stark contrast to his dirty face. Kasian in contrast was frowning as if he was trying to break free of the entrapment. Magik did not control the Wergend officer as it should have done.

Sounds of footsteps filtered through the cave, seemingly coming from all directions as the Tivorhelm grew closer.

'Release!' Meloc ordered.

A wave of amber flashed in front of Kasian and Anders.

Anders blinked and stumbled backwards as he was hit by the wave of magik. 'What happened?' he frowned suspiciously.

'It's a trap for the galdorless,' Meloc said. 'To stop them venturing too far into the caves.'

Meloc waved his hand in front of Anders' face. 'Hmm… still under. How strange.'

Kasian examined Anders' face. The naturally ruddy complexion had turned ashen white, and his bright blue eyes had faded to a dull grey.

'His life force is being drained. We need to get him out of here,' Kasian pushed Meloc to one side, grabbed the transfixed Anders by the arm, and pulled him from the cave into a sheer faced, ragged tunnel. A natural fault in the rock, the sides of the tunnel towered above them and shone with running water. Meloc ran his hand over the wall and flicked the icy water at the still dazed Anders. The captain shuddered and blinked the spray from his eyes.

'Are you going to wake up anytime soon? I'm not carrying you out of here,' Meloc declared.

Anders' face folded into a frown. 'How did I get in here? Where are the Tivorhelm?'

The warlock tutted; memory loss was a common side effect from entering the Cave of Hands.

'They have slowed but are still following,' replied Kasian grimly. 'I hear them climbing over the boulders. There are fewer now.'

'You must have bloody good hearing,' replied Anders, his colour fully restored. 'I hear nothing.'

'Yes, your hearing is very good,' Meloc replied, 'Almost magikal in fact.'

'It is the blessing of the goddess,' Kasian said, glaring at Meloc, 'a power bestowed upon me at my initiation into the order.' He walked ahead.

'You should not make such comments,' Anders said shaking his head.

'I know but I sense a magikal undercurrent about their order,' Meloc stared at the offended Wergend officer.

'Of course, they are blessed by their goddess with holy powers,' Anders shook his head and strode after Kasian.

The smile dropped from Meloc's face as he felt his left arm begin to tingle as the icy water droplets ran down his fingers. Meloc rubbed his hand against his ragged woollen trousers, but it remained icy cold. He pulled up his sleeve and cursed as he saw the black vine curse had twisted around his forearm and was gradually spreading its dark touch throughout his body. Azrael had not managed to break the curse of the fossegrim, only subdue it, and his extreme use of galdor had awoken its poison. He touched the bite on his neck, it felt wet as green water began to drip from the wound. The curse was slowly corrupting his body, changing him into a fossegrim.

'Your curse will not take me. I will find a way to break you,' Meloc whispered under his breath as he hurried after Anders.

The narrow tunnel twisted through the rocky pillars, folding in on itself until it almost formed a circle. Many larger, straighter tunnels peeled away from the narrow main, but Meloc ignored them. The better-looking tunnels were alluring decoys designed by the ancient Warlock master, Elder Drykind, and Meloc had had been warned on previous visits not to explore them. The mirror-like pools in these forbidden passages plunged deep into the heart of the cave system, drowning anyone who touched their waters. While other, drier decoy passages were cursed with a living death, *Soffet Toadstools* filling the stagnant air with invisible deadly spores which sent the unwary into an unending sleep. Any invaders following these larger passages would be marching straight into the Sumorlands.

Meloc wiped beads of sweat from his forehead and prayed they had not wandered onto a branch path. The narrow path twisted again. Light from the rising morning sun touched the twisting tunnel walls and Meloc smiled with relief.

The tunnel surfaced through a large crack in the boulder piles adjacent to the circles of silent monoliths. Anders groaned as he squeezed through the narrow exit, while an amused and much thinner Meloc watched.

'*Leigfaira*,' Meloc commanded and the surface of the boulders either side of the crack began to pop and bulge until the exit was filled.

'And so ends our Tivorhelm problem,' Meloc smiled.

'I knew you were not as useless as you look!' Anders said happily as he thumped the warlock on the back, making him gasp.

'But without the use of magik we would not have had a magik problem in the first place,' Kasian muttered as he followed after Meloc and Anders.

They followed an overgrown mud track through the boulder piles and onto a steep, jagged stone slope. The spirits of the fractured boulders growled in warning every time the companions stepped on them, and the companions looked at each other in alarm. The angry stones were broadcasting their presence to the sharp ears of the searching svinnar.

They nodded and ran down the slope, the stones shifting under their weight and cascading noisily after them. High pitched howls screamed through the air as the svinnar herd ran from the monoliths.

The slope opened onto a vast expanse of dark, flat wetlands crisscrossed with grey gravel paths that shone white in the early morning sun. An eerie silence hung over the wetlands. No birds sung or flew there. Kasian felt for the amulet that hung about his neck and found nothing. He shook his head sadly. 'This place is dead. Something evil lives here.'

Meloc scanned the horizon, squinting into the blackness. 'Don't worry, it's always been dead but never lifeless. Welcome to Fensalir, the sinking marsh.'

THIRTY-NINE

Name - Meloc

Location - The Fensalir Marsh

Allegiance - The Mercian Warbands

'Talk about jumping feet first into a raging fire,' Anders frowned as he squinted into the still waters.

'This place is cursed by death, we should not enter here,' Kasian said shaking his head.

'Oh nonsense!' Meloc sighed. 'Every piece of ground we walk upon is tainted by some memory of death. This marsh is no better or worse than any other ancient place in Mercia. Trust me… there are no curses at work here. I am rather an expert on the subject.' He winked at Kasian who muttered a prayer of protection under his breath.

'I see…' replied Anders unconvinced.

The Fensalir was infamous throughout Mercia. It was a place cursed by death and suffering. Only the desperate would willingly enter the marsh. According to the Mercian legends, the waters of the Fensalir had darkened on the eve of Lord Leofwin of Aebleakan's wedding.

Lord Leofwin and his attendants had been delayed by a daemon; fearing that he would be late, he decided to risk crossing the treacherous marshes rather than upset his beloved Ceolwyn. Neither he nor any of his men had ever been seen again. Ceolwyn, maddened by grief and loss, had searched the marches for months, desperately trying to find out what had become of her love. Until one day, she too became one of the lost.

The local Mercian farmers had become convinced that

either something in the marsh, or the very marsh itself, had killed the two lovers. In time the legend had spread across the Midheim and the northlands and now the marsh was shunned by all who knew its sinister history. Only those excused of the most horrendous crimes ventured into the marches, usually as an alternative to immediate execution, and none were ever seen again.

'I think if it were that dangerous, our warlock companion would find a different route,' he whispered to Kasian.

'Si… yes,' nodded Kasian as he watched the warlock jog slowly to the edge of the grey, muddy plains.

The sounds of squeals and muffled cries rang down from the hilltop.

'Hurry up!' Meloc shouted over his shoulder, 'the svinnar must have caught our scent. They will be upon us soon.'

The gravel covering the slope begin to tremble and trickle down the hillside as the earth moved under the tread of heavy feet as guttural shrieks and shouts sounded across the hillside.

Kasian and Anders ran into the sinking marsh.

The marsh, true to its name, consisted of thick, black peaty water speckled with islands of fields of thick green moor grass enveloped by a veil of mist. On first appearance, the black waters of the marsh slept peacefully. Many unwary travellers and animals had been seduced by this calm exterior only to become one of the disappeared, lost beneath the marsh's black waters. Hidden beneath the black mud was an underground thermal source heating up patches of the sticky peat, so that large bubbles would appear on the water's surface and burst, spraying mud high into the air as it collapsed with a dull pop.

A clawing mixture of rotting eggs and damp earth hung across the marsh.

'The last time I smelt something this bad I was in lodging rooms above an alehouse in the northlands and there was a dead dwarf in the bed next to me,' Anders frowned, rubbing his stubble. 'To this day I cannot remember why I was in bed with a dwarf.'

'Umm,' said Kasian rolling his eyes disapprovingly.

Dark clouds hung heavily in the iron-grey sky circling the marsh whereas the sky glowed brilliant blue over the rest of the outlands. Most of the marsh lay hidden beneath the low brooding clouds and the dense white fog that oozed over the marshlands. Anders shivered. Dressed only in his cream undershirt, he was ill-prepared for the sudden plunge in temperature.

They had only been wandering slowly through the marsh for a short while when Meloc found a tiny mud bank covered in thick marsh grasses. He collapsed panting on the mound, his breath wheezing with exhaustion. 'We should be safe here. I think.'

'You think?' Kasian raised an eyebrow.

Meloc groaned and looked sheepish. 'Well, we are slightly lost. I just need to sit for a while and get my bearings.' His face had turned sickly grey; the deep black circles around his eyes betrayed his exhaustion. He could feel the touch of the fossegrim curse spreading through his veins.

'Your injury was worse than it first appeared?' Anders frowned staring at Meloc's arm.

'Magikal injuries usually are,' Kasian nodded, 'let me see the wound I have some training in trauma healing.'

'I don't think a fossegrim curse can be healed by galdorless medicine,' Meloc said grimly.

'Nonsense,' replied Anders. He grabbed Meloc's by the

shoulders and Kasian carefully rolled up the warlock's sleeve. Meloc's entire arm was covered in black vines their leaves flickering, pumping the curse through his body. Kasian pushed Meloc's hair back from his neck to reveal the deep, watery bite mark.

'Wergennis protect us.' Kasian muttered as he examined the wound. 'This is a mark of walking death. He will last no longer than three days. If only I had my bag, I have antimagik healing salves blessed by the goddess.'

'Everything will be fine!' Meloc replied quickly rolling down his sleeve. 'I just need a rest.' He shook himself free from the Wergend's grasp and stumbled forward, falling onto a grassy bank.

'Good idea. I could do with a break myself,' Anders said, sitting down on the grassy bank.

Kasian nodded and sat down beside him.

Instantly, tall marshrushes closed around them. Even Anders, who stood a full head taller than his companions, could not see over the tops of the marshrushes. They were completely concealed from the gaze of the herd. They lay down amid the luscious grass, sipping a potion from the leather water bag offered by Kasian containing water from Mímisbrunnar, the well of light, renowned for its healing properties.

From far behind the walls of grasses they heard curious, discordant noises: squeals, screams of panic, groans, and fragmented orders as the svinnar desperately tried to escape the marsh.

'Get out my way!' Antik roared. More high-pitched squeals shattered the silence of the marsh. 'Leave them! We return to our woods. The marsh can eat the Mercian scum!'

Gradually, the squealing quietened until a crushing silence descended across the marsh. The companions looked at each other and breathed a sigh of relief.

Meloc scanned the marshrushes and watched as they swayed gently in a silent wind. Then, very slowly, he felt an amber haze fall across his vision and the sky began to stretch and widen as the curse spread.

Four black flames appeared above the grassy mound and the marshrushes turned brown and withered. Anders and Kasian looked at each another, the heat from the flames burning their faces.

'He has lost control of his magik, he has become a skrimsli, a danger to Mercia,' Kasian said solemnly.

Meloc stared blankly through the amber haze. He could not decide whether he was back in his small garret house or in prison. His bed seemed more uncomfortable than usual, bumps and knots prodding painfully against his back. His stretched out his fingers, finding his sheets were hot and crumbled under his touch. Something was very wrong. The smell of burnt grass caught in his throat and choked him. He tried to cry out but could not.

A series of memories flashed through his wandering brain.

'Beware the hunger of Dunmuirlun,' the sealed warlock had shouted from the benches at the Star Council at last summer's meeting. He had been taken by the Wergend to be unmynistered.

Meloc shouted 'No!' but the words died on his lips, his mouth covered. He struggled violently, trying to tear the hands away from his face. He bit down into dirty stained hand covering his mouth.

Anders squealed and slapped Meloc hard in the face.

'You need to wake up now!' Anders shouted in the warlock's face as he shook his badly bitten hand.

Meloc sat up.

The four black flames floating above the grassy mound disappeared.

Kasian stood up behind the warlock, shoving his hands in his trouser pockets.

'Did you just hit me?' Meloc demanded looking suspiciously from Kasian to Anders.

'Of course not,' replied Kasian.

'I think the curse is confusing you,' Anders said.

'I see,' said Meloc as he rubbed his face 'I just didn't realise curse dreams left bruises.'

FORTY

Name - Meloc

Location - Fensalir

Allegiance - The Mercian Warbands

Thick yellow mist oozed from bursting mud spots, which had appeared on the muddy black path next to their grassy mound.

'Danger. I can feel it coming!' Meloc whispered.

'I see nothing,' Kasian said, 'If only I had my bag. The *leitandi* would warn us of any approaching danger.'

'Oh, I think we will be able to see the threat soon enough,' replied Meloc standing up and shuffling behind Anders.

The mud exploded. An enormous tentacle raked across the mound, narrowly missing Ander's head before being snatched back into the swirling white waters.

'What the hel is that?' shouted Anders.

'The Hafgufa has awoken. She lives in a cave on the edge of the marsh. She's usually quite friendly, don't hurt her,' Meloc replied.

'Are you sure?' replied Anders crouching next to Kasian.

Three more tentacles flew from the water and two sliced through the air just above their heads. The last one aimed lower and smashed straight into the soldiers' midriffs and hurled them into the air. Anders both landed in the sticky, greedy waters of the marsh, while Kasian seemed to hover in the air for a moment before he slowly fell feet first back onto the mound behind Meloc.

'Think of a spell, quickly!' Anders screamed at Meloc as he grabbed hold of a marshrush and began to pull his way onto a bank of grass.

Meloc muttered a spell under his breath.

The wind screamed across the marsh. The marshrushes whipped from side to side, rattling against each other. The browned grasses bowed and whispered as they hid from the gale which raged over the marsh, dragging a wave of bubbling white water behind it. The wave crashed into the mound, Meloc was knocked onto his back as Kasian staggered under its force. The wind howled and ran onwards.

'Thanks, for the wash,' Anders shouted from the grass bank as the cold water dripped from his shirt.

'And that's why you should never cast spells in a hurry!' Meloc sat up, smiling sheepishly.

Two huge black tentacles whipped out from the surging waters; the earth shook and recoiled in terror. The grassy mound jumped and bowed as the crashing force of the tentacles rippled through the ground. Anders clawed desperately at the bank, grabbing hold of two marshrushes as his lower body sunk into the vice like grip of the misty waters.

'Help me... I'm sinking!' he screamed over to Kasian and Meloc who were lying prostate on the mound. Tentatively,

Kasian stood up and ran lightly across the grasses to Anders.

A massive black tentacle arced across the swirling black waters. The tentacle cracked through the air and crashed into the grassy mound. Meloc saw it coming directly towards him and dived across the mound. The tentacle whipped around him, the tip connected, and Meloc was flung into the air, landing heavily against a wall of marshrushes.

'Til Valhal!' a guttural yell sliced through the mists.

Anders saw the marshrushes cleaved in two as a wild-haired, ragged wildsman leapt through the spiralling mists, a wooden staff circling powerfully above his head. The staff smashed down against a black tentacle which went rigid and quickly retracted back into the water. A series of ear splitting, high-pitched wails sounded from the depths of the turbulent, churning waters. Then an eery silence descended across the marsh. The waters levelled and the yellow mists evaporated. The stranger stood inspecting the destroyed grassy mound.

'Help us!' cried Kasian as Anders fingers slipped from his grasp.

'Grab onto this!' the stranger yelled unfurling the hemp rope he used as a belt. He knotted one end forming a loop and tossed it towards Anders.

'Put this over your shoulders and we will pull you in,' the stranger commanded.

'Hurry, I'm sinking, and I think something is licking my leg,' Anders shouted as he slid the rope under his arms.

'Yes, that will be the creepers, tasting you. They are partial to fresh flesh,' the wildman nodded. He turned towards Kasian. 'Right then Wergend pull as hard as you can but gently mind. We do not want to awaken the creatures of the deeper marsh. I see your warlock is spent and will be unable to help us.'

Kasian rolled his eyes. 'He is not that much help even when he is fully charged either,' he muttered.

The wildman laughed. 'Spoken like a true Wergend.'

'Now, let us retrieve your fallen lord. Heave slow,' he said as Kasian took the end of the rope. They braced their feet into the marsh and pulled, their hands slipping and burning on the rough rope. Anders inched slowly out of the clutches of the marsh and slid over the top towards the safety of the grass, landing by the feet of the wildman. He looked up and gasped as he recognised the ornate golden trim of the green robe hidden beneath a layer of ragged blankets.

'The green field of the warband of the west. I knew I recognised that voice. Lord Vestar, I thought you were dead,' Anders bowed his head.

'You and the rest of Mercia,' Lord Vestar replied grimly. 'And for the sake of my surviving family it is best that remains so.'

He strode over to Meloc. 'City folk rarely walk in the wilds, and none so ill-prepared,' Vestar spoke in a low, quiet voice that warned of hidden anger. He ripped a piece of his undershirt and threw it at Meloc.

'Bind your cut tightly the smell of fresh blood will attract too many creatures.'

Meloc picked up the filthy shirt with a mixture of alarm and disgust. 'I'll just use this creeping moss thank you.' He took his knife from his boot and scraped off some of the moss which was growing over a rock. Then he rolled the moss into a ball and blew onto it, enthusing it with magik. The moss glowed amber and melted to form a black paste.

He swore and winced as he plastered the paste over his cut. The bleeding stopped instantly.

'Your warlock has good tricks,' Vester commented.

A huge grey bird screamed loudly as it soared over the marsh heading north.

'Come, we must be away before news of the svinnar drownings reach Fastness. I know a safe place you may stay a while,' he said pointing to the middle of the marsh. His arms bore signs of heavy manacles with raw bands of red circling his wrists.

'What happened to you?' Anders asked. 'Last time at court you were dancing with the Lady Drifa and then you disappeared. It was rumoured that you had been taken by the warlocks.'

'Why do warlocks get blamed for everything?' Meloc sighed, rolling his eyes.

'Because they are daemons,' Kasian said solemnly. 'Umm… no offence intended.'

'And some taken.' Meloc growled.

'What happened? Where did you go and why help us?' Anders asked.

'I know what it is like to have everything taken from you,' Vestar said grimly. 'I did not choose this life. My old life was stolen from me by the King.'

'I see,' said Kasian frowning. 'The King is anointed to the throne by the gods. If they have deemed this your life, then so be it. This is the will of the gods.'

'The gods were never a part of this. It was the King that brought ruin upon my family.' Vestar stopped and turned his face towards the orange of the setting sun. 'Four months ago, I came to him with rumours of the Dunmuir invasion. I even had proof of hidden correspondence involving the use of *sejoin* mirrors, between a high-ranking traitor in the Mercian court and Alfarin, King of Dunmuirlun. I did not know the name of the traitor only his callsign - Eirikir – the eternal ruler.'

'The claws of Dunmuir treachery run deep into Mercia,' Anders growled. 'Did you find the name of this traitor?'

'Yes,' replied Vestar turning and staring at the companions as if to challenge them in combat. 'His name is King Athelstan.'

'Huh!' laughed Kasian. 'You are insane the King would never destroy his own kingdom.'

'Unless he was offered something greater,' Vestar growled.

'Wait!' replied Meloc. 'Do you have any proof of this?'

'I caught him unawares in his antechamber before his *sejoin* mirror which he had linked to another such mirror in Dunmuirlun. The next moment I was surrounded by Purple Guards and then I was bound and thrown into the marsh. While here I learnt that a mystery illness had affected my family. My parents, Gudrun my wife, and Vestarin, my beloved heir, have all perished. It was not a coincidence.'

'If these claims are indeed correct. Why not take them to the Star Council or Grand Master Heilagan? In matters of morality the Wergend are stalwart,' Kasian replied.

'My daughters are now under the protection of the King, and I am trapped here. If the King knows I am alive I am in no doubt my daughters will die,' Vestar replied.

He strode off through the maze of grass and mud. Vestar's path was even more narrow and treacherous than the one conjured by Meloc. It was not actually a path, just patches of the marsh that were shallower than the main. Meloc waded through the knee deep black, sticky mud. His mud-splattered face glowed red with the exertion of fighting against the marsh for each step forward. Even the wild stranger seemed to be breathing more fiercely, although his pace did not slacken.

'Hurry you do not want to wander the march once darkness has fallen,' Vestar hissed.

Meloc let out a deep sigh and forced his legs to move through the clinging mire, each step marked by a squelching, gurgling sound which magnified a hundred-fold in the empty silence. He pulled himself through a wall of marshrushes, their stems cracking under his weight, and smiled in relief as the sticky blackness of the marsh was replaced by dark scrub grass. The stranger quickly strode off into the thick rolling greenness of the open moorland. He tumbled forward, grabbing hold of the flowing grasses as he struggled to pull his feet from the clutches of the moor.

'You should be safe here for a while,' the wildman stated in his quiet, restrained voice, as he pointed to a ramshackle collection of stone boulders haphazardly piled at the bottom of a sloping, lazy hill.

FORTY-ONE

Name - Vestar
Location - Hallar, the Leaning Hills
Allegiance - The Mercian Warbands

The slopes of the low-lying hills were speckled with gigantic grey granite boulders which cast heavy shadows in the fading light. Hidden in the darkness was a little stone hut, its sides made from dark granite blocks. A slow green moss climbed up the walls, merging the hut with the sleeping stones which surrounded it. The roof was a timber structure hidden beneath a heavy fringe of grassy turf, which sloped downwards joining the surrounding tufted grass. From a distance, the only evidence of its presence was the narrow smoke trail which spiralled upwards from a tiny chimney poking through the grassy roof.

Vestar opened a narrow, twig woven door set in the lower right-hand side of the building. 'Welcome to the remains of the hunting lodge of the Westhelm. Today it is our sanctuary, but soon it will be our base of vengeance.'

'Surely there is enough blood running through Mercia?' Kasian said shaking his head. 'There is no salvation in vengeance.'

'No, but a warbandman must not live without honour. Honour lost must be reclaimed. The Wergend cannot understand such things,' Anders said.

Vestar frowned and looked up at Anders. 'How is Lord Hamarr?'

'He has fallen to treachery along with the whole of

Stonefall,' Anders replied.

'Scitte,' replied Vestar. 'Is there any honour left in Mercia? Perhaps a country so corrupt deserves to fall in flames.'

Anders nodded.

'God save me from men of honour and poxy tarts,' Meloc tutted loudly and walked into the shelter.

The hut appeared empty. It consisted of one living space, with a small fire enclosed in a circle of stones, in the centre of the room. Above the fire swung a battered black cooking pot. It simmered gently, scenting the air with promises of a warm, rich 'forever' bubbling stew. The smell brought back memories of hearty meals and Meloc's stomach growled with longing.

'So, what about this hospitality the west is famous for then?' Meloc asked staring at the bubbling cauldron.

'Even diminished we can still offer a fine stew,' Vestar laughed and handed the companions wooden bowls.

'May the goddess reward you!' Kasian said as he took his steaming bowl and began to offer prayers to the goddess.

Anders and Meloc nodded their thanks and sat on the pile of furs next to the fire, hungrily devouring the first cooked food they had eaten since leaving Welfasten. Meloc felt his body sink into the soft furs. He struggled to keep his eyes from closing but lost the battle. 'Beware the raven flies north,' he whispered as the empty wooden bowl fell from his hand. It rolled noisily across the stone floor and crashed into the ring of blackened stones which surrounded the leaping fire.

'Your warlock seems a little too sleepy,' Vestar said standing over him.

'He was bitten by a fossegrim,' Kasian said standing over Meloc.

'He bears a curse mark?' Vestar said his eyes widening in alarm. 'He will attract the searching darkness. You cannot stay here. I have sent word – my loyal followers will be gathering soon. Your very presence here endangers them.'

'Our warlock needs to rest. Let us stay here awhile and we will be away before nightfall. You have my word,' Anders promised. He wrapped Meloc in a fur and muttered,

'Bindweed for mind's need. It will slow the spread of the curse through his body. Do you know of any?'

'Ah, you seek the cursed weed. Since the invasion, the bindweed infestation of the Leaning Hills had become a hidden menace threatening to strangle crops and starve the smallholders. I will take you further south to where the bindweed grows. It will not cure your warlock but may give him time enough to create his own remedy,' Vestar said staring down at Meloc.

'Yes… but you will have to carry him,' Kasian said looking at Anders. 'Strangely I seem unable to touch him.'

'I see...' said Anders rubbing his stubble. 'Not two weeks hence King Athelstan had decreed that no magikind may touch each other and the Grand Warlock Kochab was forced to cast the *Osnert* clause, the unjoining spell. Any touch between magikind within the kingdom will cause severe pain. The casting of the spell caused riots across the Midheim and the Sunderfell and many magikborne had fled to Dunmuirlun. The timing could not have been worst, one week later the Dunmuir forces attacked their ranks swollen with Mercian magikborne.'

'A fortuitous coincidence,' Vestar tutted as finished the last of his stew.

'Such a law would not affect the Wergend,' Kasian sighed. 'The eight selections of Wergennis expose anyone with magical infections before they join the order.'

'Of course not,' Anders replied raising one red eyebrow.

'Let us go before the night creatures start to hunt,' Vestar nodded and opened the door.

Anders stood and pulled Meloc to his feet.

'I can walk unaided, I'm not dead yet!' Meloc growled as he pulled his arm from Ander's grip.

Kasian frowned at the grey warlock, a shadow of fear and doubt passed across his face as they left the safety of the hut. After an hour's walk, they reached the first smallholding of the Leaning Hills. The farmhouse and outbuildings lay consumed by the bindweed, which twisted up their walls and burst through open windows like skeletal fingers searching for their prey. A grey stone chimney pierced through the seething mass of serpentine vines in a last forlorn hope of escaping the suffocating weed. Cautiously, they approached the silent farmhouse. Its vegetable garden was lost amid the spiralling vines.

Hugging the shadows of the garden wall, they crept up to the farmhouse building. Its great wooden door stood ajar; a huge, twisted mass of vine blocked most of the doorway. Its trunk felt eerily warm to touch.

'This bindweed had been cursed by myrkir,' Anders muttered.

'Try not to touch anything,' Meloc whispered as they entered the building.

The kitchen was cold. Its windows broken by the encroaching vines. Storage jars had been dislodged and lay smashed against the wooden floorboards. Anders crossed over the trailing vines and broken glass making for the larder. He brushed past the bindweed and the huge green leaves stirred and fluttered, revealing the body of the lady of the house lying prostrate on the floor. Her eyes and mouth were wide open, frozen in a timeless, surprised expression. Vines had wrapped around her legs, and her body seemed to melt into the leaves. The vine leaves had plate-sized white blossoms which seemed to glow in the shadows of the kitchen. They had grown much larger than the vines outside the farmhouse and trailed across the floor. The huge green leaves quivered as they walked past them. The white flower by the open window turned slowly. A sickly-sweet scent filled the master bedroom and clawed at their eyes.

They moved carefully around the vine, not wanting to become its next victim.

'There should be dried bindweed powder in the cold room,' Vestar said. 'We should not pick the bindweed vines which have wrought so much damage to this farmhouse. They have been cursed and corrupted.'

Kasian nodded and drew his sword as he cautiously opened the cold room door.

The vines began to rustle. Their tentacles began to unroll slowly like the tongue of a green lizard tasting Mercian flesh in the air.

'Be quick!' Anders called out, 'the bindweed is waking.'

Kasian reappeared with a small brown storage jar which he slipped into his shoulder bag.

Heavy hooves clattered to a halt in the courtyard below. The sounds of heavy boots and squeaking leather saddles echoed as a group of ragged horsemen gathered. Anders cursed under his breath and signalled to the others to disappear. He moved stealthily towards the window.

'The entire Northeast has fallen. We must ride west and

protect our rearguard!' A dishevelled warband sergeant shouted.

'No! We must go to Steinnhelm Fortress and hold the eastern line,' a blood splattered young officer shouted back. Their horses began circling and rearing, their nostrils flared, and hooves clattered against the cobbles.

'Syr Haukel, the men are defeated, and hope is lost. We must resupply and regroup at Fastness.'

'What's the point of running west when the Dunmuir will just follow? Steinnhelm is the last eastern stronghold. If that fails, all the lands from Stonefall in the north to Austurgate Tower in the east will have been lost and most of our people will be under the Dunmuir whip. Then the might of the Dunmuir army will sweep across the Midheim like a wind of death. The Midheim fortresses will fall one by one, and we will all be put to the sword, have no doubt of it!' he hissed into the sergeant's face. 'We ride to support the garrison at Steinnhelm.'

Vestar peered at the young captain and grimaced as he saw his right arm tied in a blood-stained sling.

The leaves shivered under his accidental touch and coiling vines began to slide towards him.

The sergeant bowed before barking orders at the rest of the battered warband to fall in. Armour clinked, leather groaned, and the sounds of circling hooves filled the courtyard as the last of the Eastern warband vanished from view.

Vestar punched the wall and cursed.

The leaves hugging the window frame quivered. There was a darkness behind them. Vestar drew his sword and used the blade to gently move a giant leaf aside. He gasped. He was used to death, but this was sorcery. The master of the house stood bound in vines, motionless beside the window. His eyes and mouth were open wide in a speechless terror. His arms were outstretched and inches from the open window, while his legs, body and neck were held fast by the green trailing vines. Strange grey shadows and purple whip marks covered the man's face and arms.

'What is happening?' Vestar cried out as he felt his right ankle tingle. He looked down and cursed. Small green vines had encircled both his ankles and were climbing up the bands of his black leather calf coverings. He wriggled his toes, testing the vine's response; instantly he felt the vines constrict around his lower legs. A large vine whipped across the room and cut across his face. Caught unawares, he was knocked sideways by the blow and fell halfway through the open window.

'The vines have awakened,' Meloc warned. 'We need to leave *now*.'

'I agree with your warlock!' shouted Vestar. He circled his sword and brought it down hard against the entrapping vines. As the vines halved, they released puffs of green gas which disappeared into the wind.

'And make haste!' Anders shouted as he crashed through the open window, closely followed by Vestar.

An overgrown rose bush broke their fall and they tumbled onto the path below. Anders lay there for an instant, dazed by the fall, and then brushed the shattered wood and vine from his body. He sprang to his feet, fierce blue hunter eyes scanning the garden for danger. He saw the big bindweed leaves by the window begin to tremble and heard rustling sounds, as the bindweed covering the garden began twisting towards him. Seconds later Kasian jumped feet first through the window, while Meloc appeared panting heavily next to him. Anders leapt to his feet.

Kasian opened the jar of bindweed powder. Then he shook the remaining drops of water from his drinking bag into the jar and mixed it to form a paste. Solemnly, he handed the jar to Anders explaining, 'I fear the goddess is unhappy when we touch.'

'I wish my god Tyr was that particular,' Anders grimaced as he smeared the pale green sludge onto Meloc's neck. Meloc squealed, and two amber spheres pierced through the darkness. Anders touched the runes on his forearm and without taking his eyes from the warlock, backed slowly away.

'It's alright. I'm still full of the stew. I'm not going to eat you... just yet!' Meloc grinned as the bitemark on his neck glowed and repaired itself under the bindweed enchantment. He blinked and the amber magik left his eyes.

'Enough frivolity,' Kasian said. 'Let us leave this cursed place.'

'Well...' grinned Meloc. 'Perhaps an accursed place is just what we need? It will definitely keep prying eyes away!'

'True!' laughed Anders, 'but may I suggest we sleep in the stables up there.'

He pointed to a large stone structure used for housing sheep or cattle overwinter. It rose from the stones which the bindweed seemed unwilling to cross.

Both Meloc and Kasian nodded.

'And I will take my leave,' Vestar bowed to Anders. 'May Tyr protect you!'

'May Tyr protect you too,' Anders bowed. 'And if not, I will drink with you in the halls of the mighty fallen in Valholl,' he grinned gripping Vestar's forearm.

'The path of revenge only has one destination,' Kasian said grimly.

'And I am happy with that,' Vestar nodded to the Wergend as he strode down the farm track.

FORTY-TWO

Name - Meloc
Location - Hallar, the Leaning Hills
Allegiance - The Mercian Warbands

Meloc woke to the delicious smell of dried pork and freshly baked rye cake permeating through the kitchen of Fregna Tower. He yawned and rolled off his wooden bed crashing onto the cold stone floor. He frowned. The floor of the warlock novitiates' or apprentices' wing had turned to mud. Confused, he peered into the grey shadows, which danced around the fading room as he felt his dream world shatter. He was a fugitive travelling with a wanted warbandman and a disgraced Wergend. All his old potion masters' warnings had come true. Meloc cursed but the smell of pork was undeniable.

'Here put these on,' Anders whispered as he tightened a cracked leather belt over an ancient mail coat. 'I borrowed them from the farmer. He will not be in need of warmth this winter.'

Meloc eagerly grabbed the warm looking clothes. Meloc eagerly grabbed the warm looking clothes. He kicked off his remaining boots and pulled on an old grey pair of woollen trousers and a thick green woollen jacket and secured a large leather belt. He then slipped on some leather shoes and tied leather bands up to his knee for protection against the mud and cold. It was something he imagined his maternal grandfather would have worn while out sowing corn. He looked longing down at Anders newly acquired leather boots.

'How is your neck?' Anders asked, frowning at the black bitemark.

'It's fine,' Meloc lied, the light of the morning sun searing through his brain.

'Hmm…,' Anders said shaking his head as he shoved a plate of sizzling pork and rye cakes at Meloc, who devoured it.

'Where is our faithful Wergend brother this fine morning?' Meloc asked between mouthfuls.

Anders nodded over to a rock formation facing the rising western sun. Kasian was on his knees praying devotedly to his goddess. 'It is as well he prays now for where we are heading the sun rises little. Two weeks have passed since refugees came to Stonefall from the eastern borderlands. They carried little but their clothes and tales of slaughter and fire. Now the Easternlands lies silent.'

'It may be silent but I'm sure it's not empty,' Meloc said grimly. 'Anyway, we will soon find out. Before we cross the border into Austurlun we need to make a slight detour east. I need to borrow a small magik token from Ableakan City,' Meloc said turning his back on the sun and starring into the eastern shadowlands.

Kasian came up to them dusting the dirt from his knees and looked at Meloc. 'And what is this small token you need to borrow from Ableakan?'

Meloc smiled and Anders shifted his feet uneasily.

'At present, no Mercian warband can defeat the Dunmuir invaders. Mercia has subjugated its natural magikal resources and developed great warbands, while Dunmuirlun has exalted their magikborne. They have used their natural supplies of galdor energy to enhance their forces. Mercia will never defeat Dunmuirlun unless their warlock legions are destroyed and the flow of magik is stopped. Only when the invaders are reduced to mere mortals again,' he paused for effect, 'can our warbands unite and destroy the invaders.'

'And this small magik token will stop the Dunmuir warlocks?' Anders frowned. 'It does not sound so small and harmless to me.'

'This is like a horror unfolding from the warnings of Hugues de Payne, our beloved first Grand Master,' Kasian groaned. 'The unchaining of magik and the ending of the world.'

'And my father said I would amount to nothing and yet here I am at the ending of the world,' Anders winked at Meloc. Meloc giggled and Kasian scowled at the two.

'So …what is this small thing? I have a feeling it will not be small or easily acquired,' Anders said rubbing his stumble.

'Oh, just a magik pebble,' smiled Meloc, 'of little consequence or value.'

'If only I could believe that.' Kasian shook his head.

A cloud moved across the morning sun and a grey shadow lengthened across the clearing.

'I think we should leave now,' warned Meloc. 'We have stayed here for too long.'

Anders and Kasian nodded and grabbed their things, then began their trek southeast across the rolling hills. Anders walked at the head of the small band of dissidents, an ancient, battered round shield from the days of King Awain strapped to his back; his sharp eyes hunting the horizon for prey ready for the opportunity to avenge his fallen comrades.

The crumbling silhouette of the farmhouse stood dejectedly on the horizon. During the night, tendrils of the bindweed had spread across the plains covering both grass and stone in thick wooden vines and huge, green leaves which rippled in the winds.

Shooting out from amid the leaves were large white trumpets of flowers. The trumpets stood tall and alert, their heads twisting around seeming to sense that they were being watched.

Kasian pointed to the flowers. One of the white trumpet heads opened to reveal large yellow stamens which rippled in the breeze causing clouds of green spores to burst into the air. The spores were carried away by the wind to seed throughout Mercia and the flower snapped shut.

'The seeds of death. No doubt a gift from the Dunmuir warlocks,' Kasian said grimly as he decapitated yet another bindweed seedling. His haunted expression changed to one of fleeting satisfaction at the death of every cursed plant. He sheathed his sword and marched off, his long strides carrying him through the undulating land.

'Watch out Kasian, we are about to mount the 'Sleeping Sisters', Anders winked to Meloc.

'There is no need for such talk,' Kasian blushed and glared at the warband lordling.

Meloc grinned. The Wergend Order were a strict religious group who had forsaken the daemonic demands of the mortal flesh for the purity of love for their goddess whom they worshipped with blood and death. '

'Do you know the story of the sleeping sisters?' Anders asked.

'We have no time for folk stories in the sacred temples,' Kasian replied a little too quickly.

'Then I will tell you,' Anders grinned. 'The locals had named the southern hills the 'Sleeping Sisters,' as from a distance the series of flattened hills resembled reclining ladies, with pinched waist paths and long interlocking legs. According to Mercian legend, the hills had indeed once been sisters whose beauty was unsurpassed. They were greatly admired, and people came from the four corners of Mercia to try to win their hands in marriage. The sisters, in turn, spent their days lying in bed, combing long golden hair, and watching their reflections in golden hand mirrors for signs of imperfection. They would do no work about their farm in case their bodies grew hardened and rough with the toil. Their aging father had become so desperate with their slothful behaviour, that he sought an audience with the witch who lived in the stone lair hidden within the lower stonefields of Mount Ableakan. He offered the witch a tribute of three golden coins and asked her to enchant his daughters to make them useful and important. She had twisted a single blond hair from each sister into a braid and placed them on her rocky altar at the back on the shack. Next to the hair she placed a large black raven father and some springly moss. Then she sprinkled a small vial of drek's blood from her cupboard across the offerings. A large amber cloud exploded across the altar and the braid vanished.

'It is done,' said the warlock. She looked back but the farmer was nowhere to be seen. For to avoid payment, he had spurred his horse across the fields as soon as the spell had begun because he was as mean as his daughters were vain.

However, you cannot outrun a curse and the warlock's anger at being tricked was terrible and so she cast her second spell.

At the day's end, when the farmer arrived home, he found his house was silent. There was no laughter and song inside the house. He walked outside hoping to find them at work in the back fields only to watch in horror as his youngest daughter lay down to join her elder sisters and transform into a grassy hill. His daughters had become as he had wished but not as he had hoped. They were indeed of great importance. They had been transformed into the sleeping slopes: the primary defensive line between the Mercian and Austurlun borders.'

'Enough of your blasphemy,' Kasian frowned. 'Everyone knows the land was created by the mother goddess Wergennis,' and he quickly walked on.

'I wonder which sister I'm mounting,' Anders smiled as he walked along the path that ran along the waist of the first hill, dwarfed on either side by sheer grass banks.

'I always heard he had sons,' Meloc grinned.

'Hmm…' Anders as he strode ahead and busied himself decapitating the bindweed, squashing its flowerhead under foot. Anders touched his forearm tattoo for good luck and scurried after the disappearing figure of Kasian, keeping his green eyes fixed firmly on the worn round shield strapped to the Wergend captain's back.

Meloc was soon left far behind.

Kasian and Anders stood at the crown of the first sleeping sister and watched the solitary figure of Meloc pick his way painfully through the thick grasses that covered the slopes, stumbling over hidden potholes and coughing as he climbed. From the corner of his eye, Anders caught sight of a bindweed vine stretching across the first sister as they watched the warlock's painful progress. In one deft movement he sliced the vine in two, bringing his blade within two inches of a horrified Kasian's face. A small green mist hissed from the broken plant. A disgruntled toad caught hidden in the shade of the vine leaves, glared at the captain. Slowly, Anders backed away. The toad croaked menacingly, turned its back on the retreating captain, and hopped under the cover of one of the grey rocks which lay scattered carelessly over the hills.

Anders looked at the horrified expression on the Wergend's face and bit his lip, desperately trying not to laugh.

A loud cursing rang out through the hilltops as Meloc caught his foot in a hidden pothole and fell face first into the cutting grasses.

'Do you think I should carry him? He cannot weigh more than a daypack,' Anders suggested, his composure regained.

'You can ask but you might end up like your friend over there,' Kasian smiled innocently and nodded to the rock where the disturbed toad lurked.

'I see your point,' said the captain stroking his stumbled chin. 'Then, we had best wait while he catches up.'

FORTY-THREE

Name - Meloc
Location – The Outskirts of Ableakan City
Allegiance - The Mercian Warbands

On the fifth day of their slow trek southeast across the sleeping sisters, Anders let out a whoop of joy and shouted, 'I see Ableakan City! Thank the gods! I could do with a drink!'

'From where I'm standing,' said a dry voice from behind, 'you could do with a bath…'

The three companions burst out laughing, their spirits soaring at the sight of the city. From their vantage point on the rolling hills above the city, they saw Ableakan City had remained untouched from the ravages of the Dunmuir invasion and still hummed with life. Built into one of the mountains of the southeastern border range, the city and the mountain blended together, a great orange sandstone monolith soaring high into the clouds.

The southern face of the mountain had been carved and hammered into a many tiered cityscape. Its entrance was marked by a series of elaborately carved arcades with high columns and archways. The camouflage of the city was so complete that at first glance, these entrances appeared as mere black shadows thrown against the mountain. Its second tier was comprised of heavy towers with slit windows and onion shaped roofs, catching precious sunlight and sucking it into the dark recesses of the city. While between the towers, the untamed mountain rock face bulged and cracked, casting protective shadows across the fortifications. Above the spires, faint decorations had been carved on the rock which merged into the very mountain itself.

Mount Ableakan did not seem to mind the ornamentations placed upon it. It seemed to revel in the attention, standing taller and prouder than the other eastern mountains. The confidence of the mountain radiated into its inhabitants and in the failing light the mountain seemed to twinkle and glow, pulsating with life.

To the west of the city, a high spired tower stood haughtily aloof. The rest of city seemed to veer away from its touch, huddling together, trying to avoid all contact with the iridescent, silver tower. At the very top of the spire was a huge silver lightning rod.

By day and night, white streaks of lightning cracked through the hanging clouds, exploding from the silver rod before arcing wildly across the city. Whispered rumours told that the rod was pure neodymium, creating such an intense magnetic force that it drew galdor dust from across the kingdom. The narrow spire supposedly filtered the precious dust as it fell through the tower, gathering it into an iron conduit which funnelled the galdor powder into hidden subterranean vaults. Meloc could not understand why the vaults had remained sealed during the Dunmuir invasion but thought they would be opened soon enough. Elding Tower, the lightning tower, was the home of Grand Protector Olmur and more importantly, *Hedenddorm*, the Galdor Stone.

Meloc shivered in the chilled winds that blew across the valley floor. He would have to enter the forbidding tower, wrest the stone from Olmur's grasp, and substantially increase his galdor energy reserves, if they were to have any hope in defeating the magik of Dunmuirlun.

He looked unhappily at the thriving city and wished he

could be anywhere but here. Anders pushed past the warlock and marched excitedly under the torch lit archway. Kasian had disappeared into the crowd following the long, brick vaulted corridor which led to a small stone doorway: the entrance to Ableakan City.

The doorway was manned by two city guards. They flashed lanterns into the faces of everyone who entered the city, demanding papers and asking questions. Meloc wrapped his cloak tighter around his body and tugged the hood down low over his eyes so most of his face was lost in shadows. He had never ventured outside his small garret without the cursed magikal restraints. His iron wrist guard had been left in the Welfasten, while his borrowed clothes were devoid of the downward facing coiled snake which warned the normal citizens of Mercia that a monster walked among them. Meloc knew if he was found travelling without these, only a dungeon and a noose waited.

He wiped beads of sweat from his forehead; Anders gasped in horror. His hand felt odd, icy cold, against his forehead. Meloc looked at it and cursed. The leaves of the black vine curse were spreading across his hand. Meloc cursed again, muttered the *faest* under his breath, and the vine disappeared. He stuffed his hands in his pockets, lowered his head and shuffled into the shadows.

'Do not use your magik here, warlock!' Kasian whispered in alarm.

'It was an emergency!' Meloc whispered.

A noisy group of travellers cluttered past. A child stared at Meloc and pointed. 'Look, mama, he's orange!'

Anders grabbed the warlock by the shoulders and forced him to kneel by the wall. Kasian stood over the warlock, blocking the child's view.

Meloc peered from behind the huge warrior's legs. Two gate guards pushed through the silenced crowd. Meloc closed his eyes, covered them with his hands, and willed his magik to sleep once more. Anders pressed against him, pinning his body to the wall.

'Don't do anything unnatural!' Kasian warned.

'And just who is orange?' Meloc heard a martial voice and held his breath.

Anders slowly removed his hood. Waves of unkempt russet hair fell against his shoulders, 'It is from my mother's family,' he replied in the quiet tone of one capable of sudden violence.

'Well…well… A strong man is it. And yet not strong enough the join the armies fighting against the Dunmuir?' the guard slapped Anders' face.

Meloc felt every sinew in the warrior's body grew taunt, but Anders said nothing.

The guards laughed. 'Be about your business, red, but be sure of this: I will be keeping a close watch on you. I have no doubt that you will end this night in chains.'

The footsteps marched away, and a surging crowd filled the silence.

Anders wiped the blood from his lip and stood glaring after the guards. His hand tightened around the grip of his great sword, which lay hidden beneath the folds of his dull brown cloak. He put his arm around Kasian's shoulders and whispered, 'We will never pass him off as normal. We must fight our way through the gate and go to ground.'

'Very well,' said Kasian drawing his sword, 'We fight.' He shook his head, 'I never thought I would die defending a warlock.'

'Your goddess has a fine sense of humour,' replied Anders unclipping his cloak and letting it fall to the floor revealing a rusted mail coat.

The crowd gasped and stepped backwards pressing themselves against the walls.

'All praise the goddess,' murmured Meloc. His eyes turned amber, and an explosion flashed through the pathway. Everyone within the radius of the spell's shockwave fell to the ground unconscious. By the time they had staggered to their feet; the three companions had disappeared.

Unseen by the Ableakan masses, the shadow cast by the guardhouse retracted back towards the gate, its darkness taking on the form of a giant ravenling. The ravenling flapped its wings and soared into the sky hovering above the city. It cawed quietly, its message taken on the wind as it whispered, 'Welcome to Ableakan warlockling. The city of your doom.'

To be continued.